# THIRST FOR SIN

Touch of Evil
Book One

KENNEDY LAYNE

**THIRST FOR SIN**

Copyright © 2021 by Kennedy Layne
Print Edition

Cover Designer: Sweet 'N Spicy Designs

ALL RIGHTS RESERVED: The unauthorized reproduction or distribution of this copyrighted work is illegal. Criminal copyright infringement is investigated by the FBI and is punishable by up to 5 years in federal prison and a fine of $250,000.

All characters and events in this book are fictitious. Any resemblance to actual persons living or dead is strictly coincidental.

# Dedication

Jeffrey—We begin another adventure with a brand-new series! I love you!

Cole—Never be afraid to try new things, because you never know where the adventure might take you! Love you to the moon and back!

**USA Today Bestselling Author Kennedy Layne brings you a page-turning thriller that touches evil in a way that you couldn't imagine...**

Brooklyn Sloane works as a special consultant to the FBI as one of the most adept profilers in the agency's history. She had been recruited at a relatively young age from her career in academics, but her colleagues have no idea the disturbing motive for her success.

While her current investigation into a cold-blooded serial killer garners the attention of the media, Brook is able to discover the unsub's first kill. When a tragic shooting takes place involving one of the agents assigned to the case, Brook finds herself unexpectedly out in the field searching for evidence that will eventually lead her to a viable suspect.

As Brook moves closer to her target, her own troubling past is breathing its familiar breath down the back of her neck until she finds herself at a crossroad with the very transgression that shaped her moral fiber. As her past and present collide, which one will rid her of the sin that stains her soul?

# CHAPTER ONE

**Brooklyn Walsh**
*September 1997*
*Sunday—4:36pm*

THE STEADY RHYTHM of rain that beat against the bedroom window had become more violent with every passing minute. It was as if the weather had sensed this day was going to be a horrifying revelation, of sorts. The flashes of lightning and ominous rumbles of thunder that occurred seconds later only added to the intensity of the storm.

"Brooklyn, have you seen your brother?"

"No, Mom," Brook replied, purposefully not looking up from her book. She slowly turned one of the thin pages and wished her hands would stop shaking. She'd never been very good at lying to her parents. "I just got home from Sally's house a few minutes ago. She gave me a book to read about a boy wizard who just discovered that he could do magic spells."

Brook hoped that her mother wouldn't come any closer to the nook inside the bay window of her bedroom. It was her favorite place in the whole wide world. Right now, she'd have given anything to be anywhere else but home. She fought back the tears that threatened to spill, not wanting her mom to see her cry.

This wasn't how she'd pictured spending the last day of her summer vacation.

The branch that her father had promised to cut down for the last few months clicked threateningly against the window. It was almost as if the tree was reminding her to keep quiet. She didn't think her mom saw her jump at the frightening sound, but she'd brought her feet up underneath her just in case. Maybe her mom would think she was simply getting more comfortable on the long wedge-shaped pillowtop.

The violent storm had cast dark grey shadows across the backyard. Huge drops of rain cascaded down the multitude of beveled windowpanes projecting colorful prisms into the corners of her room. The tree branch reminded her of long, creepy fingers trying to reach through the glass, ones like she'd seen recently in a scary Halloween advertisement on television.

Was Mother Nature trying to tell her that she wasn't safe inside her own home?

"Your brother left his bike in the middle of the driveway again. The chrome rims are going to rust, and then I'm going to hear from your father about how irresponsible Jacob is being about his belongings. Is this clean?"

Her mother came closer, picking up the shirt that Brook had changed out of when she'd first reached her bedroom. She held her breath, not taking her eyes off the words in front of her. The printed black letters seemed to have blurred together and were no longer recognizable.

How was she going to explain the stain?

"Jacob is lucky that I didn't run his bike over with my car."

Brook tried to swallow around the lump in her throat, but the saliva backed up in her mouth. She was still praying that her mother hadn't noticed the red smudge.

A promise was a promise, especially ones between siblings.

She had even taken the extra step of pinky swearing with Jacob to prove that she wouldn't say a word to anyone.

"Dinner will be ready in about an hour."

Brook didn't reply.

She couldn't.

Instead, she flipped another page to mimic the act of reading.

Her stomach was nauseous, like when she had to take a hard test at school or when she had an appointment at the dentist's office to tighten her braces. She tucked her legs in tighter against her body. She didn't care that the rubber on the bottom of her running shoes dug into the back of her legs. The slight discomfort took her mind off the fact that her mother wasn't leaving the bedroom.

Had she seen the red stain on the shirt?

Why had Jacob's hands been covered in blood?

Brook had been so scared when she'd caught sight of her brother staring blankly down at his fingers, but his face had twisted into a mask of rage when she'd asked if he was alright. He hardly ever yelled at her, and it was so unlike him to get so mad. She'd run away from the kitchen as fast as she could, wanting only to reach the safety of the bay window in her room.

Only Brook didn't feel safe anymore.

Not in her bedroom, not in the house, and not around her brother.

"Do you have all your school supplies organized for tomorrow?" her mother asked, tossing the shirt into the hamper. Relief poured through Brook over the fact that her mom hadn't asked about the blood on the sleeve. It was the spot where her brother had grabbed her by the arm as she was trying to pass him in the kitchen. "Don't forget to put those erasers we finally found at the pharmacy into your new pencil case."

"I won't," Brook reassured her, tossing a forced smile her mother's way.

Brook was finally able to swallow now that her mother wasn't asking anymore questions about Jacob. She'd mentioned that he had left his bike in the driveway. He might have simply wrecked it on his way back from the basketball courts, falling onto his hands and getting a bad case of road rash. Maybe he'd been embarrassed when he'd fallen off his bike.

Brook got that way sometimes, too. Her mother constantly reassured her that she'd get over her awkward stage soon enough.

Falling off his bike would certainly explain why he had so much blood on his hands.

Brook's mother smiled back at her before she walked out of the room, probably thinking about what she was going to make for dinner.

Brook didn't like to keep things from her parents, but Jacob had threatened to tell them about the time that she'd snuck down to the creek all by herself if she didn't keep quiet about what had happened in the kitchen.

Had Jacob gone to see the girl who he liked from school?

Their parents didn't know that he had been messing around with Pamela Murray, but Brook had heard him on the phone asking if she wanted to go to the drive-in movie this weekend. She lived on a gravel road, so maybe his tires had lost traction and he'd ended up on the ground.

Little by little, Brook finally relaxed after thinking about

Jacob's bike lying in the middle of the driveway. It made sense that he would be bleeding if he fell onto a cement surface or crashed on a gravel road. He must have simply overreacted due to all the adrenaline running through his system when she saw him. He probably didn't want her to say anything to their parents that could get him grounded over the weekend.

"Brook?"

She dropped the book that she was supposed to be reading. It landed with a thud against the soft carpeted floor after bouncing off her leg, most likely creasing one of the pages.

Sally was going to be mad.

Brook finally looked up to find that Jacob was standing in the doorway, wearing different clothes from when she'd last seen him in the kitchen. His wavy brown hair was slicked back, and she could tell that he'd taken a shower to clean up.

He wasn't smiling.

Brook couldn't stop her gaze from slowly lowering to his hands. She searched for any kind of scratch or cut, but there was none to be found.

"I didn't tell Mom," Brook said quickly, shaking her head back and forth hastily so that he would believe her. She didn't want to get grounded, either. Alice Jacobson's birthday party was this weekend, and both of her best friends were going to be there. "I swear. Pinky swear."

"Good."

Jacob continued to stand in the doorway as if he wanted to say more, but they just stared at each other in silence. It was like he didn't believe she could keep a secret, not one this big.

She could, though.

Brook hadn't told their parents about Pamela or that Jacob

had been sneaking out of the house at least two nights a week for the past few months. She was honestly surprised that he hadn't gotten caught yet.

She wasn't sure what had happened this past summer, but Jacob wasn't the brother who used to laugh with her during Sunday morning cartoons. He'd gotten moody. He no longer colored with her, he didn't like her coming into his room to ask questions anymore, and he hated when she asked him about his friends. Scotty and Daryll weren't coming around the house like they had before, and her parents hadn't even noticed their absences.

Brook wasn't sure why the need to cry overwhelmed her, but her bottom lip trembled at the thought that he was still mad at her. She'd kept quiet just like he'd asked, but it didn't seem to matter to him. His hands had curled into fists at the first sign of her tears. His nostrils flared wide. For a brief second, she thought he was going to break the barrier of her threshold and walk into her room.

Then she blinked, and her brother was back.

Sort of.

The shift in his stance was enough to make her believe that he wasn't angry with her anymore.

Jacob tried to smile, almost as if he knew she was still on the verge of tears. Unfortunately, the corners of his lips didn't lift all the way up. The second he turned from the door to head downstairs, she couldn't stop the tears from spilling down her cheeks.

Something very bad had happened to her brother, and Brook couldn't tell anyone—not her classmates, not her best friends, and not her parents.

Not a soul...ever.

# CHAPTER TWO

**Brooklyn Sloane**
*November 2021*
*Tuesday—5:28am*

THE INCESSANT RAIN had been coming down steadily for days, making it difficult to tell if it was day or night. According to the weather report on the eleven o'clock news, threatening clouds would continue to accumulate in the sky overhead for several more weeks to come. It wouldn't have been so bad if the temperature hadn't fallen into the fifties and the rain hadn't gained that biting edge.

Unfortunately, there was no stopping the cold dampness from settling into one's bones this time of year. It was just another precursor of the upcoming brutal winter that was expected to hit the D.C. area sooner rather than later.

Brook pushed aside the real reason that she hated the dreary month of November, expertly guiding the steering wheel of her car so that the tires were even with the curb. The crime scene in front of her was so chaotic that she wasn't worried the assigned police officers would notice another vehicle in the mix.

As a matter of fact, she was far enough away from the excitement that the distance afforded her the privacy she needed in order to survey the surrounding area without becoming part of the frenzied circus.

Rows of two-story houses in an upper-middle class neighborhood were positioned on either side of what was normally a quiet, residential cul-da-sac. Streetlamps illuminated every other manicured yard, while porch lights shed golden hues on all but a few of the front doorsteps.

In contrast, there were a few pumpkins that had been left out to soften on the numerous stoops, and bundles of cornstalks sagged under the thick veil of moisture that soaked everything exposed to the outside elements.

Halloween had come and gone without too much fanfare, leaving behind only the cleanup and what was sure to be a few stomachaches from the varied collections of sugarcoated treats. Brook didn't have to worry about throwing out rotted pumpkins, storing away decorations for the holidays, or gorging herself on chocolate.

At least, not for the foreseeable future.

She worked twice as many hours in a given day than she spent at her condo, which was an excellent excuse in and of itself not to decorate for the season. Christmas was right around the corner, and she doubted that she would even have time to put up a pine wreath let alone a tree with all the trimmings.

The rhythmic movement of the windshield wipers did nothing to deter her from scanning the curious expressions of those who were currently huddled together underneath their umbrellas or under the relative security of their front porches. No one stood out as if they didn't belong in the area, but occasionally it took a moment to spot the odd man out. Often, the killers who she tracked had above average intelligences. They weren't the average criminal mugging random pedestrians or robbing liquor stores.

Two members of local law enforcement were currently standing in front of the yellow cordon tape strung between a street sign and a streetlamp. The officers were there to restrain the small, gathered crowd from encroaching on the crime scene. The group was most likely comprised of neighbors who'd gotten up early to head into work. They had almost certainly noticed something wrong outside of their living room windows after they'd fixed their first pot of coffee for the day. No one could resist the temptation of getting a closer look prior to departing for their daily grind.

Of course, there would be the random retiree. They tended to hang in the crowd a bit longer, gathering whatever gossip they could for their daily breakfast with their pals at one of the local diners.

Bottom line was that the inquisitive residents had allowed their curiosity to get the best of them. There was no denying that something bad had happened to one of their collective flock, and it was human nature to be curious about any activity inside their small community that involved anything more than a single police vehicle.

They most likely thought one of their neighbors had been involved in a domestic dispute of some sort. Maybe even a burglary gone wrong. People tended to think the worst once the obvious didn't pan out, but violence thrusting itself from outside of their bubble was usually their last guess. They equated such crimes to the chances of being struck by lightning. No one wanted to believe that their homes could be targeted by an evil presence.

How wrong these folks were with their naïve assumptions.

Lightning was more than just a random encounter.

Brook's sole purpose was to hunt the very evil that society denied existed in the form of a cold, calculated human being who had evolved into something more than a mere predator. Out of the multitude of cases that she'd worked over the years, only two killers consumed her every waking thought—one who might be the cause of all the commotion in front of her, and the one from her own past.

Who was she kidding?

The one from her past had invaded her dreams every night for the past twenty-four years, two months, and four days. He was always on the edge of her thoughts, and never very far from her immediate future.

If required, she could even count the minutes and seconds from her realization of how her life would ultimately be shaped.

The red and blue swirling lights from the numerous police cars reflected off the wet black asphalt and the windows of every house in the neighborhood, thus highlighting the bystanders brave enough to stand out in the rain. She glanced over at the neon green numbers on the radio, noting that it was going on five-thirty in the morning. It was early to have so many spectators, another indication that there were many more upper-middle class working families in the neighborhood than retirees.

Another long day was on the horizon.

Unfortunately, these people had no clue that one of their own had been brutally murdered, possibly by the same individual the press had dubbed the Princess Killer. A few of the residents might have fleetingly waved off the possibility that a homicide had taken place, but none of them wanted to accept the reality that was going to be their new paradigm.

Was the unsub—unknown subject—watching from nearby, taking delight in the subsequent turmoil that he'd inflicted on these residents in what he assumed were their mundane lives? Was he sitting inside a parked car two spots down the road, much like herself, so that he wouldn't miss even the slightest bit of excitement when they finally wheeled out the body of another mutilated woman through her own front door? Or was he watching the scene unfold before him on a television set from the comfort of his own home while his dutiful wife cooked him a hardy breakfast, completely unaware of the real reason that her husband had been out so late on a weeknight?

A sigh of exhaustion escaped Brook's lips as she shifted the vent toward her face, needing the added warmth to take the chill out of the air. She continued to study each and every expression of those willing to stand out in the cold rain for some news to share around the watercooler this afternoon.

Talk about an odd, stagnant life.

Their world was about to change.

What they didn't know was that this particular serial killer remained close by his victims, admiring his fantasy as it carried out until the very end. The casual observers were part of that fantasy, too. The adrenaline rush from watching the events in person and witnessing the reactions of those around him were just too much to resist.

He had a thirst.

It was almost as if he perceived the viewers as readers, soaking up each word from the pages so that their imaginations would run wild. If he had committed this murder, he was somewhere nearby.

He'd be drawn to the flame like a moth.

Of that, she had no doubt.

Brook's previous sigh of exhaustion turned to irritation as she caught the slightest movement of a shadow on the street next to her vehicle. The dark silhouette elongated as the light overhead followed the individual about to interrupt her examination of the scene. She reluctantly pressed the button to lower the driver's side window.

"You're messing with my process, Fritz."

"I brought you coffee. I was attempting to forestall your annoyance from getting a call from me in the middle of the night. It's the least I can do for asking you down here this early in the morning." Roger Fritz was careful not to drop the umbrella in his grip as he handed her a large to-go cup. It was from the convenience store located right outside the front entrance of the neighborhood. She would know, especially since she'd observed the logo on their sign as she'd driven past. "Black, though. I couldn't remember if you took cream or sugar."

The hot air blowing from the vent caused Brook's eyes to water, but that didn't stop her from accepting his ninety-nine-cent bribe. She tried not to be offended that her opinion wasn't worth at least a bagel to go along with her large cup of coffee. She'd seen the price of the gas station's beverage highlighted in their window. A bargain was a bargain, even if it was solely intended to ply her to aid in his investigation.

"You didn't go through proper channels. Egos will need to be soothed on both ends." Brook took a tentative sip of the bitter brew. It was hard not to grimace at the burnt aftertaste of a pot left on a burner for far too long, but the heat immediately infused her body. "I'm going to hear about this when I get back to the office sometime this morning."

"Since when have you ever cared about the Bureau's official procedures?" Fritz's trench coat was already wet, so she wasn't surprised when he leaned up against the car to give his back a rest. He'd been having trouble with a lower strain after stopping a robbery in progress, one he'd been unfortunate enough to walk into while off duty. At least, that's what the news had reported a few weeks ago. It didn't take a genius to connect the dots as he shifted his weight for a more comfortable stance. "You know, there's a pool going on in the office for when those fed buddies of yours are going to fire your ass. The thing about being a consultant for the FBI is that they can rip up your contract at a moment's notice for anything they want."

Brook worried about a lot of things, but her being released from her current contract wasn't one of them. Besides, as Fritz had so eloquently put it, she was a consultant, not an agent. The worst they could do was not renew her contract when it ran out, though she doubted that would ever come to fruition.

She'd heard the scuttlebutt.

According to her closure rate, she was one of the best and brightest profilers in the FBI's history—and that included those within the agency.

She didn't put too much credence in water cooler gossip, though.

The only thing that mattered to Brook was that the higher-ups had graciously given her a bit of leeway to work cases to the best of her ability. Sometimes, it was more beneficial to be an outsider than it was to be on the inside. It had been their intent to allow her the latitude as long as she colored inside the lines. Institutional bias at the FBI was only a problem if one failed to produce results.

She didn't want to question the length of her leash, either.

Her supervisor did his best to clean up the paper trail after the fact, and Brook showed her appreciation by accepting the next case that he threw across her desk without being a primadonna, like so many of the more senior profilers and actual agents inside the Bureau. She and her superior had a system that worked, and the only thing that mattered to her was that these brutal monsters were taken off the streets.

Unfortunately, Fritz might have gotten ahead of himself this morning.

"What makes you think this is the work of my serial killer?"

Brook didn't miss his sideways glance of curiosity at her verbiage, but she'd stopped worrying about what others thought of her methods a long time ago. It was an issue that was brought up in therapy quite a lot, but she didn't let that concern her, either. She used it for what it was worth, giving it due consideration and no more.

"You'll see," Fritz warned, shoving his free hand inside the pocket of his coat.

Brook couldn't help but wonder if the coffee she was enjoying hadn't been his, but it wouldn't have mattered anyway. She was a caffeine junkie, and she wasn't picky about where it came from, either. Honestly, she'd have taken an IV at this point.

"Are you done sitting here twiddling your thumbs?" Fritz asked, nodding toward the heart of the crime scene. "I've got one of my officers recording the crowd, and the third shift forensics team wants to head home before the next shift kicks off. This is their third body of the night, and they are more than ready to hand this one off to your people."

Brook wasn't so sure his presumption of the situation was

how this meeting was going to end, so she fell silent as she switched her attention to one of the local blonde reporters holding up a large, bright red umbrella as she talked in front of a camera. The woman had a somber expression on her face, although Brook wasn't quite sure that wasn't due to the Botox and her inability to smile convincingly. It was honestly hard to tell from Brook's current position inside the warmth of her privately owned vehicle.

The reporter almost certainly had her audience on edge, stirring their imaginations of what could possibly have happened in such a quiet neighborhood. Given that it was taking Fritz so long to make a statement, the anchors back at the news station were probably speculating to the public that it might actually be another of the Princess Killer's victims.

Anything to bump up the ratings.

There was no need to have facts to back up one's assumptions in today's journalism. That was blatantly illustrated by the use of the title commentators rather than true reporters in the industry.

Brook really hated the nickname that the media had come up with for her unsub, knowing full well that the killer enjoyed the moniker. It grated her that the press intentionally stroked his ego, but there wasn't a damn thing she could do about their bias and quite often unethical reporting.

"Who called this in?" Brook finally asked, giving Fritz what he wanted when she turned the key toward her to shut off the ignition. The heat from the vent immediately ceased, and the chill from outside began to take its place. She should have been used to it after all these years, but she couldn't stop the shiver that washed over her body. "Neighbor? Lover? Daughter?"

"Anonymous. Something else for you to look at," Fritz replied with a frown. He stepped away from the car door, but Brook had to turn the ignition back on to roll up the window. Her day certainly hadn't started out in the best possible manner. He continued to fill her in on the details once she'd finally joined him underneath the umbrella. "I have people back at the station tracing the 911 call, but you'll probably have better luck. Unless it's a one-time use burner."

Fritz's assumptions were most likely going to ruin his day. Brook had already caught two details that weren't a match to her unsub, and she never jumped to conclusions.

It wasn't that Fritz didn't have the knowledge or experience, but she'd been dealing with these kinds of serial killers day in and day out for years. Hell, she practically breathed in their rancid scent every time she opened another file.

Brook lifted the hood of the black raincoat so that it covered her head. Fritz wasn't too steady on keeping the umbrella above them.

Besides, the last case that she'd profiled had received national attention, and somehow her picture had been leaked to the press. It was only a matter of time before she faded from memory, but there was no reason to stir the suspicions with the media standing guard as she and Fritz approached the crime scene.

Scott Larson and his crew from a local news station were pulling up now, and two crime vloggers had their phones at the ready to video anything they could use in their podcasts later today.

Matt Henley and Brian Sinclair, if she remembered correctly.

She'd already been contacted by all three, but she made a rule never to give interviews to the press. The broadcasting gods had already drawn their own conclusions, although they might have missed their mark with this one.

It would be nice to turn the tables on them this time around.

"What do you have so far?"

Brook could see the gazes of the crowd monitoring their movements as one of the officers nodded them through the area. There was an undertone of bated breath, as well as caution over what travesty had been committed inside the four walls of this residential home.

"Victim's name is Claudia Brown."

Fritz graciously allowed Brook to walk up the sidewalk first, though she purposefully slowed her pace. Her decelerating stride had nothing to do with the black high heels she'd chosen to wear today, and everything to do with the fact that something might have been overlooked in all the foot traffic through the area of the crime scene.

"Fifty-three-year-old Caucasian female, divorced with two grown children who no longer live at the residence. The daughters have been notified, and I figure you have around twenty minutes before one or both of them arrive on scene."

"Any sign of forced entry?"

"None." Fritz nodded at the lone officer recording names of those who entered as he stood next to the front door, which was made from solid, heavy oak wood. Sturdy, with thick beveled glass windows. Brook quickly confirmed there were no signs of tampering on either the lock or the deadbolt using her own small Maglite that she kept in the pocket of her jacket. "Not even the windows. Brooklyn Sloane, consultant with the FBI."

After the officer had jotted their names on a piece of paper secured to a clipboard under a plastic cover sheet, she lowered her hood and then grabbed a pair of blue shoe covers and a pair of latex gloves from the container beside him. Fritz had closed his umbrella and leaned it up against a wooden railing. It didn't take either of them long to ready themselves before entering the house, ensuring that nothing they did would contaminate whatever physical evidence was found at the crime scene.

Soft murmurs of conversation drifted down from the second story upon her entering the foyer, but the otherwise blanket of heavy silence was quite stifling. The presence of death was unmistakable, and one that Brook was unfortunately very familiar with in her line of work. That didn't stop her from tuning out even the slightest of noises as she canvassed the main floor, room by room.

Her procedures were methodical and well-practiced. She observed everything in sight, with an eye for small details. Comprehensive notes would be made if this murder turned out to be attached to her case.

The victim had done her best to make sure that her house was inviting, ensuring that the décor was rich with warm hues so that unique fabrics and antique furniture complemented one another. Family photos hung on the wall in either wooden or decorated frames to signify unity and love. The kitchen was spacious and obviously served as a gathering place for friends to enjoy food and drinks. The organization of her utensils was purposeful, and it showed that she was well-versed in the kitchen.

Brook noted all of it, but she wasn't looking for the normal scheme of a loving home. Instead, she was searching for the slightest oddity that would set itself apart. She was well aware of the likelihood that every single room might hold a clue as to why the owner had been brutally murdered in her own residence.

Brook made mental notes that would help Fritz later on down the line in his investigation, because she'd already ruled out her unsub by the time that she'd done her first pass on the lower level. Never one to make a decision too early, she waited until they were standing in the doorway of the victim's bedroom to make her final call.

Brook accepted the usual blow to her stomach upon setting her gaze onto the pale, muted body of what had once been a beautiful, vibrant middle-aged woman. The graphic details of the scene before them weren't something any of these law enforcement and forensics officers would easily forget. She doubted any of them could ever erase the memories of the victims whom they strived to seek justice for on any given day.

The body had been dressed postmortem in what looked to be a formal dress, possibly taken from her own closet. There was substantial bruising around her neck. The darker, bluish tint around her lips and the burst blood vessels in her sightless eyes were additional indicators to the fact that she'd been strangled. Some blood had seeped from the victim's abdomen, although the drying stain wasn't too extensive around the fabric of her waist. It suggested that she hadn't died from blood loss, and the wound had quite possibly been done postmortem.

Brook would stick with strangulation for now, but official cause of death was for the autopsy report to reveal.

"Cinderella?" Fritz asked quietly, having been silent the last twenty minutes that she'd used to canvass the house. The only tell in the man's seasoned authority that conveyed his unease with being in the presence of a murder victim was the tapping of his fingers against his brown trench coat. "I don't have kids, but even I know that Cinderella lost her shoe."

Brook had noticed the missing accessory as well, but she'd put money on the matching red heel being somewhere in the woman's closet. It was clear to Brook that whoever had killed this woman suffered from remorse, though Fritz would likely disagree with that sentiment. She'd learned long ago that handholding wasn't good in these situations. It was best to stick with cold, hard facts.

"Fritz, this case has nothing to do with my unsub." Brook slipped her gloved hands inside the pockets of her raincoat, not needing to take another step inside the bedroom. "She's all yours."

There was no missing the communal groans from the members of the local forensics team who thought they'd get to close out their shift at a reasonable hour. Fortunately, it wasn't her problem. The wave of despair from being surrounded by death began to release its restrictive grip with every step she descended toward the entryway.

"What the hell do you mean *she's all yours?*" Fritz spit out after the shock of her statement wore off. He was only two steps behind her now. "The victim is wearing a ball gown, a tiara, and missing a shoe. It's got the fingerprints of your case written all over it."

Brook had a full day on the agenda of combing through old case files in search of that elusive first, sloppy, inexperienced murder that almost every serial killer had in his or her past, and she wasn't looking forward to the resulting migraine from the endless hours ahead of her.

"Fritz, I've viewed every piece of media footage from the previous crimes associated with my unsub over and over these last couple of months. There wasn't one piece of live footage that was conducted in the rain." Brook finally stepped onto the marbled landing, giving herself a little breathing room. She regretted leaving that ninety-nine-cent bribe back in her car. "Do you know why?"

Brook caught sight of herself in the wood-framed mirror hanging on the far wall. The exhaustion of a day that had yet to take place showed in the blemishes underneath her blue eyes. She made a mental note to add more concealer before entering the FBI offices. At least the cold air from outside had given her high cheekbones some color, and she'd used a clip to contain her long, dark hair. The last time she'd let even the slightest hint of fatigue show in her appearance, her supervisor had brought up the fact that she was under contract and could take time off whenever she wanted.

Well, that wasn't going to happen.

What was going to take place was a conversation that Fritz wasn't going to appreciate, but one that might actually help his investigation.

"No, I don't know why, but I'm sure you're going to tell me," Fritz replied in agitation. He was probably wishing he'd kept his kickback, but nothing he said or did was going to change the outcome of her assessment. "Convince me that what I just walked away from isn't a scene straight out of some fucked-up Cinderella fantasy."

"My unsub is meticulous. He's been at this a very long time, and he plans his fantasy down to the finest, miniscule detail as if he were painting a Van Gogh." Brook waved a hand toward the front door. "He's not due to kill for another three weeks. Besides, it's raining. Some of the neighbors across the street are probably watching us from their living room windows. There are some residents who probably can't afford to be late to work, even with all the excitement. While some of these people are huddled across the street, my unsub wouldn't be satisfied with such a meager turnout. He feeds off their reaction to relish in his fantasy."

"That's reaching, Sloane. Even for you."

"You already told me that the victim is divorced, but did you know that she was currently in a committed relationship?" Brook walked over to the entryway table, reopening a drawer that she'd already searched on her first pass. "The victim recently broke up with this man, whom you should bring in for questioning. There's a thin layer of dust on this table, but you can see the spot where a picture frame used to be positioned next to the other photographs. Ms. Brown stored the frame away in this drawer within the last few days, most likely because it hurt her to look at it every time that she walked through her front door."

Fritz glanced over her shoulder in annoyance, making eye contact with the officer manning the entrance. They both probably thought she was only guessing as to who murdered Claudia Brown, but she wasn't done pointing out the most obvious clues.

"Her ex-lover was actually here, if the second wine glass in the dishwasher is anything to go by. My guess is he came to the house last night to try and make amends. Things didn't go well according to the broken wine bottle that is currently in the kitchen trashcan underneath a paper plate. The suspect tried to clean up the pinot noir with her good kitchen hand towels that are also in the garbage. Something the victim would most likely never do herself. They were a gift from one of her children, if the handstitched embroidery is anything to go by—*World's Best Mom.*"

Fritz didn't want to hear the rest, but Brook wasn't close to being done with her analysis. It wasn't that he'd missed anything. He'd just been too hung up on the details of the bedroom to see beyond anything else that had been staged by what was looking more and more like a desperate man.

"The gown your victim was dressed in after she died had blood seeping through the fabric, but not enough to indicate that she'd been alive at the time of the stabbing. There was bruising around her neck. My unsub doesn't strangle his victims, Fritz. Someone took great care to stage this murder so that you'd have reason to look elsewhere." Brook finally gestured toward the kitchen. "The dishwasher was warm, because whoever was here had run it before leaving the residence. Did you look inside? There are two wineglasses and a butcher knife. You're either looking at the ex-lover or the ex-husband, but my bet is on the former. The previous husband is a lawyer, and one who is almost certainly smart enough to know that he'd need to do a better job at getting rid of any evidence. Your unsub isn't the sharpest tool in the shed, and this was most likely a crime of passion."

"How did—"

Fritz almost certainly had been going to ask Brook how she'd ascertained the ex-husband's profession, but she stopped him before he dragged her into an even longer conversation in his attempt to convince her this murder was tied to her investigation.

"Fritz, we've worked together on a few cases. You know me well enough that I don't come into any crime scene blind." Brook was saved from having to continue when two crying women were being stopped from walking up the small path to the front porch. Fritz was about to have his hands full. "You might want to check the security camera at the gas station, too. Twenty bucks says that you'll see the ex-lover driving in and out of the neighborhood sometime in the wee hours of the morning. He may have even used the telephone outside the convenience store to make your anonymous 911 call, if the thing actually still works."

Fritz was a good detective.

As for what kind of man he was in his private life, she didn't know. She didn't want to know. She kept her professional and personal life separate. Some would argue that she didn't even have a personal life, because she was obsessed with her own failings.

They'd be wrong.

Brook did take time for herself now and again, but it factored in at around ten percent. The other ninety? She focused on her current investigations and the one that haunted her dreams until they were menacing nightmares.

Every.

Single.

Night.

"Officer," Brook acknowledged, walking past him and then the two women before they had a chance to ask her any questions.

It didn't take her long to take off the blue shoe covers and latex gloves. She threw them in the second bucket that the officer had made sure was at the end of the walkway.

The drizzling rain had at least lessened to a faint mist, but she still grabbed the hood of her raincoat to pull it over her head.

No need to feed the nest of vipers who were no doubt getting impatient while waiting for Fritz to make a public statement. She also didn't want to get pulled aside by the vloggers who would love to have some guest on their next segment to provide insight to the case involving the Princess Killer.

Even though Brook was confident in the new direction of Fritz's investigation, she still swept her gaze across the gathered crowd that had somewhat dwindled in size since she'd been inside the residence.

She was actually looking for someone in particular, though no one stood out to give her pause.

She did her best to swallow her disappointment, but that was hard to do when the acid in her stomach threatened to come to the surface. Upon reaching her vehicle, she wasn't surprised in the least to find a small business card tucked beneath her windshield wiper.

As a matter of fact, she'd come to expect them at crime scenes, though they were few and far between. She was hardly ever in the field. Her role in the Bureau didn't require her physical presence at any given crime scene.

The individual leaving his or her number had to be listening in on the police dispatch scanners, but she didn't want to alert her superiors quite yet.

What if the identity of the individual was revealed to be who she believed him to be?

What if the man who had been trying to reach out to establish contact with her was, in fact, her biological sibling?

Her big brother.

A serial killer in his own right.

Her own personal brush with evil.

If that was the case, Brook wasn't going to just hand him over to the authorities on a silver platter. Not a chance.

Justice was for her, and her alone.

As was her usual routine, she swiped the evidence from underneath the blade with a bit of frustration, not worried that she'd already thrown away her latex gloves. There no evidence to be had on the small card, of that she was certain. She ended up stashing it with the others in her glove compartment once she'd settled herself behind the wheel.

The original business card with only a cell phone number printed in bold font on one side was in an envelope inside her top desk drawer, having already been processed by someone in forensics who owed her a favor. She'd spent many years collecting those favors, knowing there would come a day when she'd need to call in those chips.

Brook had accepted long ago that her soul and the dark stain that existed inside of her brother would forever remain intertwined until she ended his existence and absolved herself of her own sin of omission.

She was the reason Jacob Walsh still walked among them—the brother whom she'd loved and now reviled with every breath that she inhaled into her body. The man who'd been her protector, but who could snuff out her existence without a sigh of regret.

Her first brush with evil had turned her life into a canvas of torment, and only she had the ability to alter the grotesque image into something else that she could live with on a daily basis.

# CHAPTER THREE

**Brooklyn Sloane**
*November 2021*
*Tuesday—10:44 am*

"ARE YOU SAYING that you disagree with my profile?" Brook asked, not bothering to look up from the file in her hand. She'd made sure that her tone indicated her thoughts on the subject. "It's a simple yes or no answer, Ann. You know me well enough that I won't be offended. If you believe that I've missed something, I'd like to know."

It was now mid-morning, and she'd ended up being the first one into the office. That was usually the case, but she'd been an hour later than her usual start time due to her detour to Virginia. Special Agent Frank Lyle and Special Agent Ann Nelson were seated at the conference table, reading over the changes that she'd made to her profile after the last murder.

The small conference room table was littered with sugar packets, coffee stirrers, and numerous case files that Brook had already combed through in her quest to find the unsub's elusive first kill. They'd kept the blinds open that faced the cubicles in the main area, as well as the door, in order to capture some of the heat blowing down from the vents in the ceiling. The draft coming off the old windows facing the street was just a bit too much for the small room to handle.

The larger conference space across the way was currently occupied by numerous federal agents working a counterintelligence case, so Brook had no choice but to take the cramped, smaller room that had been used mostly for storage until she'd decided to clear it out years ago.

"You're assuming that the unsub lives in the tristate area, but we have no proof he isn't traveling to his hunting ground," Ann replied after she'd closed the manila folder in front of her. She leaned back in the chair and attempted to get Frank on board with her opinion. Brook didn't have to look up from the somewhat interesting crime report to know that he was shaking his head in warning. "Do you agree with this? If she's wrong, then we'll have wasted days searching through old crime reports that might have nothing to do with our case."

"There's always a first kill, and I haven't seen Brook get a profile wrong yet," Frank hedged as he leaned back in his seat until the wheels complained. He tried to smooth down the edges of the mustache that he'd been growing out, but the coarse hair had some greys in it that had a mind of their own. "We've been after this unsub for five months, and her profile has basically predicted the next time he plans on taking the life of another so-called princess. If Brook is right, we'll have another body on our hands the first or second week of December. Other than that, we have nothing. It can't hurt to focus our search for the time being."

The one benefit that Brook had taken away from being the sister of a serial killer was the ability to camouflage what she was thinking at all times. It didn't matter if she experienced anger, remorse, irritation, or even sadness. She had the capability to cover up a multitude of emotions without anyone being the wiser.

"Let's start from the beginning," Brook said before picking up one of the pens that had been left behind from the last task force that had previously used the space. The small room might not be the most ideal, but it would be theirs until this case was either solved or shelved. As of three months ago, this was an active serial murder case. "So far, we have four victims—Chrissy Aper, Selma Diaz, Jessica Monroe, and Beth Lindsey. We reasonably suspect there are more out there, but I'm still combing through case files to match up the similarities. Their bodies were all staged as if they took part in some fairytale setting."

Brook scanned the victims' faces that were taped to the first white board, noticing all the differences between them. Such a thing only made their job harder.

"Our unsub doesn't seem to care about race or age. Nor does he prefer a woman with a specific hair style, eye color, or any other physical trait that we've been able to deduce." It was unusual for a serial killer to not have a type of some sort, which could only mean one thing. Well, it could technically have several meanings, but she was focused on one in particular. "I believe he's subconsciously going through the various princesses in the fairytales that he was read to as a child."

"Your profile states that the unsub inserts himself in their lives, but we've seen no evidence that these women were dating anyone who fits the profile," Ann pointed out as she grabbed another sugar packet. The first three must not have been enough. "As a matter of fact, Selma Diaz was actively dating a prominent lawyer."

"Beth Lindsey was also dating a college junior," Frank interjected after looking at his notes. He was closest to the case since he'd been the one to visit the family right after the young woman's murder. "Is he simply picking these women based on how closely they resemble a fictional character?"

"I believe our unsub meets them and establishes some kind of minor social connection." It was clear that neither Ann nor Frank were too keen on her theory. "In his mind, though. The victims wouldn't necessarily believe it had any significant meaning. Anyway, we're looking for a Caucasian male, thirty-five to forty-five years of age, and manipulative in nature. He would be employed somewhere that doesn't notice his lack of dedication to anything other than searching for his ideal woman, and in a position that doesn't allow his colleagues to monitor his movements closely. We could either be looking at someone who travels or works remotely, giving him the ability to come and go as he pleases. Something that gives him free reign to pursue these women."

"Princess," Frank inserted, gesturing toward the crime scene photos on the first white board. "He views his victims as princesses from a fairytale."

"The unsub lacks empathy and even sees himself as a victim of circumstance. It can be assumed that his mother is the reason for his obsession with fables and myths." Brook didn't comment on Ann's lack of contribution. "The fact that his kills are getting closer together indicates that he's on the verge of losing control of his impulses. The first murder that we have managed to connect to the unsub was Chrissy Aper, three years ago. The consecutive murders each took place roughly a year apart, though one month earlier than the previous. He's nowhere near done with his search. All these case files in front of you have been gathered from field offices across the tristate area. Each one fits within a specific set of parameters that I established in my original profile."

Brook had spent most of the morning rearranging one of the three whiteboards that she'd had delivered by maintenance up from the basement last month. Currently taped and visible to them were crime scene photos of four murders that had basically spanned a four-year period. It wasn't until five months ago that a local police department located in a small town of Ohio had discovered the connection that their case might be connected to the one in West Virginia.

The timeframe that Frank had mentioned had been pulled from Brook's first profile upon receiving the case. It took the unsub close to nine to twelve months to find, monitor, and then kill his victims. He was getting more skillful and mindful of his methods with each murder, but she suspected that he'd been working under the radar for many, many years.

He was perfecting his process.

Ergo, his first attempt at taking a life had probably been less refined, and he may have inadvertently left evidence behind at the crime scene.

The unsub was going to have to alter his usual habits now that the cases had been linked and the FBI had been pulled into the investigation. The media had basically been splashing his work all over the national news. He wasn't used to the attention.

"It's the Monroe case where the unsub utilized what you could consider a fairytale taken from a local urban legend about a miner who created a shrine out of coal for the woman of his dreams that had me narrowing down his location," Brook reiterated from last week's meeting. Jessica Monroe had been murdered over two years ago, but it was her case that had been the reason for Brook's decision. "I don't believe that the unsub spent much time researching this fable. No matter how hard that I personally tried to find this particular urban legend, it just hasn't been posted to a site that would make it easy for just anyone to find. As we know, some tales are retold over and over again by generations of families within a specific region."

Brook didn't want Ann or Frank to believe that there had been no mention of the coal miner's legend online, because that wasn't technically accurate. She could still be wrong in the foundation of the profile that she'd written up previously, but as Frank had already disclosed…those moments were rare.

She wasn't being smug or arrogant, but she was confident in the skills that she'd honed while being employed by the Bureau.

"There were a few social media sites created by some local teenagers that referenced the tale, but the details are really only ever shared in small towns within these three states, especially coal mining areas. Besides, the unsub likes to spend his free time looking for his perfect princess. This fable had to have been told to him sometime during his childhood, and he did his best to reenact one of the core scenes."

Brook had already gone over these details with Frank and Ann, but it didn't hurt to go over the information again. These agents had other cases that they were working on, although she preferred to concentrate on one at a time until either the unsub was caught or the case had come to a complete dead-end with no end in sight.

Being a consultant gave her that leeway.

"The three states that you listed are Ohio, Pennsylvania, and

West Virginia," Ann replied in a rather resigned manner. "I take it all of these new files that you've gathered are from the smaller police departments that are struggling to get their older cases online?"

"Yes." Brook wasn't going to sugarcoat it, because it was going to take all three of them to search through numerous murder investigations that might have been overlooked to be in connection with something bigger. "We're searching for the unsub's first murder, thus his initial mistakes. No one is perfect the first time that he or she takes someone's life. Our unsub's first foray is somewhere in these case files, and we just need to find it."

Brook rubbed her eyes when one of the fluorescent bulbs overhead began to flicker. It reminded her of the one in her office, in spite of her having put in a work order for building maintenance days ago. They hadn't gotten around to fixing it, but she probably wasn't high on their list of priorities. Not having a title within the agency tended to knock her status down a bit.

There actually *were* some drawbacks to being a consultant.

Technically, she was nothing more than a mere professor who had taught classes in criminal profiling and psychology. It had been one of her case studies that she'd written for an assignment given to her students that had garnered interest from a local detective. The profile that she'd put together had been in regard to a string of murders that had taken place on a university campus.

The local police had apprehended the suspect based on her paper, given to them by one of her students. One thing had led to another until a federal agent had shown up after one of her lectures and requested a bit of her time.

Supervisory Special Agent Matthew Harden had taken her to lunch, explained that he was interested in hiring her as a consultant for the Bureau, and ultimately ended up being the one who'd convinced her to leave her field of studies for something more satisfying.

He hadn't been wrong, in the grand scheme of things.

She had wondered countless of times if he hadn't regretted such a personal vested interest in her career, though. He'd known about her past, the reason that she'd changed her surname before entering college, and why profiling had become an obsession, of sorts.

Matt had even agreed to her caveat of keeping her past a secret from those who didn't need to know anything about her during the hiring process. She hadn't wanted to be known as the sister to a serial killer. One who still remained at large yet had oddly been forgotten about over the years. Matt had kept his promise, with the exception of the agent who'd conducted her background check, two other supervisory agents, and the director.

"Brook?"

She quickly realized that she'd been caught staring at the whiteboard for longer than she'd intended. She cleared her throat and squinted her eyes, as if she'd been preoccupied with one of the photographs that she'd taped to the hard surface. It took her a moment to realize that Frank had been warning her of someone approaching the conference room. She finally caught the shadow moving across the greyish blue carpet right outside the door.

She didn't much care for the sense of déjà vu, but at least she hadn't been caught off guard when her supervisor filled the doorframe.

"Sloane."

"Yes, sir?" Brook replied, closing the case file that she'd been reading earlier. There were details inside that had her wanting to take a second look at the crime scene photos. Apparently, they would have to wait. "We were just going over the profile that I left on your desk last night."

"My office," Supervisory Special Agent Matthew Harden said without mentioning the reason the why. "Now."

Harden didn't wait for her to follow him.

Brook took her time in replacing the file on top of one of the numerous stacks that she'd claimed for herself. She'd sort through them later this afternoon. She'd be able to pick up right where she'd left off, provided that Ann and Frank respected her domain.

"I know that you both have other cases, but the boxes on the floor are arranged by state. The two of you have a choice between Ohio and West Virginia," Brook said as she ignored the two of them exchanging glances with one another. She didn't have to be a psychic to know that she was most likely about to get an ass-chewing. Their minds weren't even on the case at the moment. "I've already started on the criminal reports from Pennsylvania. A few have caught my interest, and I'll look more into them later today."

Brook pushed her chair back and reached for her suit jacket. The good thing about switching from academia to the agency was that her wardrobe hadn't needed to be changed. She still wore pantsuits with buttoned down blouses. She envied those women who could wear skirts, but not even pantyhose or tights could keep the chill she continued to experience at bay.

Hell, she was always cold and had been since the day that she'd discovered her brother had taken the life of her best friend.

It was the day that her life had ceased to move forward.

# CHAPTER FOUR

**Brooklyn Sloane**
*November 2021*
*Tuesday—11:01 am*

"Anything I need to know before I meet with Harden?" Brook asked as she buttoned her suit jacket. "One of you has to testify in court sometime soon, right?"

"I'm following up with the Lindsey family and their neighbors," Frank replied after he'd taken out a small notebook from the pocket of his dress shirt. He flipped it open to the first page. "The brother of the victim mentioned that the next-door neighbors were having plumbing issues. It's probably nothing, but I'd like to get the name of the company. Maybe they do contract work for other vendors in surrounding cities across state borders. I'll place some phone calls to them this afternoon."

Brook nodded her agreement. The Lindsey family was located in West Virginia. Unless Frank had more than a few follow-up questions, a trip wouldn't be warranted or signed off by the supervisory agent.

She'd already ruled out truckers and those with similar professions, including a blue-collar job such as a plumber. The unsub who they were looking for would much prefer a desk job of some sort that allowed for travel. He'd want to be able to impress his victims, most likely in an attempt to garner their attention. It was when they refused his advances or didn't cast a glance his way that the rejections would eventually lead to their deaths.

"Ann? What about you?"

The other federal agent grimaced, and Brook refrained from saying anything that could be taken out of context. She and Ann hadn't seen eye to eye on many things, although they'd only ever worked one case together before. They had completely different personalities, and Ann wasn't fond of working with consultants who bucked FBI procedures. She'd made that abundantly clear, but Brook wasn't at the agency to make friends.

She had no friends, and it would remain that way until Jacob was lying six feet underground.

"I'll start going through these files as soon as I get back from New York," Ann replied as she checked the time on her phone. "My flight leaves in three hours. I should be back by Friday."

Frank began to rub his mustache again in clear amusement.

Brook didn't even bother to reply, because Ann should at least have had the courtesy to say something about being gone for the rest of the work week. There were some profilers who only wrote up their reports and sent them to the assigned agents before moving onto the next.

Those were the profilers who Ann preferred to work with on her assignments.

Those agents had their credentials, and Brook was nothing more than a mere consultant who had been given a bit of latitude regarding her involvement with investigations.

"Have a good trip, Ann," Brook replied curtly, picking up her own phone before walking around the table. She wasn't going to give the female agent the satisfaction of a rebuke, which would then be taken up with Harden. Brook was already about to be on the receiving end of a lecture, and she sure as hell didn't need another one. She nodded toward Frank with mutual respect. "Let me know what you find out about the plumber's van."

As Brook began to walk across the main area, she could hear Frank chide Ann for being adversarial and completely unprofessional. The two of them had worked together for a lot longer than Brook had been with the agency, and she was envious of their ability to be themselves with one another.

Images of her best friend's lifeless body flashed through her mind.

After further thought, Brook wasn't envious.

There was a reason that she kept people at a distance, though that pretext could be coming to an end. Was Jacob the one leaving her business cards at random crime scenes?

It wasn't his style, though she wouldn't be his lab rat if it turned out to be him. She wouldn't be lured to follow the scent of cheese into a trap. If Jacob was finally reaching out to her, then he would literally have to show his face before he could solicit a reaction.

Matt occupied a corner office.

His door was still open, and she braced herself for the reprimand that she was about to receive for going against the Bureau's policy on dealing with local departments. It was the only thing she'd done in the last few days that would warrant Matt's attention.

She and Fritz had developed a professional association that she had spent time cultivating over the years. It had taken her a long time to stack the building blocks that she needed to flush out Jacob, and she wouldn't apologize for the quid pro quo that she'd established with local law enforcement. There was bound to be a time when she needed a favor from Fritz, and she wanted him on her side for when she made that inevitable call.

"Is there a reason that I didn't get notified about the walkthrough that you made in Virginia this morning?" Supervisory Special Agent Matthew Harden asked the moment that she had walked through his office door. "I had to hear from Ann that you were out in the field earlier today without prior authorization. We've had this discussion more than a few times. That's not the way we work around here, and you know that."

Brook stood just inside the doorway, not bothering to take a seat. They'd been through this rodeo before, and she'd fully expected this lecture before her second cup of coffee. Besides, he was tidying up his desk, and that was something that he only did when he was leaving his office for more than fifteen minutes.

"I apologize, sir. I was simply returning a favor."

Brook had always addressed him with respect. Just because he was the one who had lured her through the agency's doors didn't mean that there wasn't a line drawn in the sand. She wanted to draw the discussion to a close before the lecture dragged on longer than necessary, though. It was clear that he had places to be, and she had case files to look through.

"Detective Fritz thought there might be a chance that our unsub could have claimed a victim in Virginia. I was already on my way into the office when I received the call. I didn't see any need to go through official channels when I was relatively certain his murder case had nothing to do with our investigation. He was simply informally collecting on a chip that I owed him from an earlier case."

Matt was just doing his job, and she could respect his position. She'd basically ignored procedure in favor of personal convenience, leaving her department head in the dark before conducting a field operation.

Add in her use of a personally operated vehicle to conduct official business, and she had formally violated of her professional security training agreement that she'd been required to sign upon her employment. The agreement was something similar to the one that the cadets had to endorse after their training, though she'd spotted a loophole or two in the addendum to her consulting contract.

Brook would save those clauses for when they really mattered, meaning when the time came that it was her ass on the chopping block. She understood that interagency guidelines were put in place for a reason.

In her defense, it had been a simple homicide case that had nothing to do with any federal investigation. It certainly hadn't come as a shock to know that Ann had been the one to rat her out, either. Ann resented having to follow the recommendations of a non-FBI resource.

Brook didn't bother to add on that she'd been right in judgement at the crime scene, confirmed by a voice message that she'd received an hour ago from Fritz explaining that the ex-lover of Claudia Brown had spilled his guts on record after they'd escorted him into the interrogation room.

Hell, the man had even broken down without asking for a lawyer.

Brook had no doubt that a twenty-dollar gift card for the steakhouse down the block would show up in the mail by the end of the week. It was standard practice amongst local agencies to reward anyone instrumental in clearing a murder case with a steak dinner. She had a pile of them in a candy dish on her breakfast bar.

She routinely re-gifted them whenever possible.

"We've taken some pretty bad hits in the media recently. I really don't want to get pulled into another meeting about you not following protocol. Nor do I want you get popped out on your own playing Clarice and adding yourself to this scumbag's list of victims."

Harden appeared to want to say more on the subject, but he brought himself up short.

She did the same when it was on the tip of her tongue to remind him that she wasn't an official agent. She also wasn't a cadet, fresh out of the Academy and investigating homicides on her own. At least he hadn't brought up the fact that Virginia was quite the detour from her condo in the heart of D.C.

"I'm heading out for the day," Harden said with a frown. "I overheard some of the other agents say they were meeting for a few drinks after work. Why don't you join them? You could use a little social interaction with your coworkers. You know, ease some the tension that's been hanging in the air."

Harden's push to get Brook to join her colleagues for some after-work bonding sessions had become more frequent lately. He understood perfectly well why she wasn't the social type, but something had him ignoring the limitations that she'd set forth a long time ago.

"I'll be pulling a late night, so I don't think that's going to fit into my evening plans." Brook's standard reply had Harden jiggling the keys in the front pocket of his trousers. It was his one tell when he was agitated, and he'd recently been doing more and more of the annoying habit. "Matt, what's going on?"

Brook rarely used Harden's first name in the office, but they'd cultivated an odd pseudo-personal relationship over the last seven years, ever since he'd asked her to lunch that fateful day. He'd taken her under his wing and become a mentor of sorts. He wasn't the type of supervisor who micromanaged, but he was rather easy to read.

Matt didn't reply right away, so Brook stepped closer to his desk until she was around two feet in front of him. It was then that she realized he'd yet to look her directly in the eyes. That had only happened once before, and it was when it had to do with one of her past psych evaluations. She'd managed to tread very carefully after that incident, and she hadn't been required to see the agency's shrink for close to eighteen months.

Harden's uneasiness had to do with something else.

Besides, she had her own therapist that no one in the department knew about under a manufactured alias that couldn't be linked back to her. Working for the agency had taught her a thing or two that hadn't been covered during any of her college classes. The rest, well…she wasn't too proud to admit that she'd learned a thing or two from her brother.

Therapy with Dr. Neil Swift wasn't technically helping, but it wasn't hurting, either. One couldn't be too careful in this day and age with an individual who knew all of one's secrets, especially with the sensitive topics brought up in her sessions.

They certainly weren't for the faint of heart.

"Where were you last weekend?"

The question had come out of nowhere.

Brook didn't like to be caught off guard, and she always went the extra mile to make sure that it didn't happen too often. Their conversation could have gone several ways and in regards of about a hundred other issues, but what she did on her time off wasn't one of them—ever.

"Since when did my personal time become a point of concern for the Bureau?" Brook hated that she'd been put on the defensive, and she needed a minute before turning the conversation around. "If you're asking me, then you already know I flew into Peoria, Illinois before driving over to Morton. What? A daughter can't visit her elderly father without official inquiries being made?"

Harden jiggled those keys of his again, but this time he would just have to deal with his own agitation. She'd been patient with him. She'd done nothing wrong, and she wasn't going to give a recount of every second that she spent in her childhood hometown.

It appeared that her leash was getting shorter by the day, just as Fritz had mentioned earlier this morning. She didn't appreciate her movements being restricted or questioned, especially when it involved her personal time. She thought that she'd made that abundantly clear a long time ago.

Apparently, she was wrong.

"You and I both know that you didn't go to Morton, Illinois to visit your elderly father," Harden declared, almost as a challenge.

It was one that she wouldn't take without being better prepared.

She did her best not to fold her arms in a manner that he would take as a defensive gesture, just as she refused to be the one to break eye contact. What she did with her weekends had no bearing on how she performed the professional responsibilities of her job, which was the sole reason she'd made sure her that closure rate was the highest of any field agent inside the agency.

No one could question her dedication or work ethic.

"Feel free to call the nursing home, Matt."

"Jackson knows you've been using the agency's resources," Harden finally revealed, causing her to question who had been the one to disclose that bit of information. "He wouldn't give me details, but he was confident enough in the accusation that I would say he heard it firsthand from someone familiar with your daily activities."

She was always so careful when calling in certain favors, which meant only two people could be responsible for the fact that she could potentially have her contract revoked. She sensed that Harden would do what he could to ensure that wouldn't happen, but even she was aware that some things were out of his hands.

"I was able to get him to let it slide this once, but I can't keep him off your back if you continue to go down this road," Harden warned with a grimace. "Jackson has always had a beef with me bringing you into the agency, and you know why. You've got to let this go. It's a professional conflict of interest."

Brook bit the inside of her lip to keep from arguing with him, because she would never stop searching for her brother. Arguing about her situation was pointless, though. Jacob was out there somewhere, and she was the one most likely to find him. The lesson here was to choose her utilization of resources a little more carefully.

It wasn't like she had any right to be angry with her boss. He was simply doing his job.

Matt was only looking out for her, and he took it personally when his department got caught underneath the magnifying glass of anyone outside of his department, including the higher brass. They'd been on this merry-go-round before, and he was about to launch into his positive mental health speech about how one should live life to the fullest and not dwell on the past.

Well, he didn't have to personally live with a guilt that continued to devour her soul in spite of the circumstances that her brother hadn't been seen or heard from in close to seventeen years.

She was to blame for Jacob escaping justice.

No one else.

"You know what? You're right," Brook said with a half-smile. "I should listen to your advice."

It was a hasty decision, but the unsub dubbed the Princess Killer by certain salacious media outlets could wait until tomorrow. If her profile was on point, he wasn't due to kill another victim for another three to four weeks.

She could make up for lost time tomorrow.

Right now, she had to pay a visit to someone who was no longer on her list of individuals who she would owe favors to after allowing her to be served up on a silver platter. It was best to sever ties in person. She certainly wouldn't want there to be any misunderstandings.

"I think I'll take some personal time this afternoon," Brook said, mostly just to get Harden to back off until she had time to clean up a few loose ends. "Ann is flying out to New York in a few hours, but I might meet up with Frank and some of the other agents after a much-needed shopping spree. You know, to make some of those interpersonal social interactions a little stronger."

"Brook, I didn't mean—"

"You don't get to have it both ways, Matt."

Once again, she'd used his first name to make this personal. It was, and he knew very well that her brother was the sole reason she was so good at her job. Matt didn't get her without getting a piece of Jacob.

It all came back to her brother.

Every.

Single.

Time.

"You have a good rest of your day."

Brook left her supervisor standing in his office. She fully believed that she'd made the right choice to walk away without delving into her past as he was so eager to do on these rare occasions. The end result would most likely have left her without a job.

She was angrier with herself that she'd let her barriers lapse in her search for Jacob.

Given the vast universe, spending twenty-four years with pure malevolence was nothing more than a mere speck of sand in an eternal desert. She would continue to be a patron of that hellish, desolate place until she forged that fragment of sand into a crystal-clear looking glass devoid of imperfection or flaw.

Brook had made that very promise to herself the day that she'd discovered her best friend's body lying dead in a pool of blood…all at the expense of Jacob's evil whim. What he didn't know was that her thirst for revenge was just as relentless as his thirst for sin.

# CHAPTER FIVE

**Brooklyn Sloane**
*November 2021*
*Tuesday—11:12 am*

B ROOK DIDN'T LINGER after she'd grabbed her purse and dress coat off the small oak coatrack that she'd purchased at a quaint antique shop on Georgia Avenue. With her office being so small, the hardwood stand helped her keep things organized.

She didn't like clutter.

It was one of the very few traits that she shared with her brother.

Her office hadn't rated windows at the Bureau. The HVAC vent only worked about half the time, regardless of whether heat or cooling was required, and the space was cramped. All three reasons were why she usually left her door open most of the time.

With that said, her office was still her private domain. That never stopped her colleagues from wandering in to engage her in conversation about a profile without the standard courteous knock, but she wouldn't be here the rest of the day, so it didn't matter.

By the time that she'd made it to the elevator, she was already regretting not swinging by the conference room and grabbing some of the files that she had so painstakingly sought for the last few weeks. However, she could spend the rest of the afternoon mulling over what she'd discovered in Illinois last weekend over a glass of wine…or two. After, of course, she made a pitstop to let a certain someone know that his services would no longer be required.

One thing was for certain, she wouldn't be joining any of her colleagues at a bar this evening. What an inane custom—meeting in a dark social venue and proceeding to drink alcohol until they blurted something out that they would never disclose if they were sober. Brook had never been the social butterfly, nor was she a person who would stab a colleague in the back. Two attributes that she counted in her favor.

With the rest of the day's plans laid out before her, it took her less than four minutes to reach her vehicle in the attached parking garage and even less than a millisecond for her to realize that someone was waiting for her. She came to an abrupt halt around three feet from the back end of her car. The obscurity of the darkness was unfortunately enough to conceal the man's face.

"You never called the number that I gave you. One that I provided on numerous occasions."

The man didn't seem too pleased that his persistence hadn't paid off, which was the exact reason she hadn't made the call. It was a point in her favor, and she now considered herself to have the upper hand. Whatever he'd instigated between them wasn't a competition, but she obtained satisfaction that he understood she wouldn't be made anyone's puppet.

Brook took her time answering as she purposefully relaxed her stance, even taking the time to casually survey the area around them. The silver sedan ten spaces away was the only vehicle out of place, and she'd promptly memorized the license plate number. Harden wouldn't be able to give her another lecture regarding using federal resources if it were due to her safety, especially since she was still technically on Bureau property during said encounter.

The deep voice that had come from within the shadows was older than she would have initially guessed, and not the one that she'd been hoping was the individual trying to contact her. Truthfully, the disappointment was rather overwhelming, but that didn't mean Jacob hadn't sent a hired hand or possibly an acolyte do his bidding.

She quickly discarded that thought, though.

Her brother was a loner.

He'd never ask anyone to do anything for him.

"I wasn't in the mood to talk over the phone," Brook replied without a hint of fear in her tone. For one, he wouldn't have been allowed access to this garage without some type of clearance. Two, she could easily draw her weapon before he could reach her. "Mr…?"

Brook had left her raincoat in the backseat of her car before heading inside the building, having exchanged it for her dress coat. The long overlay, plus her suit jacket, concealed her firearm without leaving an imprint. Unfortunately, that meant she had to brush aside two layers to have access to her weapon, thus reducing her response time to any perceived imminent threat.

She didn't take her gaze off her target as she slowly slipped her right hand underneath the fabric, fully prepared for him to make a move. One might need authorization to enter the garage and building, but that didn't mean this individual had gone through the proper channels to obtain appropriate credentials.

"Graham Elliott."

The name meant nothing to her, but Mr. Elliott wouldn't be here unless he needed something from her. Considering he'd spent the last couple of months baiting her in some type of cat and mouse game to demonstrate his importance and skill level, his request must be quite impressive indeed.

Brook wracked her brain once more for even the slightest familiarity.

There was none.

She'd never heard his name before, even in passing.

The one thing she had to her advantage was that she'd held her ground and forced him to come to her in person. He didn't seem pleased that she hadn't given in to the overwhelming curiosity that had only continued to build over the last three months.

She didn't participate in mind games with subjects who weren't part of her investigations.

"You obviously have something to discuss with me. I suggest you use your time wisely," Brook instructed, having time to brace herself when he finally emerged from the shadows. After this cloak and dagger pursuit, she'd expected to recognize him from either a case or the local coffee shop, but he was a complete stranger. "What is it you need, Mr. Elliott?"

There was no mistaking that Graham Elliott was former military or possibly a serving member. The straight posture and the close-cropped hairstyle stood out like harbor beacons on a moonless night, but it was also the way his tie was perfectly knotted with a full Windsor at his neckline and the manner in which his shoes were freshly shined without a hint of scruff.

She'd also accurately predicted that he was older than her,

and his voice matched his appearance—authoritative. The methodical way he spoke gave way to his intelligence, but it was his intense gaze that had her altering her earlier supposition about generic military service. He hadn't just been in the service, rather he had most likely been a commanding officer of either the Navy or Marines. Given his age of around fifty-five, she presumed he'd retired within the last year or even more recently.

"I hear that you're the best at what you do."

Brook wasn't the type of woman who needed to hear praise or be given compliments to feel any sense of self-worth. One would think she'd be in short supply of any dignity given her tragic past, but it was the complete opposite. He was beginning to come across as a headhunter for one of the other alphabet agencies. She wasn't interested in working for a clandestine agency for any amount of money.

Brook was damn good at profiling serial killers precisely because of her past. The FBI was the best fit for her personal situation, given her priorities. She was confident that Mr. Elliott was wasting his time, as well as her own.

The intuition that she'd spent honing over the years was all but screaming that this was some sort of tentative approach to poach her from the FBI's ranks. It was obvious that Mr. Elliott was keeping his cards and those of the agency that he represented close to his chest. He seemed to be under the illusion that she was playing his high-stake poker game when she hadn't even stepped into the room.

If she had to guess correctly, he was studying her in the same way she was him in order to come to some kind of decision.

"I have somewhere to be, Mr. Elliott. State your purpose." Brook's suit jacket fell back into place when she moved her hand, reaching for her car keys in the outer pocket of her purse. She always stored them in the side for easy access. "If you have a crime to report, I suggest you call your local police department."

The only indication that Brook had hit a nerve by not showing more interest in what Mr. Elliott had to say was the slight compression of his lips. He'd grown impatient that she hadn't appeared more curious as to the reason he'd sought her out.

Again, there was no need to continue the conversation.

She had the upper hand.

She wasn't about to give up her position, especially when he was going to reveal those cards that he was still holding so close to his chest in under five seconds.

"You don't like small talk. I can appreciate that, but I'm not exactly what you suspect."

Mr. Elliott seemed to have come to some conclusion that she wasn't privy to, but her stance against making small talk succeeded in moving this meeting along.

"You'll find a case file in your personal email, along with a job offer that I believe you'll accept. The salary being proposed is double what you're making as a consultant for the Bureau. You'll have full reign to hire a professional support team of your own specifications, your choice of location for the office space, and you'll get complete access to my list of contacts. I can assure you that they are as good as your own, if not better. Finally, I don't work for any of the intelligence agencies that you are currently picking over in your mind."

Brook had gone the last few months believing that her brother had somehow been trying to reach out to her, maybe playing a game of tag like they used to do back in the day.

Hell, maybe that was why she didn't like playing these types of games.

She also wasn't much in the mood for participating in a childhood memory, especially after all of them had been tarnished by the blood of Jacob's victims.

To be standing in front a complete stranger and be offered a job in the private sector hadn't even crossed her mind as to the reason this man would want to speak with her. She had her own government assets at her disposal. What would make him believe that she would give up her career to work as some private detective?

"Mr. Elliott, I—"

Brook's refusal was cut off when he reached into the inner pocket of his dress coat and pulled out a folded piece of paper.

He very precisely laid it down on the trunk of her vehicle.

"Supervisory Special Agent Matthew Harden has done his best to protect you from those who were opposed to your contract," Mr. Elliot said of information that he shouldn't have been privy to as a civilian. "While he's succeeded so far, those up the chain would rather you be relegated to a field office somewhere in Wyoming where you aren't tempted to use their resources to search for your brother. It's bad press, and it's only a matter of time before they get their way. They'd much prefer that Harden immediately cancel your agreement with the agency, thereby limiting the risk of it getting out that they hired the sister of a serial killer. Harden is unlikely to do that considering that he's the one who brought you onboard. The bottom line is the brass doesn't want a potential stain that they can't clean off their reputation, but they also don't want to be breach your contract in case you decide not to go quietly. You are a needless liability as far as they are concerned."

Brook remained silent, wondering just what information that piece of paper held about her potential future. Was this Mr. Elliot's way of proving he had high level contacts within the Bureau itself? Or was this his way of persuading her to work for him in some unusual job position?

She hadn't been spontaneous since the age of ten, and with good reason.

Brook would wait until she was in private before reading whatever was printed on the letterhead. Maybe what caught her most off guard was the fact that he didn't seem to mind that she had the familial blood of a serial killer running through her veins.

She remained silent long enough that it prompted him to end the conversation.

"You don't strike me as the type of profiler who'd be happy in Wyoming screening vanilla carbon copy reports of government separatists. This is your chance to leave the Bureau with your head above water and your professional reputation intact. This is a very small community when it comes down to brass tacks." Mr. Elliot began to walk toward the silver Mercedes with very purposeful strides, as if he had someplace else to be. It wasn't until he was a few feet from his vehicle that he stopped and looked back over his shoulder. "My offer is sincere and a step forward in your own career progression, Ms. Walsh. I look forward to hearing from you soon."

Brook did her best not to wince at the sound of her biological surname.

He was quite aware that it would get under her skin, but she'd be damned if she gave him the satisfaction of soliciting a reaction. She purposefully remained where she was until he had settled in behind the steering wheel of his car.

She wasn't surprised when he backed up his vehicle and met her gaze in the rearview mirror. Was he expecting her to stop him from driving away? He'd have to wait until hell froze over, but he didn't seem so inclined as he finally shifted the gear into drive and slowly pulled away.

Cautiously, as if a snake was coiled and ready to strike, Brook made her way to where the piece of paper still laid on the trunk of her car. She unfolded the crease and held her breath as she perused the contents. Sure enough, it was correspondence between Jackson and the director about the authority of reassigning her out of D.C. per her contract.

There was no mention of Wyoming, but Mr. Elliot's point was still valid.

Brook had no doubt that she'd be working some counter-intelligence investigations far away from D.C. that kept her from her sole purpose—hunting her only brother.

Jacob Matthew Walsh was somewhere on the East Coast, and her time to find him was running out like tiny particles of sand in an hourglass. She really hated being just another tiny speck among many identical grains. Mr. Elliot somehow had known all about her brother, and yet he was still offering her the ability to pursue Jacob while working in the private sector.

That kind of proposal came with a high price, though.

Was she willing to pay it?

Brook didn't care for someone else to have the upper hand. Now that she had Graham Elliot's name, she'd put out some feelers with those she could trust. Hopefully, she'd have enough information on him within the next forty-eight hours to figure out who she was dealing with and what his motives were for wanting to retain her services.

In the meantime, Brook needed to pay a visit to the one person who was responsible for the letter currently in her possession. Technically, she had no one to blame but herself. She also wasn't going to be the only one doused in gasoline when the building burst into flames.

# CHAPTER SIX

**Brooklyn Sloane**
*November 2021*
*Tuesday—12:24 pm*

"Was it worth it?"

Brook hadn't bothered to stop by her condo to change clothes. She would have gone unnoticed in this seedy bar had she worn ripped jeans, a pair of knee-high black boots, and a matching leather jacket.

That particular outfit was currently hidden away in the back of her bedroom closet.

She'd learned along the way that fitting into her surroundings gave her the advantage to go unnoticed, and it was something that she'd picked up before her days with the agency. She'd been hunting Jacob a very long time, and Matt wasn't some young naïve agent who couldn't sense those things about a person.

As for the clientele of this fine establishment, they were already giving her a few sideways glares that told of their annoyance at her intrusive presence. Good news for them. She wouldn't be sticking around long enough for anyone to openly convey their irritation.

"What the hell?" Bobby "Bit" Nowacki exclaimed as he came

out of a bathroom that no one could pay her to enter, let alone use.

His alarm at her sudden appearance was evident when he pulled back in surprise. He worked as an informant for one of the agents in the FBI's cybercrime unit, and it had taken her a good eight months of investigation into Bit's personal history to gain some leverage on him, if needed.

Today was that day.

The man's blond hair always seemed to appear a bit greasy, and he had an oblong face with a rather long nose. The pallor of his skin made it known that he didn't like to be out in the sun too much, and he somehow lost even more color when he recognized who had ambushed him outside of a urinal.

"Are you trying to get me killed? Jesus Christ, you can't be here."

The bass of the music drowned out most of his words, but she didn't have to be a lipreader to know what he was trying to convey. She jerked her head to the side, grateful that she'd had the forethought to pull her hair away from her face. There was a specific criminal element who preferred to hang out at this bar, and it wouldn't be wise to let her peripheral vision be hindered by anything.

The fact that she had dark brown hair with a black dress coat was the only thing that helped her blend in with the heavily lacquered tables and chairs that had been set up against walls that had probably never been washed. She walked with purpose over to an empty table and kicked a chair out with the toe of one of her high heels.

"Sit."

Brook didn't care who heard them, and he was smart enough

to know that she wasn't about to get sucked in by his innocent routine. He was the type who would look twenty when he hit his fifties. Right now, he was only twenty-four years old and didn't look old enough to be served without a bartender asking for identification. She'd come to realize that he wasn't as easily manipulated as most.

They were obviously drawing the attention of others, so he quickly did as she instructed.

"You think that I don't know you've been mining Bitcoin for the last year under the direction of Kuzmich so that he can buy illegal weapons on the dark web?" Brook's question had certainly garnered his full attention. "I'm guessing that Agent Calabro hasn't been fully informed of what you've been up to, but I have a mind to return the favor that you've apparently done for me. I mean, it's fairly clear to me that you disclosed to him the nature of our deal."

"I didn't have a choice," Bit replied quickly, leaning forward so that their conversation didn't travel too far. That was highly unlikely with the low bass still coming out of the speakers overhead. "Calabro was getting too close to figuring out that I've been helping Kuzmich. I don't mind snitching on the local thugs, but I might as well dig my own grave if Kuzmich thinks that I'm ratting him out to the feds."

Brook wasn't a cold-hearted bitch, though others might disagree with her own self-assessment.

Bit had been making extra money on the side by working with a Russian racketeer who'd moved into his territory a couple of years ago. The under the table transactions were helping Bit's sister stay afloat while she underwent expensive rituximab enhanced experimental anthracycline chemotherapy treatments for a rare form of blood cancer. Primary Mediastinal B-Cell Lymphoma, to be exact. More commonly known as PMBCL. His sister's insurance wouldn't cover the extensive regiments required due to it being considered experimental.

While she could empathize, it was that element of his life that had led her to have something on him should the tables be turned. Well, he'd decided to turn the tables. Not her.

"So, your answer was to tell Calabro about my request and throw me on the chopping block?" Brook shook her head at his foolish choice. He'd just lost out on a new stream of income. "We had a mutually beneficial deal, Bit. It's a shame that you had to go and ruin it. Just hand over what you've found, and then we'll call it square."

"Square?" Bit seemed taken aback by her resolution, but he didn't seem to realize that she was offering him a lifeline. "The deal was five grand upfront, and then five grand after I delivered you the intel."

"That was before you went and told Calabro that you were looking into something for me, and he decided to go to one of my superiors." Brook didn't miss the way that his nervous gaze kept drifting to the individual sitting at the end of the bar. She'd already been aware that Kuzmich's righthand man had entered the establishment about ten minutes before she'd made her way through the front door.

Anyone Brook had worked with at the university would have sworn on their life that she would never be caught dead in a place like this. The same went for the agents who she worked with side by side on a daily basis. What they weren't aware of was that she'd acquired a skill set to blend in anywhere at any time if she so desired.

Unfortunately for Bit, there was no longer any need to keep her dealings with him on the downlow. As far as she was concerned, he could handle the fallout of his short-sighted behavior any way he damn well pleased. He was about to learn that she was only loyal to those who returned the favor, and she didn't take even the slightest of betrayal lightly.

After all, she'd dealt with enough deceit to last her a lifetime.

"Our so-called deal changed the moment you told Calabro about our arrangement," Brook pointed out, ensuring that the chair she'd chosen had a clear view of the front exit as well as the back. "Either hand over what you've dug up, or I'll place a call to Calabro inside the hour, informing him of your arrangement with Kuzmich. Your choice. I could care less."

He hadn't failed to notice that Kuzmich's righthand man was getting ready to stand up from his spot at the end of the bar and head their way.

Bit began to shake his leg up and down in panic.

"I can either say that I'm a friend of your sister or I can show him my FBI credentials." Brook met Bit's fearful gaze to let him know that she wasn't bluffing. "Your choice. Spin the numbers."

Brook had locked her purse inside the trunk of her car before venturing inside the bar. Thieves didn't take a lunchbreak, and she didn't like to be burdened with additional baggage when she might need use of her hands. Who she was when she was at the Bureau wasn't the same woman she was when hunting her brother.

"Fine," Bit muttered with a good dose of apprehension as he quickly hoisted his backpack over his shoulder and into his lap. It took him less time to retrieve the USB drive than it had for Dima Vinokurov to make it halfway across the filthy floor.

"Here. Take it. It's all yours."

"Bit. Is there a problem?"

"No, no problem at all," Bit replied as he flashed a nervous smile up at Dima, whose Russian accent was quite thick.

The man had to be at least six feet and four inches tall, while weighing in just over three hundred pounds. He was dressed all in black, as was much of the usual clientele. The sheath for his knife was attached to his belt on his left side, indicating that he was righthanded. Such a position made it easier for him to draw his weapon of choice, plus she'd seen him nursing a beer and using his right hand to pick up the mug. His relatively meager training showed, because a cross body draw was clumsy and slow, especially if one had a gut big enough to obscure one's line of sight.

Paying attention to detail made all the difference in this type of situation.

"I'm so sorry, Bit," Brook said as she discreetly slid the small USB into the pocket of her coat. She shot Dima an apologetic smile before feigning the topic of her conversation with the hacker. "I didn't mean to bother you. Your sister was just worried about you, and I was in the neighborhood when I saw you walk inside."

The tension in Dima's shoulders relaxed somewhat, and Brook was very careful to make sure that her dress coat was fastened before she stood from her chair. It wouldn't do for him to notice that she was carrying a full frame firearm. It also wouldn't be wise for her to make eye contact with the man, though she had been tracking his every movement with her peripheral vision. He'd only take it as a challenge, and Bit had enough trouble on his hands without her adding more to his plate.

"Tell Paula that I'll give her a call this weekend." Bit wiped his nose before slinging his backpack over his shoulder, doing his best to be nonchalant in his movements. He failed miserably to appear calm, and Brook didn't have to wonder why Kuzmich kept such close tabs on his financial windfall. "And also tell her that she doesn't have to worry, because I didn't go into detail when I was speaking with her ex. She's safe."

Brook didn't say another word as she nodded toward Dima and made it appear that she was more than ready to leave. He would simply take it to mean that his close proximity made her nervous.

So be it.

She'd gotten what she'd come for, and all without having to shell out the remaining five thousand dollars for it.

Calabro had obviously taken a guess that she'd been using Bit for business not related to the Bureau. The agent had no idea that she was related to Jacob Walsh, and it would be best for all involved if he remained in the dark. Her associations weren't germane to Calabro's investigation.

She could spin this situation to her advantage, if needed.

Ideas were already forming, and she could easily say that she'd touched base with Bit regarding her current case. Granted, she hadn't listed Bit as an official informant, but she wasn't usually out in the field. She could disclose that she simply hadn't gotten around to filling out the forms.

There was a reason that Calabro utilized Bit as a source, and it wasn't just for his connections on the street to underground hackers. The young man had skills and wasn't even close to living up to his full potential. It was only a matter of time before he was six feet underground, missing all his fingers so that Kuzmich could make a point to the next sucker in line who could mine digital currency for use in illegal black-market deals. The nice thing about using mined cryptocurrencies for such transactions was that it was untraceable. On the other hand, cryptocurrencies listed on the exchanges to buy or sell had transaction numbers applied, and those could be traced from beginning to end. It was an asset class that was completely misunderstood by most people.

The cold air hit her in the face once she stepped outside, causing her to blink away the moisture in her eyes upon exposure. She could have blamed the heavy smoke inside for the small irritation, but she'd been in worse places when attempting to unearth information regarding her brother.

Brook began to walk to her vehicle despite the light rain. She'd purposefully parked a couple of blocks down to monitor the building before she'd decided it was safe enough to go inside. She was advancing into the wind, so she had an excuse to turn her head every now and then to make sure that she wasn't being followed.

Dima was not one to be underestimated.

Flashes of headlights and taillights glistened off the asphalt as vehicles sped past, the overcast sky causing the early afternoon to seem almost like it was dusk. Even the smell of the exhaust from the buses were stronger than usual, as the gloomy weather seemed to suffocate the off-putting odor with its wet blanket. Her surroundings were basically the same as when she'd entered the bar.

She didn't allow herself to experience any sense of achievement or success in the fact that Bit had actually discovered something with the photograph that she'd provided him of Jacob. Scanning social media sites, hacking into DMVs, and basically searching any site that had the ability to upload photographs was a walk in the park for someone like Bit. Her previous attempts to hire other hackers had been a waste of time, but sometimes it was all about finding the right talented individual to complete the task.

"I'm one step closer," she whispered to herself in encouragement as she settled in behind the steering wheel of her car. She quickly closed the door and secured the locks, but she had to remind herself that there was no reason to hurry home. She'd waited seventeen years for a lead such as this, so she could wait another thirty minutes or so. "I'm coming for you, Jacob."

# CHAPTER SEVEN

**Brooklyn Sloane**
*November 2021*
*Tuesday—1:46 pm*

Brook had parked in the lot across from the high-rise building that housed her condo, once again wishing that she'd grabbed the files that she needed to go through from the conference room. It was still relatively early in the day, and a part of her was experiencing quite a bit guilt for walking away from an unresolved case. She reminded herself that a half a day wouldn't make much of a difference, and she wouldn't have to wait until some ungodly hour to look at the information stored on the USB currently burning a hole in her pocket.

She'd gotten used to getting only four hours of sleep at night.

Her days were busy with the current case, while her late-night hours were spent searching for any sign of Jacob. Her therapist was constantly saying that her obsession was an unhealthy practice. Brook disagreed, because her fixation on hunting her brother would result in saving the lives of numerous women who didn't deserve to die a horrid and painful death.

The umbrella that she usually kept in the backseat of her car wasn't easy to reach, but she finally managed to get her fingers on the plastic wristlet and drag it out from underneath the passenger side seat. She didn't have to open the umbrella right away, though. She paid extra in her monthly rent to park underneath one of the assigned awnings to help protect her vehicle from the harsh elements.

The rain was starting to come down even harder than before, causing the usual rhythmic sound on the tin roof of the overhang to sound more like a hyperactive kid with a pair of drumsticks in his hands.

As always, she took her time scanning the parking lot and the front of the building for anything or anyone unusual. Even consultants had been trained for situational awareness. It was a habitual task that might pay dividends should she ever make contact with her brother.

Brook hadn't even stepped up on the curb before remembering that she'd left her purse locked in the trunk of her car. She smothered a groan and quickly made her way back to the carport, all the while pressing the button on her key fob that would pop the trunk. Reaching in, she pulled out her purse only to find the piece of paper that she'd tossed inside of it had slipped out.

She gave Graham Elliot credit for the covert way he'd gone about offering her a job that he clearly had his own reasons for proposing, but she needed the valuable resources that she'd cultivated within the agency for her own search. They were professional relationships that she had established that she never would have been able to develop had she continued working at the university.

Truthfully, Harden's proposal to work for the agency as a consultant had been like manna from heaven—an unexpected windfall.

Graham Elliot could say that he would allow her leeway on whatever mysterious type of job that he was offering her, but she couldn't take the chance of losing access to federal law enforcement databases, especially since she was getting that much closer to her goal of locating her brother.

Seventeen years in the making since he'd vanished without a trace, and her answer might lie on a single USB.

Not wanting the classified memo that Mr. Elliot had provided to her floating around, she picked up the piece of paper and shoved it back into her purse before slamming the trunk closed.

It didn't take her long to reach the glass doors of her building and swipe her access key. Once through the double entrance, she nodded toward the unarmed security guard at the desk before shaking out the leftover rain from her umbrella. The older gentleman's presence was more for observation of the people coming and going than a real threat deterrent.

The warmth of the large foyer was a welcome respite from the cold, wet temperatures outside.

"Ms. Sloane, you're home early," Lou replied with his white brows raised in surprise. He was the type who had gone grey early in his life, only to then have it turn white as snow. "I hope that everything is okay."

"I used the afternoon to run some personal errands," Brook replied with ease, giving him a smile of reassurance. She might not have close friends, but she did appreciate those in her life who she kept at a reasonable distance. Lou was one of them, because he always worked second shift from three o'clock to midnight, with an hour for lunch that he always spent reading one of the classics over his brown-bagged sandwich. His routine was rather comforting to her. "It appears that I'm not the only one switching up my schedule today."

"Charlie had a doctor's appointment, so I told him that I'd come into work early." Lou shrugged, as if his generosity wasn't that big of a deal. Brook paid attention, though. The man always went out of his way for most of the residents inside the building, from ensuring that Mrs. Wield never forgot her weekly hair appointment to reminding Mr. Tomlin to take his coupons to the grocery store every Sunday. "It's more overtime for me, right?"

Brook nodded in agreement, all the while knowing that Lou didn't love his job because of the small monetary supplement it added to his pension. He was well into his retirement years, but this gave him discretionary income as well as a chance to remain social.

"Just in time for the holidays, too," Brook added, taking the time to secure her umbrella with its snap before walking across the black runner that led to one of the elevator banks. "Does your grandson still want the latest gaming console that's all the rave with the teens this year?"

"It's all he's talked about, Ms. Sloane." Lou gave a hearty laugh before he lifted his hand to give a short wave. "You enjoy the rest of your afternoon."

"You, too."

Brook held her umbrella out a bit so that she didn't get the pants to her suit wet. It didn't take her long to reach the elevator and its marque of numbers above the doors. She pressed the top call button to go up to her floor. She lived on the twenty-third level of the high-rise, her condo taking up the entire southeast corner of the building. The layout of the structure contained four spacious units on each floor, basically allowing each tenant to have an open concept with floor-to-ceiling windows overlooking the sprawling city below. Her living space wasn't one that she would have normally been able to afford had she not agreed to sign a consulting contract with the FBI. Her recruitment had included a basic allowance for quarters and a cost-of-living adjustment for the greater DC area.

The elevator doors finally slid open, revealing a gentleman that she'd seen a couple of times before but had never spoken to in their passing. As was their usual routine, they exchanged brief nods as he stepped out and she took his place inside. There were only a few residents in the building that she knew by name, and that was how she liked things. Once again, she thought back to her therapist's opinion of the lack of personal relationships in her life.

She was honestly beginning to wonder why she even continued to attend sessions with Dr. Swift. That was a puzzle for another time, because right now she was closer to Jacob than she had ever been before. Her personal life could wait until she'd closed a tragic chapter on one haunting failure.

"Brook!" Mrs. Upton exclaimed after the elevator doors opened on her floor. The elderly woman owned the condo on the northeast side of the building, so she was basically the only neighbor that Brook came into close contact with on a semi-regular basis. "What on earth are you doing home at this hour?"

"I had some personal errands to run," Brook explained, giving the same excuse as she had to Lou. She stood to the side so that the elevator door wouldn't close before Mrs. Upton had a chance to walk inside with her cane. "I figured it was getting a little late to head back to the office with the incoming storm—

front."

"That was smart thinking," Mrs. Upton replied as she patted Brook on the shoulder. She guessed the widow to be in her late seventies, but she'd broken her hip over a year ago, which slowed her progress some. "I tell you, I'm so tired of this rain. I never believed my Henry when he said that his bones could feel the changes in the weather, but I certainly do now."

Brook continued to hold the elevator open until the elderly woman was safely inside.

"Have a good evening, Mrs. Upton."

"You, too. I'm so happy to see that you took some time for yourself." Mrs. Upton frowned her disapproval, though. "You work too much. Life is meant to be savored, dear."

Brook stepped into the hallway with a nod of understanding and allowed the doors to quietly close and cut off Mrs. Upton's reply that consisted of an invitation to have tea together. She extended the same offer every time they bumped into one another, which was at most four times a month due to Brook's work schedule.

She reached into the pocket of her dress coat for her keys, but she didn't immediately slide it into the lock. A piece of tape with the slightest tear in the side was attached from the doorframe to the door. Three quarters of the tape remained intact. It was added reassurance that no one had entered her private domain without her knowledge.

Brook had picked up on her brother's habit of checking in with her every year or so when a copy of the first book in the Harry Potter series had been left on her bedside table in her dorm room during her first year of college. She had a box full of personal items that he'd left behind for her to find, though she was well aware that he only left them to let her know that he was keeping an eye on her.

Brook shook off the remnant of resentment and rage that always came when she thought back to her last year of college, when she'd finally allowed herself to make a few friends.

She'd never make that mistake again.

Brook quickly removed the cellophane security measure before going ahead and unlocking her front door. She automatically relocked the steel fire door with the deadbolt and a floor mounted jam that made the entrance virtually impossible to open from the outside without a chainsaw.

It had been seven years since she'd last noticed signs from one of Jacob's visits—the day before she'd moved into the building in order to start work for the Bureau. She didn't doubt that he knew the location of her residence, but the high-rise was well equipped with security cameras to monitor anyone's passage to and from any entrance of the building. He hadn't evaded capture by being careless.

Still, she would never let her guard down completely.

There *was* something about being in the safety of her own home where he'd never touched her personal items that allowed her to relax in a way that she hadn't with any other living space. It was one of the reasons that she'd ensured the building had a secure entrance with a twenty-four-hour doorman, along with a personal alarm system for each apartment, which she went about disarming before placing her umbrella and coat in the foyer's closet.

She'd made sure to collect the USB from her coat before shutting the door, reactivating the alarm, and then placing her keys and purse on the thin entryway table. It was her favorite piece of furniture in the entire place, because it had been crafted by her father for her mother back when their lives had been normal.

Back when Jacob had been a little boy without a care in the world.

The salted caramel fragrance of her favorite candles still hung in the air from last night, and the comforting scent had an immediate calming effect on her excitement.

She was a realist, not an optimist.

This urge to rush to her laptop would most likely turn to regret the moment that she viewed what had been captured on screen. She'd been down this road too many times to count, but it wasn't like she had anything to do with the personal time Mrs. Upton had been referring to a few moments ago.

Truthfully, if the elderly woman could see all the maps and white boards that were displayed like pinup art on the dining room wall, she'd be appalled.

The open layout of the condo was one of the things that had attracted Brook. Her work habits were different from others at the agency, and she found that periodically glancing at crime scene photos, grids, maps, and other various images helped her piece together every step taken by an unsub at a scene. She always tried to place herself in their shoes, look through their eyes, hear what they heard, and experience what their emotions were at the time.

It was her process, and it worked.

To say that her condo had been turned into a typical conference room from the Bureau's own playbook would be an understatement, though Brook had done her best to keep the seemingly disorganized yet personalized workspace to the confines of the dining room. She despised disorder, but there was a method to her madness.

The space was visible from nearly every area inside the condo, with the exception of her bedroom.

The small kitchen was on the far side of the dining room, while the living room took up the width directly in front of the long wall of windows. Her bedroom was to the right, as was the master bathroom. The half-bath was off the kitchen, not that she ever had any guests over to utilize it.

Still, she'd told herself time and time again when she had bought the place that she would do her best to make the condo inhabitable. She'd given herself two days to choose the furniture and décor before purchasing the two large, magnetic white boards. She would have ordered a third had she known she'd needed the additional workspace, but the wall had worked out just fine for the maps.

It didn't take her long to retrieve the half-full bottle of white wine that she'd opened yesterday and a clean wine glass from the kitchen. She even turned the knob that was located under the light switch until the soft sound of soothing jazz music filled the air. Having the rest of the afternoon and evening to continue her search for Jacob proved rather invigorating, and she might as well do it up right.

She'd kicked off her high heels as soon as she pulled out a chair from the dining room table and had taken a seat. As she poured herself some decent Moscato from the local grocery store, she lifted the lid of the laptop so that the computer would come to life.

"Show me what you got, Bit," she muttered to herself as she signed in, inserted the USB, and fired up…video footage. "What the hell?"

The somewhat pixelated video seemed to be from a personal security camera of sorts.

While she waited for whatever it was that had caught Bit's attention, she went over the details that she'd shared with him. It had become ingrained in her to be extremely cautious about what she shared with those she'd hired under the table to help in her search for Jacob. She never disclosed his name, she never explained their relationship, and she always made it seem as if she was working a legitimate case for the agency…only needing a bit of unofficial help.

All she'd explained to Bit was that she was searching for an unsub in one of her older cases. She'd given him a picture of Jacob from his sixteenth birthday. She had mentioned that the unsub had a relative in a nursing home located in Morton, Illinois. Having changed her name and disassociated herself with her old life from so many years ago, she didn't fear that anyone would make the connection.

Cold cases were tagged cold for a reason.

All she'd requested was that Bit run Jacob through the aging process and then initiate a search using facial recognition software through each states' DMV, corporation databases, and all social media sites for any sign of the man in the photograph.

Brook couldn't afford to make any mistakes when it came to Jacob.

He had always been one step ahead of her.

She didn't doubt for a second that his intelligence was well above a one-fifty IQ, if not higher. She hadn't set eyes on him since the day her best friend's body had been found in the middle of a cornfield.

Oddly enough, Jacob clearly still harbored some feelings for Brook. Otherwise, he wouldn't remember her birthday every year. The postmark of the packages that arrived in the mail were always from different states.

He loved taunting her.

He got off on it.

What he couldn't seem to grasp was that such an obsession would eventually be his downfall.

"What the hell did you find, Bit?" she murmured, leaning in closer to the screen of her laptop.

The driveway that the home security camera had recorded wasn't familiar, though the surrounding area looked a lot like a residence someplace in the Midwest. Brook continued to watch as a vehicle pulled in and up to the garage. She held her breath as the driver's side door opened and the person exited the car.

It was definitely a man, but he wasn't Jacob.

It was in that moment that the footage paused and had been altered to zoom into the street at the end of the driveway. The video commenced once more, only this time in slow motion. A nondescript dark sedan began to drive past the residence. Each frame got closer and closer until the driver's side window was in complete focus.

It had been over seventeen years since Brook had set eyes on her brother. People changed in that amount of time. She was well aware that she could have passed Jacob on the busy streets without ever realizing it, but that clearly wasn't the case.

She would recognize his jawline anywhere, because it was a staple of the Walsh family.

Her father still maintained the square facial feature even in his old age, and now she'd been given proof that Jacob had, as well. She'd taken after her mother with more of a heart-shaped face, which helped to give people the impression that she was vulnerable. She was completely fine with that assumption, because the criminal element always underestimated her inner strength.

And now, Jacob had underestimated her.

Bit must have spent hours scouring the personal security feeds of each residence near her father's nursing home. The illegal method that he'd utilized in his search wasn't lost on her, but she'd already known what she was getting herself into when she'd hired him for his digital acumen, not his moral code.

She took a healthy drink of her white wine to try and maintain some semblance of composure. After all these years, she was setting her gaze upon the man responsible for ruining any semblance that she'd had of a normal life.

She'd used the mousepad with trembling fingers to pause the footage right as Jacob had glanced to his right, probably from having caught the movement of the owner as he'd walked to his front door. It was the perfect frame, and she would print the image after taking time to comprehend the meaning behind the recording.

Jacob was somehow visiting their father without anyone being the wiser. It was the one lead that she'd spent years searching for, and her dedication had finally been rewarded by the single image that was currently on her screen.

Her opportunity to end over two decades of grief, anger, and torment had finally arrived.

# CHAPTER EIGHT

**Brooklyn Sloane**
*November 2021*
*Wednesday—7:04 pm*

"IT LOOKS AS if I owe you an apology."

Harden stood in the doorframe of her small office, which was basically a ten-by-ten square room painted in government issue off-white paint. It was without a window and had the typical dropdown acoustic tiled ceiling. To say that it had no more appeal than an average jail cell would quite accurate.

No one had ever claimed the insignificant space, and the room had been used to store some heavy fireproof filing cabinets that she had barely been able to open from nonuse and neglect. Once she'd emptied the office and lined up the cabinets outside in the open bullpen along the wall, she'd then moved in a desk and a couple of chairs. The paltry private area kept her from having to socialize with the other agents.

The fact that her boss was paying her a visit at seven o'clock at night told her that Bit had survived their encounter yesterday afternoon. He must have really wanted the additional five thousand dollars that she'd offered him before he'd gone and muddled their deal. Not that he was going to get a red cent after he'd thrown her under the bus.

Still, it wouldn't surprise her to find that he'd contacted Special Agent Calabro and made up some story about her seeking out his services for her current case. She'd have to draw up the paperwork to make it official, though.

"If this is about the florescent lightbulb that's flickering above us as we speak, I'd rather have maintenance come in and replace it instead of getting an apology," Brook replied, attempting to brush yesterday under the rug. "Not even the small lamp that I brought in for some proper light is helping my migraine tonight."

Brook wasn't embellishing the fact that she'd developed a tension headache, but it had technically started yesterday after Harden had all but told her that she should make nice with the other agents. No matter how hard he tried to push his team together, she would still be the sole remaining outcast.

She could only imagine what their reactions would be should they ever discover her true identity. It was something that she didn't want to dwell on this evening.

"All the desk lamp is doing right now is adding to the yellowish, tinted characteristic of these old files," Brook pointed out once again when Harden didn't follow her lead. "I'm probably breathing in some type of mold spore."

"I don't believe that's covered in your contract," Harden finally replied as he leaned against the doorframe. His dress coat was slung over his arm, indicating that he was leaving for the night. "Seriously, I received a call from Jackson about an hour ago. I'd asked for proof the other day to back up his accusation that you had been using agency resources. Turns out, he couldn't provide any. You are a valuable asset to our team. More importantly, you positively contribute to the closure rate of my team, Brook. It's the reason I brought you in as a consultant, and all I'm asking is that you—"

"Hey, sorry to interrupt," Frank replied unapologetically, popping his head around Harden's shoulder. "Do you have a minute? I just spoke with David Lindsey. There's something that I need to run past you."

Frank's request could not have come at a better time.

"I'll meet you in the conference room." Brook closed the discolored manila folder that she'd been perusing, tossing it into the pile that would eventually be sorted and sent back to the original city or state police records department that they had on file. "I wanted to go over the list of suspects that you emailed me, anyway. Sir, did you need me for anything else?"

Harden seemed to want to say more on the subject, but Frank had remained nearby, waiting for their supervisor to finish his conversation.

She couldn't even recall eating lunch. Having arrived at the office before six o'clock in the morning, she'd made great headway into the Pennsylvania case files. She'd also fielded a couple of calls from two reporters wanting progress on the Princess Killer, one of them Matt Henley. His voicemail message had requested exclusive interviews with whoever was involved with the investigation on a federal level. She'd already forwarded the appeal onto Ann and Frank. As far as she was concerned, Henley would die of old age before Brook gave him the time of day.

The last thing that she wanted or needed was to have her face splashed across the local or national news again.

"No, that's all. You two have a good evening."

"Do I want to know what that was all about?" Frank asked after Brook had joined him on the short walk to the conference room. He even glanced over his shoulder to verify Harden's departure. "I'm going to go out on a limb and assume it had something to do with yesterday's impromptu meeting."

"It's nothing important."

Brook turned the light on in the conference room, wishing she'd thought to bring the water that she'd had on her desk. She'd polished off the bottle of wine last night after such a startling discovery regarding Jacob, unable to get more than three hours of sleep. Every logical plan to apprehend her brother wasn't good enough, because he was way too smart to fall for some burner plate bait-and-switch setup published in the Bureau's operation and tactics manual.

She needed to come up with something original to ensure that she kept the advantage.

She'd waited seventeen years, so a few more days or weeks wouldn't make much of a difference. It was best that she continue on with her daily routine until she had something completely bulletproof to work with, which most likely meant bringing Harden in at some point once she had a firm handle on her operational plan.

She certainly wasn't looking forward to that conversation.

"What did you find out from David Lindsey?" Brook asked, getting down to business as she pulled out one of the chairs and took a seat.

"He claims that there were two plumbers that day, but the next-door neighbors—Brett and Angela Hemmer—swear there was only one guy." Frank took a seat across from her before taking the small notebook out of his pocket. He flipped the pages until he got to the notes that he had written down. "Pete's Plumbing. I called the owner, and he backed up the Hemmers' statements."

"Did you follow up with the employee?"

Brook had seen several cases solved by the simplest of follow-ups. Frank might very well have caught the thread that could unravel their investigation. She tried to tamp down the anticipation of closing this out and focusing more on her brother, but she wasn't going to get ahead of herself.

"Yes." Frank flipped to another page. "Will Ramirez. He claims that he was by himself that day. He arrived at the Hemmers at approximately zero nine hundred, changed out an obstructed drainpipe underneath their sink, and then left before eleven hundred hours."

"Were you able to speak with David Lindsey on the phone?"

The boy in question was the brother of Beth Lindsey. He was only sixteen years old and had been the one who had discovered his sister's body. She'd already graduated high school and had been packing up to leave for her second year at college.

"Yes, and the boy sticks by his story." Frank closed his notebook and leaned back in his chair. "I believe him, but the neighborhood isn't the type to install doorbell cameras or video surveillance. They all leave their doors unlocked, as if the rest of the world can't touch them. I can't prove that anyone else was there."

"The unsub would have done his homework on the victim's family, friends, and neighbors." She thought over her profile, and she wasn't ready to alter the main points. "The victim would never have been impressed by the unsub the way he desires in a plumber's uniform. She didn't know him like that, which means he used the van as merely an opportunity to gain access to the residence without anyone noticing him."

Brook stood and walked over to the whiteboard that contained Beth Lindsey's crime scene photos. They were one step closer to apprehending their target.

"How would the unsub have known that—" Frank stopped talking when he comprehended what she'd been attempting to convey. "The unsub created the diversion himself. The Hemmers did say that the sink had been fine one minute, and then overflowing the next. Damn."

"Look at the way the victim was displayed on her bed after her death. Blue top, yellow skirt. Just like Snow White." Brook tapped the apple in the photograph that had been purposefully placed in her hands. "The bite mark of the apple turned out to be from the victim herself, which means that the unsub was able to get her to eat it before he stabbed her repeatedly in the abdomen. He wasn't some plumber, but it would have been a great disguise to throw off anyone in the surrounding area. She let him into her house on her own accord."

"We checked her phone, social media, and other chatrooms that were downloaded to her computer. There was nothing that we could find that indicated she was in touch with someone other than her usual friends." Frank held up a hand when Brook turned to follow up on that angle. "And while Ann and I were in West Virginia last week, we confirmed with each of her friends the messages that had been sent the week prior to the murder. Nothing was out of the ordinary."

Due to the murders taking place in the tristate area, Brook hadn't accompanied the two agents when they'd canvassed the old murders scenes. She'd stayed behind and worked on a profile that would eventually help them piece together the case. She'd based it around the investigations they could connect to Beth Lindsey, because the lead detective of the small town had randomly remembered a murder from a couple of years prior that resembled a scene out of a fairytale.

Unfortunately, there had been some earlier murders that they had loosely linked to the unsub from something as simple as a tierra left behind, and some of the vital evidence had been ignored as nothing more than part of the victims' belongings. It seemed with each passing day that they were adding to the possible list of kills that the unsub had made over the years.

"You said that you looked over the list of suspects that I compiled from all four murders." Frank asked, moving the conversation along. He most likely wanted to get home to his wife and kids. "Zero names of the lists of the suspects crossed over into the other states or towns, with the exception of Stephen Schmidt. He travels for his job as a pharmaceutical sales rep."

"Schmidt," Brook mused, recalling that the man was questioned in the Selma Diaz murder. "Have you spoken to him?"

"Ann reached out to him, and he's agreed to an interview with her. She'll fly from New York to Ohio on Friday."

Brook and Ann might not see eye to eye on a lot of things, but the federal agent was damn good at her job. If Schmidt was a likely candidate for their unsub, Ann would be able to ferret out any discrepancies in the man's statement.

"I discovered three more cases in Pennsylvania that might be connected to our investigation. Give me a minute to grab the files."

Brook quickly made her way out of the conference room and

into her office. She'd placed the folders of the cases in question off to the side of her keyboard. Frank or Ann would be able to follow up with the local police departments in Pennsylvania or one of them would fly out themselves when there was a break in their schedules.

As she went to leave her office, the chime of her cell phone indicated that she was receiving an incoming call. She almost let it go to voicemail, especially since she wasn't expecting any calls.

For some reason, Graham Elliott crossed her mind.

She hadn't taken the time to look at her personal email. He'd stated that he'd sent her some sort of case file, along with a job offer. She had no intention of taking him up on the latter, but that didn't mean she couldn't look at the document that he'd sent her. She was under no obligation to help him, but she wasn't in the habit ignoring a possible ally with powerful connections.

After all, the secretive Mr. Elliott had gone to an awful lot of trouble to stir up her curiosity. She still wasn't sure why he'd chosen such a route. It was as if he'd been testing her, but she'd held out long enough that he'd finally come to her. He'd inadvertently let her know exactly how bad he wanted her services.

Brook gave a soft groan of irritation before leaning over her desk and grabbing her cell phone. It wasn't a number that she recognized, but that didn't mean anything. She gave her cell number out to a lot of people, especially in her bid to find Jacob.

"Sloane," Brook answered, tucking her phone in between her ear and shoulder so that she could also grab her water bottle.

There was nothing but silence on the other end of the line.

She transferred the manila folder and water to her left hand so that she could take another look at the display on her phone. Her screensaver was showing, telling her that she must have just missed the call.

If the reason was important, whoever it was would call back.

Brook exited her office and began to make her way to the conference room when she spotted Harden rushing from the direction of the elevator banks back to his office. It was late enough in the evening that the overhead florescent lights in the main area had been turned off, leaving a golden hue to shine down from the strategically placed bulbs in the ceiling. The obscure shadows caused by the lighting couldn't hide his concern.

"What's going on?"

"I don't know," Brook murmured in reply to Frank's question. He was standing in the doorway, monitoring Harden as the man entered his office. "212 area code is New York, right?"

"Yeah," Frank replied, his gaze landing on her in curiosity. "Why?"

Brook's phone chimed again, this time indicating that she'd received a voice message.

"Shit," she muttered, recognition dawning on who had been trying to call her. She quickly walked past Frank into her bid to reach the conference room. She'd already pressed the callback button on her phone and set it to speakerphone before placing her other items onto the table. "Do you remember Ethan Bell, from the New York office? He was here a few months ago helping out on that counterintelligence investigation with Robinson."

"You don't think—"

Bell answered before Frank could finish his sentence.

"Sloane, did you get my voicemail?"

"No," Brook replied honestly, meeting Frank's troubled gaze. "I called you right back. You're on speakerphone, and Frank is standing right next to me. We just saw Harden go into his office. What's going on?"

"I thought I'd give you a courtesy call after you helped me out on that one issue when I was in D.C."

Brook was grateful that Ethan hadn't disclosed how she'd helped him, nor the fact that their time spent had been on a more intimate level. That would remain between them, and only them. It had been a one-night stand kind of thing, anyway.

"Ann Nelson was shot today serving a warrant, along with Special Agent Joseph Vittore. Vittore didn't make, and Nelson was taken to the nearest hospital. The last I heard, she was in emergency surgery."

Brook hung her head as she absorbed the news, barely registering the rapid questions that Frank was rattling off to Ethan. Apparently, Ann had offered to help serve a warrant to a male unsub involved with an embezzlement scheme. She'd gone to the New York office on another case, and it was rare that she strayed from her assigned duties.

"Vittore didn't want to wait for me to finish up giving testimony in a trial, and he asked Ann if she'd go along with him," Ethan said to finish out the call. "I'm sorry. I was the one who supposed to be with Vittore."

"You have nothing to apologize for," Brook replied after Frank had left the conference room. She had no doubt that he was on his way to see Harden. Their supervisor was almost certainly already on the phone with the hospital, obtaining an update on Ann's condition. "We all know the risks involved in our line of work. Let's just hope that she pulls through."

While Brook technically carried a firearm, she'd never had to draw her weapon in the line of duty. It was rare that she was out in the field in any capacity. It was only every so often that she would walk specific crime scenes, especially when it benefited her to get a feel for the unsub.

It was how she'd gotten to know Fritz.

As for being in the vicinity at the time of an arrest, that had never happened during the seven years that she'd been profiling for the Bureau.

"I appreciate the heads up, Ethan."

"Don't worry. I still owe you. Like I said, this was just a courtesy call."

Brook disconnected the line and then sat down in the chair to take a moment, but she didn't get it. Frank immediately reappeared and gave her an update.

"Harden is catching the first flight out to New York. Desmond will step in as Acting Supervisory Special Agent in Charge."

There were other delegations that would be taking place, as well. Caseloads would need to be shuffled around, and the dynamics of the office would change. Frank would have to either take Ann's place to meet with Steven Schmidt or hand off the interview to someone from another field office, which meant that someone else would need to fly out to Pennsylvania.

"Go home," Brook instructed, pushing to her feet. "I'm sure Harden will touch base once Ann is out of surgery."

"You mentioned that you wanted to show me some of the cases that you believe might be connected to ours." Frank ran a hand over his mustache, stretching his jaw at the same time. He was a bundle of apprehensive energy right now. "Let's just keep—"

"Frank, it's okay. There's nothing that can't wait until tomorrow." Brook picked up the files in question, her bottle of water, and her phone. "We'll schedule a sit down with Desmond to see who we can pull from another case to help us with some interviews. For now, go home. Be with your wife and boys. Let's just agree to text one another if one of us gets news on Ann."

Frank finally nodded his agreement. She had a long night ahead of combing through at least a quarter of the stack of case files obtained from the main records department of the Pennsylvania State Police, and it was going to be up to her to go through the criminal reports from either Ohio or West Virginia. More often than not, the state police in each state kept a copy of every homicide, even if the case had been handled by the county sheriff or some local police department.

"Right, right." Frank was clearly having a hard time processing the shooting. He'd worked with Ann for a very long time. "Are you staying?"

"Just for a little while," Brook replied once she realized that he would experience guilt by leaving her to comb through the files alone. She'd worked hundreds of cases with different agents, depending on who had been tasked with the investigations. If she had to pick one of her favorite colleagues, hands down it would be Frank. "Seriously, go home and be with your family."

Frank didn't go directly to his desk, but instead walked back to Harden's office in what was most likely hope that some news had been given in the past three minutes. It was times like these that reminded her that she would never have the camaraderie among her colleagues the way that Frank, Ann, and the others had with one another.

She often wondered what would happen if she chose to stop hunting Jacob and attempted to live a normal life. It would be nice to cultivate friendships and foster relationships that she'd steered cleared of since the promise that Jacob had given her as they had both stood over her best friend's body.

*"You don't get to be the normal one, Brook. I'll always make sure of that."*

# CHAPTER NINE

**Brooklyn Sloane**
*November 2021*
*Thursday—7:46 am*

"I DON'T UNDERSTAND," Brook said for the third time in the past ten minutes. Her frustration had been mounting ever since she'd walked into Harden's office to find that Lawrence Desmond had already switched around a couple of assignments. "Why can't we have someone from the Pittsburgh field office go speak with the sheriff in Sutton? A routine phone call is all it would take for the agent to be brought up-to-date."

She and Frank had been summoned to Harden's office first thing in the morning to find out that Desmond was already knee-deep in the day-to-day administrations of the current investigations. His jacket had been thrown on top of the credenza in a haphazard way, and the sleeves of his dress shirt had been rolled up a couple of times as he got down to work.

As for Ann, she'd made it through surgery last night.

That was about all the good news they had on that front. The doctors had labeled her in critical condition after removing bullet fragments that had been resting against one of her arteries.

"The Pittsburgh field office is swamped with a high-profile case involving a domestic terrorist cell," Desmond explained as he clicked the end of his pen in frustration. "Harden left specific instructions that Frank is going to have to take over some of the cases that Ann was working on, which means we can't spare him this week, either. I've reached out to the Cleveland field office, and someone is awaiting your call on…"

Desmond shifted around some papers until he got to the one that had details written on it in black ink. Brook took the time to exchange an annoyed glance with Frank.

"Steven Schmidt. Give the field office a call, explain why we're requesting their help with the investigation, and you'll be transferred to the agent who can go question Schmidt this afternoon or tomorrow, at the latest. The Pennsylvania cases will just have to wait." Desmond sat back and raised both hands in a beseeching plea. "Brook, I'm only following Harden's wishes. We just don't have an agent free at the moment to drive or fly out to Sutton, Pennsylvania. It's going to have to wait until Frank's caseload eases up. Why don't you reach out to the local sheriff's department that oversaw the case twenty years ago? I'm sure that they can gather whatever information that you're looking for and report back to you in a timely manner."

Brook mulled over their choices.

For the amount of time that she'd spent at her condo last night, she might as well have spent the night in her office. She wasn't ecstatic over having discovered three more victims from cases that had been overlooked.

"Listen, I have a suggestion." Brook waited until she had the focus of both men before continuing. "We have four murders assigned to our unsub, but I believe that I found three more during my search last night. They are in addition to the other two that we think are related upon research from a few weeks ago. The reason those particular three stand out is because all of them seem to be clustered in a forty-mile radius from a small coal mining town in Pennsylvania. The first one goes back twenty years, and that particular sheriff is now retired. I really think it was our unsub stretching his legs for the first time. We *need* to follow up with the case in Sutton. How about we take the Ohio field office up on their offer to speak with Schmidt, but I personally fly into Pittsburgh myself to aid in some interviews. The unsub is due to strike in three or four weeks, and that means he already has a victim picked out. He's attempting to garner her attention right now, and if that fails…"

Desmond began to click his pen at a faster rate, which told of his concern over making such a unilateral decision. He wasn't confident that he should authorize her to go into the field, but it wasn't like he had much of a choice. Even Harden would have gone along with her line of thinking, because he trusted her judgement on these types of cases.

"Three weeks doesn't give us much time, Des," Frank pressed, basically pushing the Acting Supervisory Special Agent against the proverbial wall. The two of them went way back, and it meant a lot to her that Frank was willing to go to bat for her. "Brook is more than capable of requestioning those involved with a twenty-year-old case."

Desmond still seemed hesitant, until she followed up with a promise.

"If I feel at any time that I could potentially be in any danger, I will call for backup." Brook thought over her options on that front. She'd stop by the Pittsburgh field office and let them know the sites of her visits so that they would have addresses should something go wrong. "The likelihood of me needing additional help is almost nonexistent."

Brook might have stretched the truth with that last statement, but neither Frank nor Desmond seemed to catch the slight tension in her shoulders. She couldn't put her finger on it, but she would bet her paycheck that the three cases she'd discovered in the massive piles of folders were related to the more extravagant ones currently being committed by the unsub.

He'd perfected his craft over the years, but those first few canvasses held the key to his identity. It was the one in particular that had occurred *in* Sutton, Pennsylvania that stood out the most.

"Fine," Desmond relented, motioning that the two of them should leave Harden's office. "Go do what you need to do while I try not to drown in Harden's cesspool of instructions. Oh, the two of you need to chip in twenty dollars. The collection jar is out on Ann's desk. We're going to send her a gift and flowers when she's out of the ICU."

Brook didn't waste any time as she exited the office and made her way through the bullpen. She could sense Frank on her heels, and he was no doubt interested in what she found in Pennsylvania.

"Sloane, you have a call on line one," someone called out from the other side of the room. "It's Matt Henley from that crime podcast."

"Tell him that I have no comment," she exclaimed as she veered toward the small kitchen. It smelled of burnt coffee from the old glass carafe that had to have been used since the 1970s. Someone had the forethought to bring in one of the single cup makers, and she took advantage of the new technology. "Well, that wasn't how I thought today's meeting would go. I didn't count on having to make a trip out of state."

"It's the best we're going to get right now." Frank opened the cupboard and chose one of the standard office cups that was available. Brook grimaced when he reached for the carafe. "What has you wanting to take care of this yourself? You hardly ever go out into the field."

"You know as well as I do that we're on a three to four week timeline until the unsub strikes again." Brook took one of the coffee pods and went about making herself a cup of hazelnut coffee. She usually drank it black, with the exception of those times that she stopped at a specialty café that made macchiatos. Such simple pleasures in life were one of her weaknesses, and she usually stopped into her favorite café almost every morning. "Besides, I think this might be the one to break the case."

Frank stopped lifting his coffee cup to take that first sip so that he could stare at her in what could only be read as astonishment. The right corner of his mustache twitched as he squinted his eyes to get a better read on her.

"I'm serious."

Brook waited until the machine had finished brewing the single cup. Once the last drop had been added, she hastily picked up the mug and led the way out of the small kitchen.

"One of the three cases involved a woman who had been stabbed to death in her own bedroom. She had on a prom dress, red lipstick drawn on her lips, and a flower in her hand. The notes suggested that the boyfriend was their main suspect, but they never had any evidence to make an arrest."

"What fairytale would that correlate with?" Frank asked with a frown, joining Brook in her small office. She had one extra chair up against the far wall, but it was currently full of files. He chose to lean against the doorframe while she filled him in. "It sounds a bit too general, if you ask me."

"Which is probably the reason that the original detective didn't think anything of it." Brook carefully set down her cup before reaching for the criminal report in question. "Here. Take a look at the crime scene photos. Tell me that you don't see some similarities to our latest scenes."

Frank wasn't about to give up his coffee, so she opened the file for him and laid it out on her desk. While he began to peruse the photographs that had been included, she made sure to have the other two ready for review.

"That victim was named Chrissy Aper." Brook set down the second file, and the one she thought could be the unsub's first. "This is Vicki Anderson. Her nude body was found in the woods, but the unsub had covered her with hard tack candy. I'm not sure how this case ties in with ours, but it reminded me too much of "Hansel and Gretel". He could have thought of the sister in a sexual manner, and maybe he attempted to save her from the wicked witch who lived in a cottage in the middle of the wilderness."

"You know that if Ann was here, she'd say that you are reaching."

"And you would come back and remind her that my closure rate as a profiler is the highest in the Bureau…consultant or agent," Brook replied wryly. She could see that it gave Frank a sense of comfort to talk about Ann as if she were coming back later today. "I'm serious, though. There's something about these pictures that is bugging me, and I can't figure out why."

Frank leaned over and began to scan the numerous photos that had been included with the criminal report. He took his time, mindful of his coffee that he still wouldn't set down. She waited patiently, and she wasn't disappointed.

"It's the way her hair was brushed," Frank murmured as pointed at the picture with his index finger. He straightened so that she could lean down and inspect the image herself. "Look at the way her hair is brought over her shoulders, with both curls facing inward. It's the same way that Beth Lindsey's hair was posed over the neck of the blue blouse."

Brook experienced that jolt of elation that came when connecting cases, because this changed the way they would handle the investigation from this point on.

"Damn, if you didn't do it again." Frank took a sip of his coffee as he stared at her over the rim of his cup. He then smirked. "I can picture Ann frowning and crossing her arms, reluctant to admit that you were right about the tristate area. You know that's how she would react if she were here right now."

"You technically noticed the hair," Brook fired back, tugging the arm of her chair so that she could bring it closer to take a seat.

She had a lot to do before making flight arrangements, renting a vehicle, and contacting the local sheriff's office who had handled the original case. While a man by the name of Benny Morgan had been listed as sheriff on the criminal report, a deputy had been the one who had technically worked in cooperation with the state police. The deputy was now the sheriff—Joe O'Sullivan. Unfortunately, she hadn't recognized the name of the suspect, not that she thought it would be that easy.

"I'm pretty sure that you already saw the similarities and you were just trying to include me."

"I need to work on my reputation, then." Brook had already taken the file and flipped it around so that it was facing her. She easily located the number to the local sheriff's office. She'd start with them first, hopefully able to get a name of a hotel that would be close to the area that she would be scouting. "I don't want the others to think that I'm getting soft or anything. I have a rep to maintain."

"Never." Frank clicked his tongue on the roof of his mouth, basically announcing his exit. "I've got to go and get caught up on those cases. You have my number, so don't hesitate to call if you find anything of interest. And for the love of God, call the sheriff's office or the field office if you actually stumble across the unsub himself. The way you work, I wouldn't put it past you to try and make an arrest yourself."

Brook already had the phone in hand, but she couldn't let Frank leave without offering him some show of support.

"Frank."

He turned around to face her right when he would have walked out of her office. There was a sadness in his eyes that he had failed to hide.

"Ann is a fighter." Brook had never viewed herself as an overly compassionate individual. She couldn't be, not with what she dealt with on a daily basis, but it was more that she'd had to shove that part of her to the side in order to concentrate on one thing—hunting Jacob and making right the wrong that she'd committed all those years ago. "She'll pull through, Frank."

Her fellow colleague attempted to give her a smile, though he wasn't as successful as he probably would have liked. He lifted his coffee cup in salute as he disappeared from view. She thinned her lips, wishing that she could have come across as more supportive, but at least he was aware that she had tried her best.

After Brook dialed the number onto the desk phone's keypad, she began to sign into her computer. She would book the first flight into Pittsburgh, most likely landing at the terminal sometime this evening. She'd need to give herself enough time to head home and pack, though.

"Sutton Police Department, how may I direct your call?"

"Sheriff O'Sullivan, please," Brook replied, having already pulled up the flight schedule for the rest of the afternoon and evening. She tried not to take offense at the sardonic tone. "Tell him that Brook Sloane is calling from the FBI."

She didn't have an official title, but her employer's identification was enough to initially get her through the door. She could always explain how being a consultant worked after the fact.

"One moment, please."

Brook waited for the inevitable music that usually accompanied such an occurrence, but there was complete silence. She had to glance at the display on her desk phone to ensure that she was still connected. Apparently, the department was just as small today as it had been twenty years ago.

While she continued to wait for the sheriff to answer, she perused the flights available. There were two later this evening, but that would mean she would have to wait until tomorrow morning to drive to the town in question, which was around sixty miles northeast of Pittsburgh. She grimaced at the thought of wasting that much time.

"Sheriff O'Sullivan."

"Good morning, Sheriff," Brook greeted, noting that he didn't sound old enough to have worked a twenty-year-old case.

She'd have to do a quick fact check before meeting him in person. "I'm Brook Sloane, a consultant for the FBI. I'm the profiler on a case that I'm sure you heard about in the news, and there was a murder in your jurisdiction around two decades ago that I believe might be connected. I'd like to take a trip out your way to look more into the details."

Sheriff O'Sullivan didn't answer right away, and Brook could appreciate him taking time to think over his response. Truthfully, there was only one outcome here, but it would benefit him to work with her.

"The Princess Killer." The sheriff had stated the moniker with contempt, but she could also hear the interest in his voice. "I received a call from a Lieutenant Lawrence regarding the case, and I already sent him over the cases that we had spanning back twenty-five years. We've had nothing similar to that occur here. Not since I've been the sheriff, at least."

"Vicki Anderson." Another long pause, but Brook had a feeling this one hit closer to home. "You were a deputy assigned to the case back then."

Small towns like Sutton usually didn't have murders like the one she was about to turn over with a fine-tooth comb. Everyone knew everyone else. She should know, considering that she'd grown up in a similar town.

"Vicki Anderson was killed and left in the woods to rot like a dead animal carcass, ma'am. As you said, I should know. I was the one who handled the case."

Brook figured it was safe to assume that it had also been his first, which no doubt had left a stain on his soul. She knew all about the dark spots that couldn't be erased with time.

"Please, call me Brook," she requested, hoping that it would lessen the tension that had filled the line. "I realize that you might not see the similarities, but I assure you that they are there. I'd really like to work with you, Sheriff O'Sullivan. Seeing as you were the first deputy on scene and the one to write the report back then, your insight would be invaluable."

Brook might have laid it on a bit thick, but at least the sheriff hadn't hung up the phone. She really didn't want to have to step on his toes. Everything would run much smoother if he was amicable to her visit.

"Please, Sheriff." Brook had already made the decision that she would drive, figuring it would take her just as long if she were to fly, rent a vehicle, and find a place to stay. She'd worry about the last detail once she'd crossed the state line. "I can be there late this afternoon, and I'll show you why I believe that Vicki Anderson might have been one of the first victims of this unsub. Your case might be the key to apprehending a serial killer who has gone unnoticed for twenty years."

She was already reaching for her briefcase before the sheriff had even responded, but she'd known that he wouldn't be able to pass up an opportunity to find justice. Law enforcement officers of small towns took those types of crimes personally. It probably wasn't in the man's nature to let an opportunity like this slip by.

"I'll be waiting, Ms. Sloane."

Brook wasn't offended when Sheriff O'Sullivan disconnected the line. She'd gotten what she'd wanted, and she had no doubt that he would accommodate her requests once she'd arrived in Sutton, Pennsylvania.

In the meantime, she needed to collect the files that would tie everything together, give Des and Frank an update on her travel plans, and go home to pack for a few days. She highly doubted that she be gone longer than that, because anything she found would be followed up by Frank or whoever might be available to help close out the investigation.

After that, she'd request some personal time off that she was due in order to take care of family business. She wouldn't be working in an official capacity, either. What she had in mind for Jacob wasn't something that would be considered legal in terms of her position at the agency.

# CHAPTER TEN

### Brooklyn Sloane
*November 2021*
*Thursday—3:34 pm*

FOUR HOURS INTO the drive was when Brook had decided to stop and stretch her legs. She'd pulled off the interstate before quickly locating a gas station that wasn't too far off the beaten path. She figured that she was no more than a half an hour from her destination, and she'd made excellent time.

Brook shut off the engine before grabbing her dress coat from the back seat. She'd changed into a pair of black jeans, keeping her white dress shirt and black blazer on in order to maintain a professional appearance. The outfit afforded her comfort for the drive, yet it would display an act of respect by those at the local police station.

Her cell phone rang before she had a chance to reach for the handle on the door, and she decided to take the call before pumping gas and using the restroom inside the building. Seeing as her Bluetooth was no longer connected to her speaker, she'd had to remove her cell phone from its cup holder.

One look at the display told her that the caller had blocked his or her identity.

"Sloane."

Brook held her breath as she waited to hear who was on the other end of the line, anticipating an update on Ann's status. Another part of Brook couldn't accept that she was finally one step ahead of her brother, yet Jacob couldn't possibly know that she'd obtained footage of him driving past a random residence near their father's nursing home. The likelihood that he would also have obtained her cell phone number was miniscule.

Still, she never counted on certainty.

"You never opened your email."

The gathered tension in her shoulders faded, and she couldn't help but smirk at the irritation in Graham Elliott's voice. Between her hunt for Jacob, the investigation, and Ann's shooting, she hadn't been able to run a background check on him.

Hell, she also hadn't even taken a minute to look over his proposal.

"So, you are who they made that read feature for," Brook said, shifting her cell phone to her left ear and resting her elbow on the door. "I honestly didn't think that anyone actually used that option in their email."

"It's not nice to lie to your future employer, Miss Sloane."

Brook had to bite her lip to keep from laughing, because she had actually utilized the receipt option when sending an email to a colleague a time or two. Her smile began to fade when she realized that he was reading her the way she read crime scenes. She didn't appreciate having the tables turned on her, and it was time to end this game of tag.

At least he'd used her correct name this time around.

"Mr. Elliott, I've already explained to you that I'm not looking for another job. I do appreciate your—"

"Jackson might not be able to go after you for using an informant for personal business, but you can mark my words—he *will* find something to have you removed from the D.C. office."

"Why?"

Graham Elliott fell silent, but something told Brook that he wasn't the type of man to lie. She still believed that he'd been some sort of commanding officer in the military, and men like him put honor above all else.

"There's been a reporter by the name of Jennifer Madsen who's made it her mission to paint the agency in a bad light after that botched counterterrorism case that went down last year in San Francisco."

"You mean the one that Jackson authorized." Brook vaguely recalled the details, though the raid had taken place in California and nowhere near D.C. "I believe it resulted in the death of two FBI agents."

"One of those agents was Madsen's brother."

Brook didn't want to contemplate the similarities in that scenario right now, especially with Ann lying in a hospital bed, so she got right to the point.

"What does all that have to do with me?"

"Madsen somehow stumbled across the fact that Brooklyn Sloane didn't come into existence until around fifteen years ago. Your cover story has been compromised."

Brook had gone to great lengths to leave that young girl behind. The day that she'd graduated high school was the same one where she'd petitioned to have her surname changed to Sloane. She hadn't even known what she'd wanted her last name to be, so she'd picked one from the numerous signatures that had been on the sign-in sheet in front of her on the counter.

Not terribly ingenious, but it had sufficed at the time.

She would have done anything back then to forget about her childhood, her memories, and her brother. It had taken her all through college and her subsequent gravity toward the psychology department to figure out that she was the only one who had the capability to end her own nightmare. All she had to do was bring her brother to justice.

Well, her brand of justice, at least.

"I appreciate your honesty, Mr. Elliott. I'm actually in the field right now, but I'll address the issue when I'm back in D.C." Brook could sense from his silence that he wasn't too happy with the result of the call. She wasn't sure why she'd prolonged the inevitable, but she gave him the crumb that he so greatly desired. "When I have a spare moment, I give you my word that I will look at the file you sent me."

"Do I sound like a man who is desperate, Miss Walsh?"

Brook tensed upon hearing her true surname once again. She'd clearly offended him with her poorly aimed breadcrumb, but he was purposefully reminding her of a past that she'd tried very hard to bury from prying eyes.

He surprised her with his next statement.

"I am desperate, Miss Walsh. I've learned throughout my years when to handle something on my own and when to seek out those who can get the job done properly." Graham Elliott paused once more, but she was doubtful that it had anything to do with him choosing his words wisely. He'd already known what he was going to say, and so did she. He wasn't a man to ever admit to being desperate unless it was the truth. "You *are* that individual for me, Miss Walsh."

It took her a moment to realize that he'd disconnected the

line.

It shouldn't have taken her aback, really. He'd conveyed what he'd wanted and gotten his point across without embellishing any facts, stirring the reaction that he'd known would entice her to open her email.

What would someone in his position need her help with that he couldn't find through his own contacts? It made no sense, but she didn't have time for anything else but her own personal pursuits and the current investigation that was running down at the moment. It was how she'd always worked, and she would continue to do so.

Brook had taken around twenty minutes to fill up her gas tank, use the facilities, and to also buy a few snacks for later this evening. She'd conducted a brief Google search on the small town, and the only thing that was open twenty-four-seven was the 7-Eleven that had set up shop right on the outskirts of town.

Quite a few backroads later and less than thirty minutes after the pitstop, Brook caught sight of the town's worn blue and white welcome sign, along with its population declaration. Eight hundred and sixty-three residents lived in Sutton, Pennsylvania. She would bet that all eight hundred and sixty-three of them also knew the Anderson family.

A dark tragedy like that didn't unfold without it leaving a mark for a few generations.

Brook did her best to push her own memories to the back of her mind, refusing to allow her personal experience to cloud her judgement. She'd get to hear firsthand from the sheriff what he could recall from that time, and it would most likely not be as hard as some could imagine it to be twenty years after the fact.

The details were almost certainly branded into the sheriff's head as if the perp had used a white-hot iron.

Brook glanced at her GPS, noting that the sheriff's station was a half mile ahead on the righthand side. The main road into the town was like a gateway to the past, with old and faded brick buildings on either side. One or two even appeared to be available for lease or purchase, but there were a few mom-and-pop shops that had neon signs in the windows, signaling that they were still operating and open to the public.

The only description that she could come up with was that this area resembled a shell of what it had formerly been twenty-some years ago. There were only faint remnants of the past existing in the worn shutters, cracked glass, and faded bricks.

It really was quite sad to see a small American hometown in such a decline.

From her understanding of the town's history, a major part of the coal mine had suddenly collapsed and then flooded many years ago. The closing of what had once been the sole industry that had kept this place thriving had basically forced generations of families to seek work elsewhere. The ones who'd stayed either drove an hour into the city for work or had survived on what security had been left in their pensions.

Brook spotted the sheriff's building and flipped her turn signal on to indicate that she would be getting off the main drag, not that anyone had been on the street behind her. It was still early enough that Sheriff O'Sullivan should be able to drive her straight to the site of the murder.

Once again, an incoming call prevented her from gathering her coat, purse, and briefcase, all of which were now tucked into the passenger seat of her car. She hadn't turned off the engine, though.

"Sloane," she called out after answering through her blue tooth. She recognized the number this time around. "How is Ann doing?"

"Out of critical condition," Harden replied over the muffled voices in the background. "I'm at the field office in New York, finding out what the hell went wrong. Ann's sister is asking questions, and I want to make sure that I have some answers lined up. Des sent me a message that said you're out in the field somewhere in western Pennsylvania. Whatever you found must have been damned good to pry you out of that conference room chair."

"It's only a lead, so I wouldn't celebrate too early. I give you my word that I'll contact Frank if I find anything of interest," Brook replied, tapping her thumb on the steering wheel. She'd been scanning the front of the sheriff's office, taking note that there were only two vehicles parked out front, and neither one was the sheriff's patrol car. It was a wonder that this town still had a sheriff's position after the population went from two thousand to eight hundred. "I drove instead of taking a flight, and I already called the field office to let them know of my location. Is Ann conscious?"

"No, but the first twenty-four hour hurdle is over and done with. I hear they plan to remove the ventilator later this evening."

"That's good." Brook almost brought up Jennifer Madsen and the woman's grudge against Jackson and the Bureau, but it wasn't the time or place. They both had tasks that took priority. "I'm about to walk into the Sutton Police Station, but I appreciate the update."

"Be careful, Brook. I'm only one supervisor, and I can't be

everywhere at once."

"I'll do my best not to disappoint you."

Brook let Harden disconnect the call first, a part of her regretting not following through with her instinct to bring up the Jennifer Madsen subject. The reporter had the potential to inadvertently prevent Brook from reaching her goal, as well as having her contract nullified by the one individual who hadn't wanted Harden to hire her in the first place.

If Madsen ended up writing an exposé about how the FBI had hired the sister of a serial killer as a consultant to profile other serial killers, it would look bad for the Bureau, but Brook would be the one without the job that afforded her the tools to hunt down her brother. She wasn't really worried about a paycheck. She could always go back to the university to earn a salary, but such a move would definitely reduce the likelihood of tracking down anymore leads that she might otherwise acquire with her current access to resources.

Maybe it *was* time to look at other options, but she first had to apprehend the unsub who she'd driven all this way to find.

Brook turned off the engine to her vehicle, making the decision to leave her dress coat on the front seat. She was wearing a blazer, and anything else would be too bulky for such a quick visit. She and the sheriff could do most of their talking on the drive over to the original crime scene.

She didn't waste time exiting the car with her briefcase and purse in hand, walking the short distance to the front entrance of the police station. The building had seen better days, as with the others on the main thoroughfare of town, but the fact that it was still standing with a leader at the helm clearly meant something to this town.

The first thing that hit her was the burnt scent of coffee mixed with what could only be stale fast food. She swallowed down her acid reflux, which was saying something. She ate a lot of fast food herself, but this was something completely different.

"May I help you?" an older gentleman asked before he took a napkin and wiped the ends of his mustache. It wasn't as neatly trimmed as Frank's facial hair. She recognized the voice, though. The individual sitting down behind the counter had been the one to first answer the phone this morning. "Oh, you must be the federal agent who Joey said would be stopping by. Come right on through."

Brook had only ever seen a small wooden swinging door like the one in front of her from pictures or the movies, not that she had a lot of time for the latter. The odd entrance separated the small foyer from the main room and had no real function. Basically, the building was one large area with what looked to be a restroom to her right and a single holding cell in the back.

Walking into a place such as this was like being sent back to the Wild West. She'd been pretty good at geography in high school. As far as she was aware, Pennsylvania was a far cry from what had comprised of that specific territory.

"I'm Benny Morgan. Nice to meet you, ma'am."

Benny had an infectious smile, but she found it hard to return. It was as if he wanted her to underestimate him. She hadn't had much time before leaving the office this morning to do a thorough check on all the parties involved in the case from twenty years ago, but she certainly recognized his name.

Benny Morgan had been serving as sheriff when Vicki Anderson had been murdered not a mile and a half from the high school football field. Why would he have allowed a deputy to write up the report?

He waited for her to pass through the swinging wooden door, holding out his arm to greet her when she was finally close enough to shake hands.

"It's nice to meet you, too." Brook appreciated that he didn't go light on the handshake. "Please, call me Brook. Is Sheriff O'Sullivan here?"

Clearly, the man who she was looking for was not in the building, but it seemed an appropriate thing to ask.

"He'll be back shortly. Have a seat." Benny wasn't wearing a uniform, so Brook could only assume that he'd been kept on the payroll in some type of administrative role. Either that, or he simply liked hanging around his old stomping ground. Sheriff O'Sullivan was the only member of law enforcement listed on the town's city council. "Joey said that you're in town to see some old case files from the Vicki Anderson case."

Benny shook his head in sorrow, though any deep-rooted memories from that time didn't seem to take away his appetite. He went right back to devouring his burger that looked as if it had been soaked in grease for weeks. The soggy fries didn't appear to be any better.

"I am," Brook replied, pulling over a chair from a desk that sat empty. Out of the four desks that were positioned around the room, the only one that appeared to be in use was the one closest to the coffee pot that sat on what looked to be some type of breakfast bar. "I believe that her murder might be connected to my current investigation."

Benny nodded as he chewed a large bite of his food, though he didn't seem to be in agreement. He proved her right by following up with his thoughts.

"I wouldn't waste your time."

Benny used the same napkin to wipe his mouth again. He had a salt and pepper mustache, which matched his hair. She could only assume by the lines around his eyes and his weathered skin that he was somewhere in his late-sixties or early seventies. The murder investigation might have been Sheriff O'Sullivan's first case, but Benny had definitely been there to walk him through the motions.

"You're the former sheriff," Brook stated matter-of-factly. He nodded with a glint of knowledge in his blue eyes. "Tell me, Benny. Why would I be wasting my time by looking into Vicki Anderson's murder?"

"We know exactly who killed that girl." Benny tossed his napkin down in irritation, grimacing as if the conversation they were having was leaving a bad taste in his mouth. "His name is Francis Walker."

# CHAPTER ELEVEN

**Brooklyn Sloane**
*November 2021*
*Thursday—5:14 pm*

"You must be Miss Sloane."

Sheriff Joe O'Sullivan wasn't dressed in a uniform. He wasn't sporting a trooper's hat on his head, and he didn't even have a badge that was displayed anywhere on his body. He could fit in basically anywhere, and no one would be the wiser that he was part of the law enforcement community.

Granted, with a town the size of Sutton, Brook could only assume that everyone knew the man. There was no need for identification or anything of that sort. Still, it was odd to go from such a hierarchal agency to such a laid-back atmosphere. She was grateful that she'd changed into a pair of dark jeans to go with her blazer.

"Sheriff O'Sullivan," Brook acknowledged, returning his greeting by shaking his hand over the swinging door. It was firm, and he didn't soften his grip just because she was a woman. She wondered if Benny had anything to do with such a learned behavior. "I appreciate you allowing me to look over your old case files."

Benny made a noise that sounded very similar to a dismissive grunt, but Brook allowed it to pass. She was here for one thing and one thing only, and she hadn't appreciated being kept waiting for so long.

"You've already looked over our case files," Sheriff O'Sullivan replied pragmatically, just as she had with Benny twenty minutes earlier. "I was the one who gathered the files and mailed the hard copy off to your office in D.C. What has me concerned is what your presence here in town is going to do to Russell and Amanda Anderson."

Brook didn't care for how their first meeting was starting out, so she decided to slow things down. She wasn't one for small talk, but she was always able to acclimate to the situation when needed.

Sheriff O'Sullivan finally pushed through the swinging door, wearing a brown leather jacket over a navy-blue sweater and matching jeans. He walked directly to his desk and dropped his keys on top of a manilla folder before removing his jacket.

"Please, call me Brook. As I stated on the phone, I truly believe that Vicki Anderson's death is connected to—"

"The Princess Killer," Benny offered up from where he was still seated in a chair near the counter. His gaze followed her as she closed the distance to the sheriff's desk. "Isn't that what the media is calling him? It doesn't take a rocket scientist to connect the dots."

"Benny." Sheriff O'Sullivan waited for the former sheriff to refocus his attention. "I've got this. Isn't Carol waiting for you at home?"

Benny grimaced, but he didn't argue with the point that Sheriff O'Sullivan had made about the man's wife. She must run a tight ship.

"She's making that damn vegetarian lasagna again," Benny grumbled as he stood up. He snatched his jacket off the back of the chair in irritation before jamming his arms through the sleeves. "You sure you have this handled, Joey?"

Brook couldn't help the sense of gratification at being seen as a threat by these two men. Technically, it wasn't her. She understood that it was the agency that stood behind her that elicited such an uneasy response. Either way, she would obtain the information that she came for and maybe walk away with an arrest. She couldn't imagine that these men wanted anything less.

"I'm positive, Benny." Sheriff O'Sullivan cast her a glance of warning. It took her a moment to comprehend the reason. "You can call me Joe. I haven't gone by Joey since I was in high school."

"Quarterback and prom king, I'm guessing." Brook caught the look that had been exchanged between both men. They simply assumed that she'd done her research on them before driving into town, and she had to some extent. Those modest inquiries weren't what had her stating the obvious, though. "There's a football in the corner chair, along with a letterman's jacket hanging on an old coatrack that hasn't been disturbed in years."

"I give you points on the quarterback deduction, but there is no way in hell that you guessed his prom king status from his senior year of high school," Benny said begrudgingly, not leaving the building quite yet. "What kind of databases are you people running at the Bureau?"

Brook gave a small shrug, along with a denial. She'd like to keep the upper hand, and neither one of them needed to know that she'd spotted a reunion invitation half hidden underneath the manilla folder on the sheriff's desk. It had clearly stated the names of prom king and queen in bold lettering.

"Look at him, Benny. He is a handsome man in a small town, elected sheriff, and still pines for the good ol' days." Brook took a seat in front of Joe's desk, ready to get down to business. "No offense, Joe."

"None taken," he replied wryly, motioning for Benny to leave. Joe pulled his chair close as he took a seat behind his desk. "Say hi to Carol for me. Oh, and tell her that there is no need to activate the phone tree."

Benny could be heard complaining underneath his breath as he swung the wooden door out of his way before walking toward the exit. The interior of the large open space finally revealed the ticking of an old-fashioned clock hanging a bit crooked on the far wall. It was as if the faint noise was a warning that she was running out of time, on several areas of her life.

"I've read the case file, and you crossed every T and dotted every I." Brook wanted to make sure that they got off on the right foot. "I'm not here to question your investigation. The pieces weren't there for you to see the whole picture, but they are now. I plan to spend the night, and I'd like to speak with those involved tomorrow—Vicki Anderson's friends, teachers, and family. I'd also like to share with you what we've discovered at the other crimes scenes, and why I believe they might be connected to your victim."

"I'm sure that Benny has already told you that Francis Walker killed Vicki. Nothing is going to change our minds about that." Joe gave his opinion as he pulled a file that had been in the middle of his desk closer to him. He hesitated just a bit when his gaze landed on the invitation, but he let his suspicions go. "We couldn't prove it. There was no evidence to tie Francis to her murder. Benny handled most of the investigation, but he was having heart issues at the time. His first heart attack came two years later. I filled out most of the paperwork back then and kept in close contact with the state police."

Brook took her time replying, still attempting to keep what peace that was between them on an even keel. Joe clearly held Benny on a pedestal. She wouldn't get far in the hours or days ahead by knocking the man off it.

"I understand why you, Benny, and the state police focused on Francis Walker. He had sex with her that night. He was also the last to see her alive. Unfortunately, he doesn't fit the profile." Brook studied Joe as he opened the manilla folder in front of him. He was a handsome man, in the next-door kind of way. There was also an underlying intelligence about him that went unspoken. It was obvious from his defensive tone regarding the Anderson family that he cared about his community. "The unsub who we are looking for is a Caucasian male, thirty-five to forty-five years of age, and manipulative in nature. As I've explained to my colleagues, he would most likely be employed somewhere that doesn't notice his lack of responsibility to anything other than searching for his ideal woman. He'd want to be in a position that could impress the women he seeks to have as his own princess. Where is Francis Walker employed?"

"Before we get to that, Francis *does* check off the first two attributes on your list."

Brook allowed Joe to have his moment, but only because it was clear that he didn't want to believe that there was a chance someone else who he'd grown up with, went to school with, and even attended the same town functions could have become such a monster that they all seemed so willing to label Francis Walker.

The two men couldn't have been more than three or four years apart. Joe being older, of course.

Francis had already been a year out of high school during the time of Vicki's murder. She'd still been a senior and had last been seen by friends at a bonfire to celebrate the first football game of the season. She'd left with Francis, who swore at the time that he had dropped her off at home after they'd had sex in his car.

The home her parents swear she never returned to that night.

"Your suspect also works in a paper mill one town over, and he often works twelve hours shifts." Brook let her remarks sink in while she mentally lined up the rest of the points that she needed to make in order to get Joe to see things her way. "Francis Walker is accounted for basically twelve hours a day, six days a week. I would wager that people steer clear of him due to the stigma surrounding his alleged connection to Vicki Anderson's murder. He became an outcast, and will remain so, even if he's proven innocent beyond a shadow of a doubt. The only ones who will breathe a sigh of relief are his family members, because it will give them hope that their family will be welcomed back into the community with open arms at some point. We both know that's not how it works."

"Are you from the area?" Joe asked, leaning back in his chair as he regarded her more carefully than before, if that was even possible.

"No."

Brook didn't talk to her colleagues about her past, and she wasn't about to start opening up to a complete stranger.

"Francis had means, motive, and opportunity. He had no alibi. Vicki's friends saw her leave the bonfire with him, and he admitted to having sex with her that night," Joe stated, motioning toward what had to be statements in front of him. "He had anger issues in high school, and he was even kicked off the football team his senior year because he couldn't control his emotional outbursts."

"The unsub who I am looking for wouldn't have played football in high school. He wouldn't have even considered such a notion, because he wasn't physical in that manner. Francis' parents are also still together, which goes against the profile."

"Let me guess," Joe replied wryly. "Your suspect has mommy issues."

"Yes."

Brook wasn't going to apologize for the fact that her profile resembled a template. Sometimes, formulas worked in the way that they were intended to. Jacob had been the exception to the rule, but she'd worry about that tomorrow.

"The unsub possibly only had a father figure, who continually disparaged women. I believe that there were either photo albums or some type of old videos left behind that told of a different story. One where the unsub's parents had a fairytale beginning, only for their romance to sour. Something or someone destroyed their marriage, and the unsub wants to recreate what he feels is a happily ever after with his perfect princess."

Brook pointed toward the manila folder that Joe had shoved aside, because in those statements laid the answers that they all sought.

"Francis Walker's parents are both still together, and by all accounts, have a functional marriage." Brook had taken the few moments in between packing a small suitcase to pull up the Walkers' social media platforms. "They recently celebrated forty-six years of marriage."

Joe remained silent as he opened a drawer in his desk and began to rummage around until he pulled out an old notebook. The aging of it was evident from the curled pages and the discolored edges. She did her best to subdue her elation that he'd kept notes that had not been included in the initial criminal investigative report.

"Do you have a particular suspect in mind?" Joe asked, not sharing what he'd written down back in the day. "Someone still in town?"

"Let me ask you a question," Brook said, evading his questions. She shifted in her seat to become more comfortable. "Have you ever heard of the urban legend about a coal miner who created a shrine out of coal for the love of his life? It was as large as his love for her….only the memorial that he'd spent months building collapsed on them as they stood side by side?"

"Of course. It apparently happened near the creek down by the covered bridge. We used to tell that story around a few bonfires back in the day."

"Let me guess," Brook offered, encouraged to witness his willingness to open up about the town. "You told the urban legend around the bonfires in order to get a few of the cheerleaders to cling to you just a little bit tighter."

"I don't admit nor deny," Joe replied with a crooked smile, tapping the back of the old notebook that was still in his hand. "I'm not sure there wasn't a bit of truth to that story, to be honest. There are still rumors told that you can see their spirits walking the creek bed every full moon. Not that I can tell you what a full moon has to do with such a tale."

"I hadn't heard the full moon bit, either. The story is actually told in several surrounding towns, but with different variants to make it more fitting to the area." Brook leaned forward a bit in order for him to understand where she was going with the conversation. "Joe, a victim by the name of Jessica Monroe was stabbed to death before being buried underneath a ton of coal. The urban legend is told in a very concentrated region. It's the reason why I've been looking so closely at murders in the tristate area, and not just those that are still categorized as open investigations. Our justice system isn't perfect, so I included all cases that had certain factors that met the criteria that I've put together."

Joe remained silent, though it was evident he'd appreciated her explanation. Truthfully, all she wanted right now was to read through the notebook in his hand and have him take her to the site where Vicki Anderson had been murdered.

"Do you *have* a suspect?"

"No." Brook ignored the chime of her phone, which was currently tucked inside her purse. It was most likely Frank, wondering if she'd been able to make any headway. "That's why I'm here, Joe."

Joe sighed and leaned forward, handing her the old notebook over the desk.

"There were no other viable suspects." He pushed back with his legs so that his chair rolled away far enough to allow him to stand. She had believed that their small talk would get him to relax about her presence in town, but it seemed to have done the opposite. "Driving out to the site where Vicki was murdered will have to wait until morning. The usual road that is used to reach the area has been blocked off due to flooding. We'll end up walking a good half a mile from another access point, and the terrain isn't ideal without good lighting. We can meet back here at seven o'clock tomorrow morning."

Brook could sense that he would completely shut down any sense of cooperation if she pushed the issue, so she simply nodded and held up the worn notebook in gratitude.

"That works for me," she agreed before standing, as well. She switched the old pad to her other hand before extending her right arm. "I appreciate the help, and I'll use tonight to go through your personal notes on the case."

Brook was impressed that he would have kept such detailed information regarding a case, especially given his age at the time of the murder. She sensed that he would take her compliment as an insult had she said anything aloud. He'd been young, most likely around the age of twenty-three, and the notebook might have been some type of journal to help him cope with the fact that a girl who he'd known all her life had been left to rot out in the woods.

"There is one more thing."

Brook had paused to take out a file from her briefcase. She'd carefully exchanged the worn notebook for the manilla folder.

"This is one of our case files attached to the investigation." The information inside was basically the bare bones of Beth Lindsey's murder. "Please look this over tonight. Let me know if you see any similarities between the crime scene photos taken of the victim. Look closely to see if anything resembles what you witnessed firsthand at the site where Vicki Anderson's body was discovered."

Brook didn't have to witness the surprise written across Joe's facial features to know that she'd reeled him in to the exact spot in the water that she needed him to be for their morning hike to go as planned.

She'd pegged him as a quid pro quo kind of man, and she hadn't been disappointed.

"I'll be here at seven o'clock tomorrow morning," Brook replied as she picked up both her briefcase and purse. "I truly appreciate your help, Joe. I'd wish you a nice evening, but I do believe that you'll need a shot of whiskey or two once you make the connection."

Brook left Joe standing near the garbage can that Benny had used to throw away his leftover food. She was grateful to step out into the cool, refreshing air. There really wasn't a place to stay in town, so she would have to drive a good twenty some miles before finding anything resembling a motel.

Seeing as Benny had a good head start and he wasn't likely to be heading home to his wife anytime soon, the town almost certainly had Brook's description, the make of her vehicle, and the fact that she was determined to dig around in their sordid pasts. Without a doubt, she wasn't going to be welcomed with open arms.

It was best that she stay overnight on the outskirts of town, anyway.

Joe would have a change of heart once he got a good look at the crime scene photos of Beth Lindsey's murder, but the residents would still view her as someone who wanted to sift through their closely guarded secrets.

One thing that Brook was more confident in now was that these close-knit residents had skeletons in their closet that would reveal the identity of her unsub. She just needed to locate the right residence for which the closet belonged to all those years ago.

# CHAPTER TWELVE

**Brooklyn Sloane**
*November 2021*
*Thursday—11:08 pm*

B‌ROOK TURNED ANOTHER worn page inside the old notebook, making another annotation in her own files of an additional name to run a background check on before tomorrow morning. The data wouldn't be complete, but it would at least give her a broader idea of who to investigate more thoroughly at a later date.

It was safe to say after reading Joe's personal notes regarding the investigation that Vicki Anderson had been popular among her peers, and she had certainly caught the attention of Francis Walker.

While Brook didn't believe that Walker was the unsub, he just might have been paying close enough attention to the victim to have an idea of who else had been seeking her admiration. Those types of devotees sometimes paid a bit more attention than friends or family. Joe wasn't going to appreciate the numerous people who she wanted to speak to after their visit to the crime scene.

Another ping echoed throughout the small room that she'd secured without issue. It was the alert from her personal email, and several had come through in the last ten minutes. At least two of them were probably from her father's nursing home.

She'd checked in with management regarding any new hires within the last year once she'd accepted that Jacob had the audacity to step foot back in Illinois, though she couldn't picture him doing anything so reckless to be close to their father. The last thing her brother had said was that he'd hoped their parents rotted in hell.

Why, then, was he visiting Illinois?

It wasn't like she could ask her father. His Alzheimer's Disease had robbed him of remembering any of the immediate family, let alone recalling what had taken place months ago.

Brook had sent an email to a nurse on staff who accepted a monthly monetary gift on the side to monitor any guests who visited her father, any phone calls that he received, or if anything unusual occurred on what had to surely be a rather mundane life of staring out the windows of the nursing home community room.

Brook sighed as she set down Joe's notepad and tossed her pencil on top of it. She'd been going through each page as meticulously as possible, having already noticed that Joe had included a lot of the information in the actual criminal report that he'd typed up in the days after the murder.

There weren't that many loose ends left to tie up.

Her vision was now a bit strained, especially given the dim lighting in the room. Management certainly hadn't splurged on the lightbulbs. The out-of-the-way motel was located around twenty minutes south of town next to the entrance of the main highway, and it certainly wasn't anything to write home about.

As she stood from the bed, she gradually stretched her arms

above her head and grabbed her left elbow with her right hand. She'd taken off her blazer and hung it up in the small closet on the other side of the bed. There hadn't been a dresser or anything of the sort, so she'd left her small suitcase packed on a stand meant for large-sized luggage.

She pulled her elbow ever so firmly behind her head in an attempt to loosen the knot in her shoulder blade as she made her way over to the worn desk. Her upper back had been bothering her lately, and no amount of stretching had been able to relieve the dull ache.

Upon entering the motel room earlier this evening, she'd opened the lid of her laptop to check her emails before discovering from the sign inside a scratched plastic holder that the motel didn't have room service. What they did offer was the phone number of a small pizzeria that delivered until nine o'clock in the evening.

Brook had ordered a medium-sized pepperoni and mushroom pizza hours ago, along with three bottles of water. She hadn't eaten it all. Then again, she had experienced guilt upon asking them to deliver a small pizza. She briefly considered going there to eat, but she hadn't wanted to waste time that she could use to comb through the entire contents of Joe's notes.

She waited until she was seated in the hardback chair that had seen better days before perusing the emails that she'd recently received. Sure enough, she discovered the one that she'd been waiting for regarding new employees who had been hired at the nursing home in the last few months.

She breathed a sigh of relief at the photos of the three women who were new to the facility. Only one male individual had been brought onto the staff, and he was a sixty-eight-year-old volunteer. She verified his photograph before moving the mouse to close down her email.

Brook hesitated when she caught sight of Graham Elliott's name. The subject line was still in bold. A part of her wanted to ignore the message; make him wait a little bit longer for the notification that would be sent once she opened the email. To validate her procrastination, she also reasoned that she had a long night ahead of her on the current investigation.

Still, it wouldn't hurt to see what value that he'd come up with for her to exchange the one vehicle that enabled her to locate her brother. He'd basically promised the same, but she highly doubted that he would be able to provide the same contacts and technology that the agency had at their disposal.

Besides, she already had a lead on Jacob.

Brook debated for another few minutes, even going so far as to make herself a cup of coffee in the cheap machine that the hotel had positioned on a small counter right outside the bathroom. She took the paper cup back to the small desk and proceeded to open the message.

The first thing that her gaze landed on was the annual salary that Elliot had typed in the first line of the first paragraph.

She almost dropped her cup.

If her fixation on Jacob hadn't been the main issue keeping her from leaving the Bureau, she would have seriously considered the proposal. On the other hand, there was no explanation as to how a retired senior officer from the Marine Corps could run an operation such as this. The bulk of the email went into great depths of how he would like her to run a consulting firm based on her experience with the FBI. The only caveat was that the first case had to be the one attached, though she didn't have time to go through the files. There were too many attached, and apparently from many different police departments around the country.

"You have piqued my interest, Mr. Elliot," Brook murmured to herself, placing her lips on the sensitive skin that was between her index finger and thumb. The hot beverage had all but scalded her hand, and she would have a red mark for a day or two. "Who exactly are you?"

Wanting answers to that question before she spoke with him again, Brook made her way back to the nightstand where she'd left her phone on the charger. She used her left hand to send a message to someone in operations who owed her a favor, requesting information on one Graham Elliott. She figured she had time before he attempted to contact her again. He would see that she'd opened his message, read the contents, and give her time to come to a decision, though she already knew what her response would be to his proposition.

Right as she sent the text, the shrilling of the hotel phone reverberated around the small room.

"Sloane," she answered before finally taking a tentative sip of her coffee. There was only one person who knew that she was staying at this motel, besides those at the local FBI office. "Please tell me that there is a good coffee place in this town that's open before seven o'clock tomorrow morning."

She grimaced at the acidic taste, but she managed to swallow the bitter coffee.

"Ms. Sloane, don't hang up. Please."

"Who is this?" Brook asked cautiously, setting down her coffee before she ended up causing more damage to her hand.

"This is Matt Henley."

Brook stilled her movements as she collected her thoughts and emotions. She sure as hell wouldn't lose her composure over the phone to a crime vlogger who would more than likely publicize her reaction. Hell, he was almost certainly recording this call for good measure.

Several questions mulled through her mind, though.

First and foremost, how did he know that she had left D.C.?

And just as important, how did he know where she was staying when she hadn't even known herself?

She already had the answer to that inquiry based on the profile that she'd generated of the unsub. Nothing escaped the residents of a small town, and that meant Matt Henley was in the area.

"Mr. Henley," Brook began as professionally as she could while palming her firearm that she'd set on the nightstand. She'd taken the holster off her waistband so that she would be more comfortable on the bed. "How did you get this number?"

"It wasn't easy, but I really need to speak with you."

Brook slowly crossed the short distance to the door and peered out the small hole. Considering this was a motel, she'd been able to park her vehicle directly in front of her room. She scanned the view that was available to her, with no success in locating the so-called reporter.

"You know more than most that the FBI has a protocol for any type of statements regarding ongoing investigations, so I suggest you use them."

Brook continued to monitor the parking lot.

"Please, just hear me out," Matt practically pleaded in what could only be considered panic. She held off disconnecting the call and remained quiet to see if he would continue. A silhouette finally disconnected with the dark shadows on the far side of the parking lot. "You're going to want to talk to me tomorrow, regardless. I'm just hoping to get in front of this."

"In front of what?"

Brook debated on swinging the door open to catch Henley off guard, but she decided against it. She'd rather that he possess the impression of having the upper hand in this situation. The panic in his tone was rather profound, and it was only a matter of time before he confessed to whatever had him wound up.

"I graduated from the same high school as Vicki Anderson, two years after her murder."

Brook once again remained silent.

Matt technically fit the profile, as well as his job. He was also always reporting on current events across the nation. He traveled, reported to no one, and such a career would impress the women…for a short while.

Still, the unsub wouldn't offer himself up on a silver platter to the FBI. Her profile stated that the unsub wasn't even remotely ready for his search for a princess to come to an end.

"Stay where you are. Hands where I can see them."

Brook disconnected the call, monitoring his movements for a solid minute before she finally left her place by the door. She took her time collecting her holster and attaching it to the waistband of her jeans. Once her weapon was secure, she then grabbed her blazer off the hanger. She even made sure that the key to her room was tucked into the back pocket of her jeans before verifying that Henley was still standing in the same spot that she'd last seen him.

With his hands still half raised in the air, Brook slowly opened the door and shut it behind her before she closed the distance between them. The cold air was brisk enough that she could see his breath was uneven with every exhalation.

Matt Henley was nervous.

Brook waited to speak until she was about ten feet away from him, having already scanned the parking lot. There were only three vehicles to be found, along with a white van that she'd already taken time to memorize the license plate number, along with the company's name.

"I didn't kill Vicki Anderson," Matt replied, keeping his hands somewhat raised and away from his body.

He paused and waited for her to respond, but she didn't feel the need to in this situation.

He was a reporter.

Therefore, it stood to reason that he was recording this conversation.

"Listen, I got a call last night from an old friend. He said that an agent was coming to town with questions that might be related to the Princess Killer case. I tried calling you at the office, but they wouldn't tell me anything. So, I drove down here first thing this morning. It doesn't take a genius to figure out that the FBI is interested in Vicki Anderson's murder, but then I realized how it was going to look when my name and picture showed up in the yearbook."

It certainly wouldn't look good, but she refrained from agreeing with him. The longer she remained silent, the more he seemed inclined to talk.

"Imagine my surprise when I found out that you're here instead of one of the agent's assigned to the case. This has to do with the profile, right?" Matt's arms slowly lowered, though not to the point that such an action made her nervous. "I can help you. I know these people. You tell me who you want to speak to, and I'll make it happen. John Taylor? Luke Harris? Sam Baker? They were at the bonfire, and they all still live around here."

All three names were listed in the report, and all three boys had given their statements back then. Brook had made a list of those who she'd like to re-question. She wouldn't go through Matt Henley to do it, though. Still, she appreciated his ability to be forthcoming about his involvement, however little it might have been.

"I appreciate your offer, Mr. Henley. As I am sure you already know, I've already been in contact with Sheriff O'Sullivan." Brook didn't miss Henley's slight upturned lip upon hearing Joe's title. She let it slide for now. "I would like to know if you were at the bonfire that night."

"No. I was busy at home that night writing about the football team's first win of the season for the school's newspaper." Henley didn't disappoint her by following up on his contempt for the town's sheriff. "I can help you, Agent Sloane. Joe O'Sullivan might have been older, but he was friends with most of those guys back then. He won't tell you the truth."

The faint sounds of tractor trailers driving down the highway traveled through the night air. Other than the slight humming of their large tires against the asphalt, there were no other sounds to be heard. No crickets, no frogs, and no nocturnal birds overhead looking for food.

It was as if the wildlife in the area sensed another predator was in their territory.

"And what truth is that?" Brook asked quietly, not bothering to correct Henley on her title. He was rubbing his hands together to keep warm, and such a gesture indicated that he was becoming more comfortable as the conversation wore on. "This is a small town, Mr. Henley. Everyone knows everyone else.

That isn't anything new."

"You don't know, do you?"

Brook didn't take offense to the question. She'd already made a connection that she fully intended to follow up on in the morning, but it was to her advantage to come across as if she was still in the dark. If Henley happened to mention something else that she could use in the investigation, so be it.

"Joey covered for Benjamin Morgan, Jr.—Benny Morgan's son. He was seen with Vicki that day," Matt pointed out, clearly hoping that the intimate details got him an inside track into the investigation. "I bet those details wasn't in the initial report. Am I right?"

The fact that Henley didn't currently have the public reports on Vicki Anderson's murder told her that he'd never made the connection between his hometown and the investigation. It had only been when he had received a call regarding an agent's inquiry into the case that he eventually connected the dots.

"I can help you, Agent Sloane."

"For a price," Brook predicted, finally receiving his nod of confirmation. She looked off into the darkened distance, never one to turn away a source without reason. "What are your terms, Mr. Henley?"

He shifted his weight under her scrutiny, but that didn't stop him from forging ahead in an attempt to make a deal. He would be significantly disappointed when she didn't take him up on his initial offer, but she'd see to it that she had bargaining room if the time ever came that she needed information.

"I help you in exchange for an exclusive interview as the profiler on the case." Matt held out his hand as if a mere handshake would solidify their arrangement. "Agreed?"

# CHAPTER THIRTEEN

## Unsub
*November 2021*
*Thursday—11:34 pm*

FEAR THREATENED TO drown him, but he'd managed to hold onto his composure until he walked through his own front door. Once alone, he screamed in anguish until he landed onto the hardwood floor of his living room mentally exhausted. His knees hit first, followed immediately by his clenched fists.

Where had he gone wrong?

What thread had led her here?

What tiny detail had directed Brook Sloane's attention to such a small town in Pennsylvania? All of his carefully constructed plans had started to unravel once he saw on national news that the FBI had been called in to assist the local law enforcement officials with his version of Snow White.

He'd been so careful.

The profiler's arrival was all anyone in town could talk about, and her presence had him remembering his earlier version of Hansel and Gretel. She'd been laid to rest, though. He'd already shown everyone that she hadn't been deserving of her own story. She'd deceived him, and he'd had to rewrite the ending to suit her punishment.

Just like he had with all the others…

He'd been so meticulous and painstakingly patient in searching for a woman deserving of his love. Most of their names escaped him, because they'd been nothing but imposters. They were no longer important in the grand scheme of his eternal story.

His fairytale was simply waiting to be written.

He leaned back on his heels when he was steady enough, and then he used the back of his hand to wipe away the moisture underneath his nose. No one was going to stop him from finding his princess—not the twisted and dishonest media, not the evil stepmother, and certainly not the simpleminded Brook Sloane.

# CHAPTER FOURTEEN

**Brooklyn Sloane**
*November 2021*
*Friday—7:44 am*

THE RAIN HADN'T let up since Brook and Joe had gotten out of his forest green F-150 truck a half mile back. The overcast sky was a mixture of lighter and darker grey clouds, and there didn't seem to be hope for even a single sliver of sunshine anytime soon. While she slowly walked around the site of where Vicki Anderson's body had been found, she understood the unsub's reasoning for choosing such a remote area.

The isolated place was far enough away from civilization that no one would have heard his victim's agonizing screams. Most of the region was covered in tall dead overgrown grass and wilted weeds waist high that hadn't been cut back in decades. Most of the red maples in the area had lost their leaves this fall, and there was a row of pine trees off in the distance that had been damaged from decades of raging storms. The scent of wet dirt hung heavy in the air, while the only sound that could be heard in the distance was the faint sound of spitting rain onto the roof of an abandoned structure maybe sixty feet away from where they stood.

Joe had been good on his word and met her at the station at

seven o'clock sharp. Surprisingly, he'd even brought her a cup of coffee from the local diner. She hadn't mentioned the activities of her evening, and he hadn't bothered to ask. As a matter of fact, he hadn't said more than five words since they'd gotten into his truck.

Brook had been up since before five thirty, having fallen asleep sometime after one o'clock. She wasn't bothered by his silence, but she figured it wouldn't be long before he began to ask her questions regarding the file that she'd given him to review yesterday.

As for Matt Henley, he had left without his handshake, though she had given her word that she would take time to think over his proposition. A quick search had revealed both of his parents were still together and owned a farm on the outskirts of town. She'd submitted for a more in-depth background check, but she was relatively certain that he wasn't her unsub.

She had sent electronic requests for background checks on Benjamin Morgan, Jr., as well as John Taylor, Luke Harris, and Sam Baker. She'd also included one on Sheriff Joe O'Sullivan for good measure, though he didn't fit the profile, either—both of his parents were still married to this day, he had an older brother by one year, and his job required that he be in town on a continuous basis. She still wanted to confirm that nothing stood out to raise a red flag.

"Have you seen enough?"

Joe clearly wasn't a morning person, but Brook didn't let that bother her. She'd found exactly what she'd expected, which fed further into her theory that Vicki Anderson had been the unsub's first victim.

One of the puzzles that she couldn't solve was where the vast number of sweets had come from. The victim's body had been covered in pink, blue, and green hardtack candy. Such an odd detail meant the murder had been premeditated.

The unsub must have fantasized about such acts from a very young age. He may have even started masturbating, once reaching puberty, to thoughts of posing the bodies of his victims.

Where had he gotten his hands on so many boxes of hardtack candy without being questioned about his purchase or seen around town buying the telltale item? The age range of her profile meant that the unsub would have been of driving age. He most likely would have had access to a vehicle, which meant other towns that had carried such candies would have been an option. She'd have Frank check into it when he could, given his current caseload.

According to the criminal report, Joe had followed up with the local shops back then to see if someone had either bought or stolen the specific square hardtack candy that had used to place on nearly every inch of her skin. None of the local owners had been out of stock, nor had they remembered anyone buying it in bulk.

"Look over there," Brook instructed, though she'd kept her tone as light as she could under the circumstances. There was no reason to get his defenses up quite yet. "Tell me what you see."

"I know where you're going with this." Joe took out the gloves that he'd shoved into the pocket of his coat earlier. He wasn't even glancing in the direction of the falling down structure styled in early Pennsylvania Dutch. "I can see how the landscape could be compared to Hansel and Gretel."

"And the file that I gave you last night? Did you notice anything of significance?"

"The way the victim's hair was brushed over her shoulders."

Brook was pleased that he'd taken the time to study the comparisons.

She took a few more moments to study the area. There were remnants of a wooden cross and some frayed ribbon that someone had left behind as a memorial. It didn't appear that anyone had been out here recently, and she highly doubted that the killer himself ever ventured out this far in the years since the murder. This was the past, and his gaze was drawn toward the future.

He'd brought an end to this particular story, and he'd already moved on to another…many more, in fact.

"Francis Walker didn't murder Vicki Anderson," Brook stated with conviction. She had to close her fingers into the palms of her hands to maintain any warmth. "You can see that now, right?"

"How confident are you that the killer is from Sutton?" Joe asked, purposefully not responding to her question.

He finished putting on his gloves and was currently staring at the worn wooden cross that had been left behind by some poor grieving soul who had once loved the victim very much. If Brook had to guess, Joe wasn't even registering that the monument was there. He was no doubt envisioning what Vicki Anderson had looked like the night that her body had been found by the owner of the property.

"What's to say that the killer didn't spot her while driving through the neighborhood, abduct her from outside of her home, and then bring her out here to kill?"

"You already know the answer to that, but I'll humor you anyway." Brook adjusted the hood of her black raincoat. She hadn't bothered with gloves, because chances were that the unsub was already aware of her presence. She wanted access to her weapon if she needed it without being hampered by thick leather. "A random stranger wouldn't know how to get to this place. The unsub would have established some type of relationship with Vicki, which was the reason that she didn't put up a fight outside of her home. She went with whomever it was willingly. She trusted him."

"If the killer takes time to establish a relationship of some sort with the victims, wouldn't you already have a description of him from their family or friends?" Joe inquired with a very valid question. She also had his full attention now. "I mean, one of the victims would have mentioned a new man being in their lives to someone, right?"

"I'm not so sure the connection between them would be important enough for her to mention it to those closest to her." Brook had seen enough of the site, and it was time to head back into town. She had a long list of people who she would like to speak with this morning. The faster they got through the list, the quicker they'd be able to locate the unsub. "For him, maybe. For her? It might be someone she speaks with every morning at a café. It could be someone who jogs on the same path that he'd used while in an area, or it's possible that he's merely someone she speaks with on the phone for work. What she sees as harmless, he sees as something more."

Joe fell into step beside her, and they strolled slowly toward the area that he'd parked his truck. Brook had planned for not only walking around the site, but also the trek to and from the vehicle.

Vicki Anderson had done so herself that fateful night,

though the region had probably been full of growth back in the day. The trees would have had an abundance of leaves, the grass would have been maintained, and the structure off to the side wouldn't have been so worn down. Brook could envision the property alive with lightning bugs, wildlife running here and there, and birds flying from branch to branch. Truthfully, the area reminded her of some sites in her hometown.

Brook had laced up her black boots tight across her ankles for extra support. While the boots were functional for hiking, they weren't conducive to wearing for the remainder of the day. She considered herself lucky that she'd had the foresight to store her black flats in the leather briefcase that she'd stored in the back of Joe's truck.

"No one in town has a job that allows for travel plans like you're referring to," Joe pointed out, unable to wrap his mind around the fact that a simple week was all it took to spark the unsub's fantasies. "There are a lot of surrounding areas that could be home to this psychopath. I believe it's a viable theory that you should at least consider."

Joe might be willing to accept that Francis Walker wasn't responsible for Vicki Anderson's death, but he wasn't at a point where he could fathom someone who he'd grown up with as being a cold-blooded killer.

"Technically speaking, the unsub would be labeled a sociopath in this case. He has established emotional ties with those in this community. A psychopath is unable to do so, although they are very good at faking it. I don't see that in this situation." Brook had considered the possibility that they were dealing with a psychopath, but her profile suggested otherwise based on the way he'd staged his victims. He had formed a bond with them while they were living, however misconstrued it might have been for him. "As for the unsub's profession, it would be something that would allow him to travel across the tristate area. He hasn't gone farther based on our findings, though. As I stated before, the trips wouldn't be long. He connects quickly, and then he lets his fantasies play out while he's home. He could then stalk them online, causing him to believe that he's involved in their lives on a more intimate level."

Joe remained quiet for the rest of the walk. He kindly opened the passenger side door for her, waiting patiently while she hoisted herself up and inside the cab using the side handle. She waited until he'd closed the door to push the hood of her raincoat off her hair. She'd taken time to secure the dark strands at the base of her neck. As for her muddy boots, it would be pointless to change out of them now, so she'd wait until they were back at the station.

It wasn't long before Joe had settled in behind the steering wheel. He took his time removing the gloves that he'd technically just put on before setting them on top of the dashboard. She gazed over at him warily when he didn't automatically take the keys out of his pocket.

Brook had personally reached out to some of the individuals on her list to speak with around six o'clock this morning. Two would be at the station in under an hour, and the other would be later in the day. Joe wouldn't be pleased that she hadn't included him, but he'd unknowingly forfeited that right the moment that Matt Henley had exposed the coverup for Benny Morgan's son.

"Vicki Anderson was blonde, whereas Beth Lindsey had dark brown hair. Serial killers usually have a type," Joe pointed out, still trying to make sense of where he'd gone wrong twenty years ago. He'd only had one murder and little evidence to go by. She had multiple murders, an in-depth profile, and a vast lab of technological advancement that hadn't been available two decades ago. "What are the connections between the victims?"

"We're not completely sure." Brook had answered as matter-of-factly as she could, no longer needing to entice him along on this investigation. She wasn't surprised in the least that his first question had basically been the first of many. His mind was working overtime and attempting to connect the dots. "You're right that most victims are usually linked in some manner, whether that be their profession, the color of their hair, or the color of their eyes. The only connections between the victims in this case are that they are female. Period. No age requirements, no race requirements, nor specific body types. They have no correlation to one another, which means that we are left to sort through their lives with a fine-tooth comb in hopes of catching that one thread that could tie them all together."

Joe pondered over her reply as he finally took the keys out of his pocket. She'd already anticipated his next question, though he took his time as he turned over the engine. It wasn't long before he shifted the truck into gear, not even bothering to put the vehicle in reverse. He simply pressed his work boot onto the accelerator and drove in a wide circle until they were back on the road and headed into town.

"I'd like to see the other case files."

"I can have that arranged." Brook held her right hand in front of the vent. The air was warm enough to heat her skin, proof that they hadn't been gone from the vehicle for too long. "I'd like to speak with Vicki Anderson's parents later this morning. I'd also like to ask John Taylor, Luke Harris, and Sam

Baker some questions this afternoon about that night."

"I assume that Meg and Tasha are on that list of yours?"

Meg Beavin and Tasha Dahl had been Vicki Anderson's best friends. Brook had read over their statements, but nothing they'd given at the time had aided in the investigation. They'd been emotionally distraught and in complete shock over their friend's death. Add in living in such a close-knit community, and it was doubtful that either woman had ever gotten over such a tragedy.

They should count their blessings that they hadn't been the ones to find their friend.

Brook did her best to push down the resentment that threatened to come forward, which was unusual. She'd handled dozens of cases where she'd had to interview family and friends who'd experienced survivor's guilt. She prided herself on maintaining a professional distance. Unfortunately, being so close to her own brand of justice seemed to have her on a precipice.

As images of her own best friend's body lying in the middle of a cornfield flashed through her mind, Brook purposefully took a deep breath and held it until she became refocused on the day ahead.

"Are you alright?"

"Yes," Brook responded cursorily, letting her hand drop from the vent. She pulled her cell phone from the pocket of her raincoat. "I'm just going over the day's events in my head. As for Meg and Tasha, I've already spoken to them this morning. They'll be at the station shortly."

"I could have helped you with those phone calls."

"It was no problem. I was up early, anyway."

The rain was coming down a bit harder than before, and Joe had turned the wipers onto the next speed to keep up with the relentless stream on the front windshield. Brook allowed the silence to become somewhat comfortable before giving the name of the person she was truly interested in speaking to later in the day.

She'd purposefully waited for the perfect time to monitor the sheriff's reaction.

"There is another individual of interest who I'm meeting at three o'clock this afternoon. I've already taken care of the arrangements. Knowing how these small towns can be, I didn't want there to be any conflict of interest on your part. I'm sure you can understand my position."

The whitening of Joe's knuckles on the steering wheel gave credence to Matt Henley's personal observation all those years ago. She might find herself giving that exclusive interview, after all. Technically, she would pass the buck off to Frank, but Henley would still obtain an exclusive for his vlog.

"And who would that be?"

"Benjamin Morgan, Jr.," Brook replied as she turned her attention to her phone. She'd gotten the reaction that she'd expected, so there was no real need to keep him in suspense. "As I already told you, I phoned him myself before meeting you at the station this morning. It's best to keep your friendship with him separate from my investigation."

"You've been busy. Look, I don't know how you—"

"It doesn't matter how I connected your friend to the investigation, but I am not going to ignore the facts of this case due to the involvement of the former sheriff. That's not how the FBI does business."

Would Benjamin Morgan, Jr. fit the profile of the unsub?

Was Carol Morgan even the biological mother of Benny

Morgan's son? If not, that alone was enough to have a closer look at the family.

Brook would have the answers to her questions shortly.

Hell, they might already be sitting in her inbox. She'd already requested a full background on everyone who she would be speaking with today. The software that she had at her disposal could give her the surface details, but hidden skeletons tended to take a bit more digging. Frank was already busy, but he'd promised to do what he could in that area.

There was one thing that she had wanted to mention to Joe in hopes of making this day easier on the two of them. It was looking more and more like it wouldn't be long before she fit a suspect with her profile, and that meant calling in an agent from the Pittsburgh field office to help her make an arrest.

"In case you missed my point entirely, Sheriff O'Sullivan, now would be the perfect time to fill me in on what you left out regarding Benjamin Morgan, Jr.'s connection with the victim."

Three to four weeks was all they had before the unsub struck again, and she wasn't going to stand by and let the sheriff run interference and make this case drag on longer than necessary. Another woman's life hung in the balance, and too many had already been forsaken.

# CHAPTER FIFTEEN

**Brooklyn Sloane**
*November 2021*
*Friday—8:52 am*

"I APPRECIATE YOU taking the time to come into the station to speak with me today," Brook said as she finished jotting down the last note of her first interview. "There is one more question that I would like to ask you, and I'd like you to know that anything you say will remain confidential."

Meg Beavin hadn't aged well.

Her weathered skin was indicative of repeated exposure to too much sun over the years or her smoking habit had taken its toll. Both, if Brook had to hazard a guess. Not even her chipped nail polish could disguise the yellowish tint on the inside of her index finger. Her dirty blonde hair had been dyed too frequently, and the bags underneath her eyes indicated that she'd not only stayed out a bit too late last night, but she'd also had one too many drinks.

The woman shifted uncomfortably in the chair that Brook had set next to one of the empty desks in the far corner. She'd purposefully chosen the one that had been positioned near the restroom, which was the farthest away from Joe's desk. The chair that Meg occupied also had the back of it facing in his direction.

Brook didn't want his appearance to influence the answers that she was soliciting from the townsfolk.

Joe was currently on the phone, and his agitation pointed to the former sheriff being on the other end of the line. There was no doubt word had already spread around town that she'd requested to speak with Benjamin Morgan, Jr.

Joe had come clean about Benny and his son. He'd explained how he believed such a detail would have muddied the waters and taken the warranted attention off Francis Walker. She figured that Joe was more worried about his reputation at the moment. There was no telling how the townsfolk would react to such a blatant coverup of a viable suspect. The resulting fallout would all depend on how well-liked Benny's son was in town.

"What do you mean, confidential?" Meg asked cautiously, crossing her arms in a subconscious maneuver to protect herself. She hadn't even bothered to take off her coat. Reliving the past wasn't something that she'd been eager to do. "Everyone knows everything in this town. Francis Walker is the one who killed Vicki. I don't know why you just don't arrest him. It's not like you'll hear anyone say anything differently."

"Tell me about Benjamin Morgan, Jr."

Brook had purposefully chosen to go with an open-ended inquiry. She was likely to get more information than had she tried to narrow things down too quickly. To make it appear that the direction of the conversation was nothing more than a mere follow-up, Brook set the pen down and reached for her coffee.

She'd had just enough time to change out of her muddy boots and into her black pumps before Meg had pulled up in front of the station. Brook once again was glad that she'd worn a pair of dark jeans, although this time she'd accompanied them with a deep burgundy turtleneck underneath her black blazer. She'd wanted the extra layer for when they were at the site of Vicki Anderson's murder, but her need for warmth inadvertently had an added benefit.

Joe kept the office slightly cooler than she would have been comfortable with back at the FBI offices. Maybe that was the reason why Meg hadn't taken her coat off to hang on the row of metal hooks on the wall near the front entrance. By making it seem whatever answer Meg gave in the next few minutes wasn't important enough to write down, the woman would almost certainly give more details on the subject than not.

"BJ?" Meg frowned, as if he wasn't important. "BJ wasn't even at the bonfire that night. He was older than we were, and he could have cared less about football."

"Why?" Brook asked, taking a sip of her coffee. She'd already asked Meg if she would like anything to drink before they had taken their seats, but the woman had turned down the offer. "I would think the son of the sheriff would have thrived in that type of atmosphere."

"You're talking about sports, right??" Meg let out a light laugh, relaxing somewhat under the guise of mere conversation. "BJ wasn't athletic in the least to the utter disappointment of his daddy. He still isn't much of a man, to tell you the truth. Benny Sr. was captain of his football team back when my parents went to high school. A hometown hero. It was common knowledge that he tried to push BJ in that direction, but he was too busy…well, hanging with his friends."

Brook noticed the break in Meg's statement.

It was common for children of those in authority to rebel. Joe's confession about BJ's proclivities outside of school was about to be confirmed, though Brook couldn't quite fathom that a town of this size had any gang relations to the big cities. Small towns such as Sutton tended to have small groups of rebels or malcontents' binge-drinking, growing weed, and using or trafficking Class 1 substances. Nevertheless, heavier drugs had found their way into every corner of the country.

If BJ had been selling drugs to the high school crowd, which it was looking more and more like that was the case, that alone would discount him as the unsub. Nowhere in her profile did it suggest the unsub would do something to tarnish his reputation with those he was attempting to impress.

Brook had to word her next question very carefully if she wanted to get any useful information from this point on. The fact that Meg had prudently caught herself before revealing too much had exposed a thread that was worth pulling, regardless that it went against the profile.

"I want to make it clear that I am only here to investigate Vicki Anderson's murder. Other offenses are not of any interest to me." Brook technically was here for a lot more than that, but she needed Meg to believe that the FBI had a personal stake in this investigation. "I don't care about underage drinking, drugs of any sort, or who was sleeping with who twenty years ago. I just need to establish a timeline in the days leading up to Vicki's death. All I need is a simple yes or no answer. Was BJ supplying Vicki with drugs?"

Meg visibly swallowed and quickly peered over her shoulder. Brook cleared her throat so that the woman's gaze didn't linger too long on either Joe or the woman standing next to the swinging door. She'd walked into the station a few moments ago and was holding a book close to her chest. It was actually a yearbook, and it had been something that Brook had requested Tasha Dahl bring with her while they'd been on the phone.

"Don't you think that Vicki's parents have suffered enough?" Brook asked softly, leaning forward before touching Meg's knee. She quickly turned back around and clutched the sleeves of her jacket a little tighter upon the physical interaction. "Did Vicki meet with BJ the day of the bonfire?"

Meg bit her lip in hesitation as stared down at the pen on top of the notepad. Brook made no move to pick it up, but instead maintained contact with the woman's knee. It was important that she experience reassurance that she was doing the right thing. Since the investigation had basically been done by one of their own, there had been no need to state the obvious back then.

"Vicki only ever bought weed from BJ," Meg whispered after leaning forward. She didn't want her voice to travel or for those inside the building to believe that she was ratting out a friend. "I swear. BJ met with her earlier that day before the bonfire and sold her a few joints. That's all."

"A few?" Brook inquired without judgement. "You mean for her, you, and Tasha."

"Yeah," Meg replied hoarsely, nervously shaking her leg the moment that Brook sat back in her chair. "It wasn't a big deal. We didn't even get to smoke them that night. Tasha was hung up on Luke, and we didn't see her for much of the night. Vicki left the bonfire with Francis, so I got stuck trying to get a ride home from Sam."

Meg's recounts of that night were the same as Joe had typed up in his report. As a matter of fact, she hadn't varied much from her original statement. Establishing a timeline days before the bonfire was essential to the case, though.

"What time did Vicki meet with BJ that day?"

"After school." Meg's knee gradually began to slow its tempo. "Maybe around four thirty, in the parking lot."

Brook reached for Tasha's statement, recalling something else happening about that time. She scanned the contents while Joe ended his conversation on the phone.

"That was about the same time that Vicki's father came to the school looking for her, correct?" Brook had noted the time only because the last bell had rung an hour beforehand. "And there was no cheer practice due to the game. Is that why the three of you were still on school grounds? Vicki wanted to meet with BJ?"

"No. Not at first. Vicki had lost one of her earrings in the locker room during our gym class. We spent a good hour looking for it after school. Her mother had given her diamond studs for making captain of the cheerleading squad our senior year. It was kind of a tradition for the women in their family." Meg had calmed down to the point that she'd released her hold on her jacket and tucked her hands in the pockets. "I can still remember Vicki panicking over losing the stupid thing. She said she needed something to calm her nerves when we couldn't find it, so she used the phone in the office to call BJ."

"Did Vicki ever find her earring?" Brook asked as she mulled over this new information.

Nowhere in any of the statements had anyone mentioned a missing diamond stud. Granted, no one had probably thought anything of it at the time.

Had the unsub been taking trophies from his victims? There had been no evidence of such a thing, but it *was* something to consider. A diamond earring was a trinket that wouldn't have been missed in the grand scheme of things. Vicki hadn't been wearing any earrings at the time of her death, and no one had even mentioned that she'd lost one.

Brook didn't hesitate to reach for her pen now that Meg had been truthful of past events.

Brook made a note to have Frank contact the families of the victims to see if they'd had anything taken or had simply misplaced an item that they couldn't locate in the days before their death.

"No, Vicki didn't find it," Meg replied with a small shrug. "At least, not that I recall, but it didn't matter after—"

The door to the station opened, causing her and the others to turn and see who had entered the building. The only other person who Brook had been scheduled to speak with over the next hour was Tasha Dahl. After her interview, Brook had planned to take a drive with Joe to the Anderson residence. The rest of the day would then be spent back at the station so that she could meet with the four men on her list…including BJ.

The man who had entered the building was wearing a pair of black slacks and a dark grey sweater. He looked nothing like Benny. There was no resemblance whatsoever. Could the man in question be one of the three boys who'd attended high school with Vicki?

Unfortunately, Brook hadn't had time to scour social media sites or to read the reports that she'd requested on specific individuals. The morning had passed by faster than Brook would have liked, and she'd planned on having Tasha wait a few more moments before beginning the woman's interview. DMV records would have been included in Brook's requests, and it would be nice to be able to put a face with a name.

While the male subject seemed very familiar, she couldn't quite put her finger on where she'd seen him. He hadn't been at the motel, and he certainly hadn't delivered her pizza last night.

He had to be a local, though.

Tasha had greeted him with a warm embrace and some small talk.

"The earring hadn't mattered after everything that happened later that night," Meg finished saying, apparently not disturbed by the man's presence. She sighed audibly as she focused on Brook. "Are we done? I have some things to do before I have to be at the diner for the lunch crowd."

Joe had mentioned that Meg waited tables at the local diner.

"I appreciate you coming into the station to speak with me," Brook replied as she stood to follow Meg to the door. "If you remember anything else, no matter how insignificant you think it is, I would appreciate a call."

Brook handed Meg a business card with a number that fed into the offices back in D.C. The extension listed was directly to her desk. She never gave out her cell phone. Ever. Then again, it was rare that she was ever out in the field.

"You should arrest Francis Walker," Meg replied with contempt. She shoved the business card in her coat pocket without a second glance. "He's been walking around free for far too long, as far as I'm concerned."

Brook refrained from commenting on the man whose life must have been made a living hell after Vicki Anderson's death. Francis Walker and his family had been outcasted by those who'd assumed his guilt without a shred of evidence. The candy that had been left on the girl's body had been stored as evidence with the state police. The first thing that Brook had done was request to have it sent to the FBI to be reprocessed for any DNA evidence.

The DNA that they had on file from the other crime scenes hadn't matched anyone currently in the system. BJ might have sold some recreational drugs, but he'd never been arrested by the police…other than maybe Joe, who had almost certainly let him go with a warning. It would take time to get the lab results, but she was confident that any evidence found at the Sutton site would match those cases that she'd already connected to her unsub.

"…give her a call, okay?" the man said softly, having already made his way over to Joe's desk. Both men were now standing on the far side of the room, but their words carried enough to reveal that they were siblings. "You know how Mom can be, and Dad called me three times this morning to see if there was a problem."

Brook escorted Meg to the front of the station.

Tasha was waiting patiently, and Brook didn't miss the way the woman scanned Meg from top to bottom with concern. According to Joe, the two women were still practically inseparable.

"Are you okay?" Tasha asked quietly, waiting to embrace Meg until the woman was on the other side of the swinging door. "Come by the house after your shift. Luke is taking the boys to football practice, so we'll have time to talk. All these memories from way back then are making me a blubbering mess."

"Tell her that Francis was the one who did this," Meg directed with a bit of scorn, sticking to what she so strongly believed happened so long ago. "He needs to pay for what he's done."

Brook was surprised that somebody in town hadn't owned and followed through with the same belief. Joe seemed to be an upstanding man, but her opinion of him had gone down a notch after discovering that he'd left out certain details regarding Benjamin Morgan, Jr. and his connection with the victim. Such a poor decision now had her questioning everything in his reports.

What else was Joe O'Sullivan hiding from her?

Every small town had its secrets.

Brook didn't bother to glance over to the men still standing next to Joe's desk. Both had turned their attention toward her, and she didn't want either of them to think that she had an interest in their conversation.

Joe's brother had already mentioned that their parents were worried there could be a problem with her presence.

Why?

Was there something more that he'd done than omit pertinent details about a murder investigation? She needed to figure out a way to speak with the brother in private.

"Tasha, why don't you go have a seat at the far desk?" Brook suggested as she opened the swinging door for the woman to enter. Instead of remaining on the inside, she stepped out and let the swinging door fall back into place. "I forgot something in my car. I'll be right back."

Brook retrieved the keys to her vehicle from the pocket of her raincoat, which she'd hung on one of the hooks to dry. Joe undoubtedly wouldn't want his brother at the station any longer than necessary. If she timed it right, she might get to speak with the man as he left the station.

By the time that Brook had stepped outside, Meg hadn't wasted any time getting to her vehicle. She must have left it unlocked, because she'd quickly opened the door and settled in behind the wheel.

The cold temperature wasn't as big of a shock had the police station not been kept somewhere in the high sixties. Had Joe purposefully set the thermostat low to make her uncomfortable? She hadn't originally gotten a sense of such cruel intentions, but she'd clearly misjudged his character. Maybe that was why she relied on her profiles so much.

Thankfully, the rain had slowed down to merely a mist. It was almost as if a blanket of fog had entered the area.

Brook had parked to the left, leaving the front of the station empty for those who she needed to interview. There were two cars parked out front, and she made the assumption that the minivan belonged to Tasha. The nondescript sedan next to it had to belong to Joe's brother.

She took her time walking around her own vehicle. After pressing a button on the key fob, she was able to open the driver's side door. Given her background, she wasn't one to leave anything of importance inside her car if she didn't plan on returning to it right away. When such an occurrence happened, she always stored things in her trunk.

The only plausible reason why she would have had to walk outside was to retrieve the long cord to her phone charger. While she always carried extra in her briefcase, Joe's brother didn't need to know that specific detail.

Brook reached in and unplugged the cord. She then opened the console where she kept the additional block to use in an outlet, palming the small white device in her hand. She straightened before slamming the door shut.

The entrance to the police station opened, finally revealing Joe's brother.

He was right on time.

Brook pressed the button on the key fob once more as she walked around the front of her car. She'd taken a guess that he was raised with the same manners as his brother, so she purposefully dropped the white block onto the graveled lot.

"Here," Joe's brother said, releasing the door so that it closed behind him. He hastily closed the distance between them. "Let me get that for you."

"Thank you so much," Brook replied in appreciation, stepping back so that he could pick up the power adaptor. "It's been quite the morning."

Brook waited for Joe's brother to stand before she studied his features. He appeared to be close in age with his sibling, though with a leaner build.

"You must be Joe's brother." Brook took the charging block from him before holding out her right arm. "I'm Brook Sloane, a consultant for the FBI, though I'm sure you already know that."

"Mitchell O'Sullivan." He shook her hand, though his grip wasn't as tight as that of his brother. "And yes, I'm aware of who you are. That's the way it is with small towns, though."

"Let me guess," Brook said with a half-smile, deciding to go straight for the jugular. She wanted to solicit a reaction, and she needed to do it quickly. "You think that I should arrest Francis Walker and call it a day."

Mitchell wasn't as easily fooled as she would have liked, and he remained silent with firm resolve as he attempted to see where she was going with this conversation. A vehicle slowly passed by the station, then another by the time he responded to her statement.

"Do I believe Francis Walker killed Vicki? Yes, but so does everyone else in town. He admitted to sleeping with her, and he was the last to see her alive." Mitchell slipped his hands into the pockets of his black pants. His dark hair had a natural wave to it, and the ends of the strands were becoming damp from the mist. "Joe is a good guy, and he loves this town. Benny was and remains real close with the Andersons. He thought it best that Joe handle the investigation, with the help of the state police, of course."

"And did the Andersons know that the former sheriff's son was selling drugs to their daughter?"

Brook didn't take any satisfaction that she was right when Mitchell looked away in concern. He certainly didn't lack intelligence. The entire situation didn't look good for Joe, but no one could comprehend that she wasn't here to put the position of either a deputy or a sheriff on the chopping block.

"Look, Mitch, I grew up in a small town myself. I know how close the residents are, and I also know the lengths that people will take to protect their own. I don't believe that BJ killed Vicki Anderson, either. The point that I'm trying to make here is that by Joe withholding pertinent information in the timeline before Vicki's death, he might have inadvertently missed something that would point toward the person responsible for her death."

"It's Mitchell," he corrected politely while finally meeting her gaze. "Look, Joe was in his early twenties, learning everything that he could from someone who he respected. We all knew about BJ. Other than trying to protect him from the staties, I have no doubt that Joe crossed every T and dotted every I on whatever forms you've been reading over."

"Is that why your parents sent you here to check on him, Mitchell?"

Brook got the reaction that she'd been hoping for, using his full name as requested.

"They didn't…" Mitchell sighed in regret before running his hand through his hair. "Look, it's not what you think."

"And what should I think of the situation, Mitchell?" Brook figured that she didn't have a lot of time left. Joe had to know that she was out here having a conversation with his brother, but she needed to exploit a small crack in this town's armor. She certainly wasn't going to get what she needed from the town's sheriff. "Tell me."

"Benny Morgan was having an affair with Vicki Anderson's mother twenty years ago," Mitchell professed rather reluctantly. "Vicki found out about it."

"That night?" Brook asked, wanting clarification.

Mitchell shook his head, clearly despondent that he'd been the one to share that piece of information with her. She wasn't sure how such a sordid detail impacted the investigation, but it did open a venue of possibilities of who Vicki might have turned to that fateful evening.

"Sometime that week, I think. Francis mentioned it to Joe during the interrogation, but he…well, he thought it best to keep it buried. Enough lives had already been ruined by Vicki's death. Why would he throw more coal into the fire?" Mitchell asked, as if she would have done the same thing to protect the feelings of those involved. She wouldn't have done the same, but that was one of the reasons that she was so good at profiling. She sticked to the facts of the case. "Besides BJ's involvement, the affair was one of the main reasons that Benny had Joe take lead on the investigation. Joe was young and inexperienced. He had to work closely with a state police detective, and it put a lot of pressure on my brother."

"Your parents were aware that Joe kept pertinent information out of his reports, and now they're worried that he could be in trouble with the federal enforcement officials." Brook wasn't going to let on whether or not their parents had a valid concern, because she might be able to use such knowledge to her advantage in the near future. "I appreciate your honesty, Mitchell. I don't want to keep you, and I have more interviews to conduct this morning."

Brook made an attempt to pass him, but his concern for his brother got the best of him.

"Wait." Mitchell waited until she was facing him to continue. "What happens now? Benny's affair had nothing to do with Vicki's murder, or else Joe wouldn't have concealed the information from his reports."

"I appreciate your concern for your brother," Brook replied, knowing all too well what it was like to experience the opposite. "I really do, but I'm not here to critique his performance. I don't know what the fallout will be, and it's honestly not an issue of concern with me. I'm here for one reason, and one reason only—to figure out who killed Vicki Anderson."

# CHAPTER SIXTEEN

**Brooklyn Sloane**
*November 2021*
*Friday—10:19 am*

THE SHORT DRIVE out to the Anderson residence had been wrought with tension. Joe had offered to drive, and Brook had taken him up on his offer, more so to give her a moment to think things over. She hadn't brought up her knowledge of the affair between Benny Morgan and Vicki's mother. At least, not yet. It would get them nowhere right now, and she needed Joe present when she questioned the Andersons.

It was evident that he wasn't sure how to broach the subject of her conversation with his brother. He had to know that they'd spoken, given how long that she'd been outside. Silence reigned for the six minutes that it had taken to reach their destination. He had even pulled alongside the curb in front of a house that had seen better days, leaving the engine running.

Brook waited patiently, not even attempting to get out of the truck. She took her time reaching for the handle of her soft leather briefcase. It resembled more of a messenger bag, and she hadn't been confident that she could leave the case files and her laptop at the station. Had it been more of a secure building, she wouldn't have lugged everything with her to an interview.

"Benny and his son had nothing to do with Vicki's murder." Joe still couldn't seem to bring himself to ask about her conversation with his brother. "I hope that your interviews with Meg and Tasha proved that and has you reconsidering Francis as a viable suspect."

"Francis Walker doesn't fit the profile, and neither do either of the Morgans."

Had Brook had the time, she would have simply gotten out of the truck and went on about the day's interviews. Unfortunately, he'd kept critical information regarding a case out of official reports for the sake of protecting those who he believed were innocent of a horrific crime. Had she not written the profile, she could have found herself wasting precious time searching for needles in a haystack.

Brook realized her view of the situation made her a hypocrite, but she was way past the point of caring about her self-image. Or his, for that matter.

"I gave you some of the other case files to review while I was speaking with Meg and Tasha. My profile of the unsub was included, so you know that we're looking for a Caucasian male whose mother either died or left the family, leaving him with his father." Brook slid the strap of her bag over her shoulder, grateful that the drizzle had finally come to a complete stop. The sky was still overcast with gray clouds, but at least the reprieve would allow them to reach the front porch without getting soaked to the skin. "You supply me with names of who fits my profile, and we can both save ourselves a lot of time."

Joe apparently didn't want to push the issue about his brother, and he nodded his agreement as he finally turned the key in the ignition. It wasn't like a simple phone call to his brother wouldn't reveal the extent of their conversation. What would Joe do when he realized that his brother had given her relevant information that could explain why Vicki hadn't gone straight home that night?

"I have three names in mind already, though none of them really fit the rest of your profile."

"Let me be the judge of that," Brook replied, following suit when he reached for his door handle. "We'll take an hour for lunch after meeting with the Andersons. You can fill me in, and we'll discuss it without any outside interference or personal bias."

Brook had caught on after the third phone call this morning that Benny had been keeping close tabs on the investigation. He'd been wise enough to keep his distance from the station, though she had a gut feeling that Joe was the one ultimately responsible for such a decision.

"Let's get this over with then," Joe murmured in resignation.

The outside temperature wasn't that much different than what they'd had to endure inside the truck. They hadn't driven far enough for the engine to create warm air blowing through the vents, and the humidity wasn't nearly high enough to make a difference.

The streets of the quiet neighborhood were dark in color due to the previous rain, and there were even thin streams of water alongside the curb that ran into the storm drainages positioned every five hundred feet or so.

Most of the old homes were made of brick, though the Andersons had attached a wooden porch to their house. The white paint had faded and curled, along with a worn path on the three long steps that preceded to a screen door. It didn't look to be latched, and upon a second glance, she realized that it wasn't hinged properly on the left side.

Joe didn't comment on the state of the residence.

Instead, he quietly opened the screen door, holding it in such a manner that the bottom corner didn't get stuck on the chipped wooden planks. He gave three solid knocks on the inner door. If she had to guess, it wasn't even locked.

Old habits died hard.

"Joe."

A man in his mid-sixties had answered the door. There was no life to be had in his dull blue eyes, and his movements could only be described as mechanical. The loss of his daughter had clearly stolen his life at a critical juncture, and she was left to look at the wreckage that remained behind.

He slowly stepped back to let them enter, and Joe motioned that she should go in front of him. Brook nodded her appreciation to Mr. Anderson before stepping over the threshold and to the side, giving Joe room to join her.

The house reeked of stale cigarette smoke.

So much so that Brook found it hard to breathe. The interior of the house was stifling, and she doubted that a window had been opened to air the place out in a very long time.

"Mr. Anderson, this is Brook Sloane." Joe had waited to introduce her until after Russell had closed the door behind them. "She's a special consultant to the FBI."

"A little late, don't you think?" Russell muttered in disgust as he passed by them without a second glance. He didn't have a high regard for law enforcement, not that Brook could blame him. His little girl had been brutally murdered and left to rot in an abandoned field next to a disintegrating cabin. "Word around town is that you aren't going to arrest Francis Walker. I don't know what you're doing here if you aren't going to do your job."

Brook hadn't expected this visit to go smoothly, but she also hadn't anticipated such a hostile reception. While her presence might have opened some wounds, she would have thought the Andersons would want closure.

They did, in their own way.

Unfortunately, the individual they believed killed their daughter was completely innocent of the crime in question.

"Russ, stop with all the insults." An older woman who appeared to be more in her seventies than sixties walked out of the kitchen drying her hands on a dish towel. She wore a pair of black slacks with a matching long-sleeved shirt. The lack of color didn't help the woman's pallor. "She's just trying to help us."

Russ grunted, though Brook doubted it was in agreement with his wife's views on the subject.

"Joey, it's good to see you," Amanda Anderson replied as she motioned us into the living room off to the right side of the house. "I saw your mother at church the other day. She's looking good."

Joe maintained small talk regarding his mother as the older couple led the way into the living room. The furniture hadn't been updated in years, and the long drapes reminded Brook of the ones her mother had up over the windows in their childhood home.

There were doilies on top of the coffee table, an old newspaper sorted by sections thrown on the floor next to the recliner, and old photographs that hadn't been updated in over twenty years. It was hard to believe the once vibrant woman with a bright smile was the same woman who stood in front of them. In one photograph, she was standing next to her daughter as they both held pom-poms into the air.

Now?

It was as if the Andersons had been frozen in time.

"Mrs. Anderson, this is Brook Sloane." Joey waited until Brook had taken a seat on the couch before he joined her. Russ had reclaimed his recliner while Amanda sat in what was clearly her favorite spot in the living room. The loveseat had a lamp behind it, and the books piled up at the side indicated it was where Amanda spent most of her time. "She's a consultant for the FBI. She believes that Vicki's murder might be tied to the Princess Killer case that's been making it into all the newspapers."

Brook winced internally, wishing that Joe hadn't started out the conversation in such a crass manner. Granted, the entire town had been filled in on the connection the moment that she'd sent the request for old case files matching certain parameters, but she still would have liked to ease into the conversation.

"Francis Walker killed our little girl."

Russ cleared his throat as if his emotions were getting the better of him. Amanda wrung the dish towel in her hands a little tighter, though she was brave enough to make direct eye contact with Brook.

"Please, call me Amanda." She sat on the edge of the cushion as if there could be an inherent need to run at the slightest provocation. "It sounds as if we want the same thing, but even Joey is convinced that Francis Walker killed our Vicki."

Russ turned his head away, almost as if he couldn't bear to hear his daughter's name.

"Mr. and Mrs. Anderson, first let me express my sincere

condolences for your loss. I realize my being here is bringing up memories that you'd rather leave in the past, but I will try my best to make this as painless as possible." Brook ignored Russ' grunt of displeasure, purposefully steering the conversation into helpful territory. "You should know that I've reordered the evidence discovered at the crime scene to be retested for any DNA evidence left behind. We've come a long way in twenty years when it comes to forensic testing. As Sheriff O'Sullivan mentioned, I do believe the individual who murdered your daughter is responsible for the other murder investigations that I'm currently overseeing at the moment. With that said, I do understand how Sheriff O'Sullivan might have arrived at the conclusion that Mr. Walker killed your daughter, but as with every investigation…new facts come to light."

As Brook had predicted, the mere mention of DNA evidence being retested had generated the interest from both parents. Now that she had their full attention, they would be eager to help rather than hinder the case.

"How long had Vicki been seeing Francis Walker?"

"We didn't even know that she *was* seeing that boy," Amanda replied, leaning back against the cushion now that her husband wasn't being so obstinate. Russ had focused on his wife while she did most of the talking. "She'd been happy that year, having made the captain of the cheerleading squad and all."

"I heard that you gave her a pair of diamond studs to celebrate the occasion." Brook had set her leather briefcase onto the floor. She thought it best not to take notes, so she was surprised when Joe took out a small pad from the inner pocket of his jacket. "Do you still have them?"

Amanda blinked, as if she hadn't thought of the jewelry in

the entire time that Vicki had been gone. She even looked to her husband for guidance, though he didn't respond.

"I assume that they are still in her room." Amanda had straightened her shoulders, as if she were about to be judged. "We...well, we couldn't bring ourselves to empty her bedroom."

Brook fought back the sense of elation upon discovering that the Andersons had inadvertently kept part of the crime scene intact. While Vicki hadn't been murdered in her own bedroom, the very heart of who she was remained behind in her material belongings.

"If it's alright with you, I would like a moment to look inside her bedroom before we leave," Brook proposed, eager to see if Vicki had kept a diary of some sort. "It will help me get a sense of who she was and maybe even give me a direction in which to conduct some interviews. I know that her best friends were Meg and Tasha. You mentioned that you didn't know your daughter was seeing Mr. Walker, but did she ever mention someone else? Maybe someone who she had a crush on?"

"My daughter wasn't some—"

"I didn't say that she was, Mr. Anderson." Brook purposefully cut off the wrong assumption that Russ had made regarding his daughter. "I'm merely trying to establish a timeline of events leading up to the day of her death, along with who she might have interacted with. Was Vicki acting strange, had she mentioned someone new in her life, or did anything strike you as odd with her behavior? The most obscure thing could be the most important."

Russ and Amanda shared a long, contemplative stare. Joe had jotted something down on the miniature notepad, but even he seemed to be anticipating what the Andersons had to say regarding the question.

"Vicki was agitated that week," Amanda replied hesitantly before studying the dish towel in her hand. "She—"

"Secretive," Russ interjected, correcting his wife's outlook. "She was keeping something from us, but now we know it was that Walker boy. I don't understand how this is going to help you. Did you say that you were having evidence tested for DNA? The results should prove that he did it. You can make your arrest, and then we can get on with our lives."

"Secretive how?" Joe asked, evidently hearing about such a behavior for the first time.

"She'd be doing homework in her bedroom, but she'd immediately cover up whatever she was writing down in her notebook. She'd come home from cheer practice a half hour late or leave for school twenty minutes early, but she would never give us a reason why," Amanda revealed with a slight shrug. "Russ is right. Once we discovered that she was seeing Francis, it all made sense."

The interview had carried on for a good thirty minutes more before Brook made the decision that there was no more information to gain from Vicki's parents. She wasn't looking forward to the next part of the conversation, but the topic had to be touched upon.

"I'm sorry that I have to bring up the past, but is there any chance that Vicki found out about your affair with the former sheriff?"

The tension in the room had built to the point that it was palpable.

Russ abruptly stood from his recliner and left the room.

Joe hung his head while Amanda placed her hand over her

mouth.

"You mentioned that Vicki had become slightly withdrawn and secretive," Brook pushed, needing to know where the affair fit into the investigation. "Could she have known about your relationship with Benny Morgan?"

"No," Amanda whispered after lowering her hand. She linked her fingers together in her lap and stared down at them in embarrassment. "Vicki didn't know. I'm sure of it."

Brook hadn't brought up the sensitive subject to berate Amanda Anderson.

There were theories that needed to be explored, such as whether or not the affair had been the catalyst for Vicki's murder. Undoubtedly, the young girl had pulled away from her parents because she'd known about the affair. The pieces of the puzzle had finally started to fall together.

Had the unsub wanted not only a young girl who fit the narrative of the perfect princess, but also deemed that her family had to be worthy? Was that the reason he'd given himself to end her life? Brook would have to look back at the families of the victims to see if there was some type of connection.

She carefully wrapped up the questioning, needing to ensure that she had the ability to look at Vicki's belongings. The fact that Amanda hadn't been able to change her daughter's bedroom in the years following her death would be a tremendous benefit to the case.

Joe had fallen rather quiet since she'd made the knowledge of the affair known. He now had the answer to the question that he'd been afraid to ask earlier. He should have been upfront with her. The sooner that he owned up to his past behavior being a detriment, the faster a path would be carved out for them to apprehend the suspect.

"May we see Vicki's room, please?" Brook asked, deciding that it would be best to let the subject drop. It would not be beneficial in any way to let Amanda know that her daughter had discovered such a secret, and one that could have destroyed their family. Vicki's death had sealed that fate. "We'll be respectful. I give you my word."

Amanda stood and sniffled as she led the way out of the living room. The staircase was rather thin, so Brook made sure that she climbed the steps cautiously, holding her briefcase closer to her body so that it didn't smack into the wall. Amanda then guided them down a short hallway to Vicki's bedroom.

It was as if the doorway had been a portal to a past life.

Brook had to close off the part of her that recalled what it was like to be so young. There would never be a time when memories of her past didn't elicit the unwanted images of her brother and his bloody hands standing in their kitchen.

She managed to refocus her energy without anyone the wiser. She made quick work of studying Vicki's sanctuary before respectfully sifting through the leftover belongings under the watchful eye of her mother. Amanda had remained standing in the doorway with tears in her eyes.

Joe stood off to the side while Brook had slowly walked around the room and took in the desolate ambiance. A sadness hung in the air, and no amount of justice would ever erase the vulnerable emotion contained inside these four walls.

Posters of Faith Hill and Tim McGraw had been hung on either side of the closet, giving away that Vicki had a penchant for country music. A white vanity with a large mirror had been positioned against the far wall, and the girl's makeup box had been full of used eyeshadows, blush, and lipstick. Brook envisioned Vicki trying to get her hair and makeup just like that of the singer who she'd clearly idolized.

From the clothes that had still been hanging in the closet, she'd had style. Not surprising, given that she had run with the popular crowd. A thorough search of the small jewelry box that had been left on top of the dresser didn't reveal any diamond studs. Most of the items had been nothing of significance. Friendship bracelets, inexpensive rings, and gawdy necklaces took up most of the space. While there was also a collection of earrings, there was no sign of the diamond stud that Vicki had in her possession after school that day.

Brook spent a good forty minutes going through miscellaneous boxes the had been shoved underneath the bed and the numerous drawers in Vicki's dresser, nightstand, and vanity. There had been nothing of interest that Brook could find to benefit the case with the exception of the pink backpack that had been hung over the back of a chair.

Brook had known exactly what to search for given that both Vicki's parents had mentioned that she had purposefully covered up whatever she'd been writing in her notebook. The bonus was the fact that the single diamond stud had been placed in a side pocket for safe keeping.

"Joe." Brook had spoken softly, though the sound of her voice had Amanda startling from her place just inside the doorframe. "I need this as evidence. Plus, there are some notebooks that I would like to look through."

Joe had understood that a request from her to take the backpack wouldn't go over as well as if the appeal had come from him. She'd made sure that he saw the diamond stud in the side pocket before she had pulled the zipper closed. It would have been pointless to keep him in the dark from the details that she'd gotten from Meg and Tasha, so Brook had been candid with him before they'd left the station.

While the earring was of utmost interest, Brook was counting on information written inside the notebooks to give them something concrete. One simple name or even a set of initials to compare to those individuals who fit the profile currently living in town could be all that was needed to close this case.

# CHAPTER SEVENTEEN

**Unsub**
*November 2021*
*Friday—11:24 am*

He stood in front of his bookshelf, staring at the leather-bound case disguised to resemble a classic novel. The hollowed-out interior held the items that had been of utmost interest to him. He'd discovered the treasure box years ago at a garage sale. The navy-blue leather spine had been labeled to resemble Grimm's Complete Fairy Tales in gold leaf lettering. He kept the skeleton key that opened the antique lock mechanism securely around his neck on an old gold chain that he'd purchased from a five and dime.

How appropriate was it for such a special case to contain the memories that he'd made of the women who had done their best to deceive him? They had merely been cloaked to hide the evil that lurked in the lives of those who didn't want to seek out the truth. They denied the eternal truth, that which was sacred before other things. They were profane, adulterers of the truth.

His initial panic upon discovering that the investigation into Vicki's death was being reopened had subsided, and he'd regained his composure. After all, his story was still ongoing.

The arrival and involvement of the FBI had regrettably prevented him from leaving town to check in on *her*—his princess. Was she the one? Was she the one who his mother had told him about when he was a child? It was a real possibility, but he was being kept from her by the authorities.

Did that make her Juliet to his Romeo?

He'd only ever spoken to her twice on the phone, but her voice was like slow molasses in wintertime being poured into a cup of hot tea. Closing his eyes, he tilted his head back as he replayed her sweet voice saying his name over and over.

Their story would have to be put on hold, though. The next chapter in his life was about someone else entirely. Someone who he should have been concentrating on from the very beginning. Evil had been hiding in plain sight all along.

One woman was standing in his way of an epic ending.

There *was* one simple solution to his problem, though.

He needed to witness her suffering and watch the life slowly drain away from her body.

# CHAPTER EIGHTEEN

**Brooklyn Sloane**
*November 2021*
*Friday—12:01 pm*

"I'll go back through the case files," Frank replied over a noise that sounded like the copier machine in the office. It had a unique squeal that made it identifiable. "I'll also reach out to the victims' relatives to see if they noticed anything missing among the belongings left behind. Oh, and Steven Schmidt? Yeah, he didn't pan out. He basically has alibis for most of the murders in question."

Brook and Joe were at the local diner, though she was standing outside near the entrance under the overhang. The break in the rain hadn't lasted long, and she'd had to put on her black rain jacket before they'd stepped out of the truck. Joe had already gone inside, leaving her to make some calls in private.

She'd had a chance to glance at the background reports that had been sent to her inbox during her interview with Tasha, and no one on the list had fit the parameters of the profile. All the same, she would keep the scheduled meetings with Luke, John, and Sam. While she doubted that they could fill in the gaps of Vicki's life that she'd kept secret from her parents and two best friends, there was still a chance that they had noticed something off in the days leading up to her murder.

Tasha had admitted to knowing about the former sheriff having an affair with Vicki's mother. Tasha had made it known that she didn't believe such a sordid detail had anything to do with her friend's murder. She still believed that Francis killed Vicki. Apparently, the young girl had been trying to figure out a way to let her parents know that she was dating the boy. He hadn't been too happy at the time that she'd been taking so long, giving Tasha enough motive to convince herself of his guilt.

"It doesn't surprise me about Schmidt. I'm close, Frank. The unsub is somewhere here in Sutton." Brook monitored a vehicle entering the parking lot, though the place was quite full given the lunch hour. The mixture of rain, oil, and exhaust was preferrable than the stale cigarette odor that she'd endured at the Anderson's residence. "The sheriff has provided a couple of names for me that could fit the profile. Once I have them narrowed down, I'll have one of the agents in Pittsburgh drive over and help me bring the suspect in for questioning."

"Good. Do you need anything else from me? Des wants to see me regarding one of my cases with Ann. She was supposed to testify next week, but it looks like I'm going to be flying solo for any near-term court appearance."

"No, nothing else." Brook stepped to the side for the couple who'd arrived in an older Chevy. They both regarded her warily as they entered the diner. "I know you're swamped, so I'll let you go."

Brook disconnected the line, wishing that she'd thought to ask about Ann. All had to be good on that front, though. Frank would have mentioned something otherwise, and Harden would have left her a voicemail. She had one message that she hadn't listened to yet, but she didn't want it hanging over her head.

It didn't take her long to reach the screen that she'd needed in order to press the call back button. The line was answered on the first ring.

"We need to meet. Now."

Brook sighed in frustration upon hearing Bit's voice as she readjusted the strap on her briefcase. She'd brought along one of Vicki's notebooks that was currently safely inside a clear plastic bag. Of course, she'd have to use gloves to flip through the pages, but she would eventually send it off for analysis. As for Bit, he'd been a personal resource, thus deserving of her cell phone. She was now regretting the decision to call him back.

Joe had park right out front of the large glass display window of the diner so that they could keep tabs on his truck. She would have had him stop by the station to drop the evidence off, but she didn't trust Benny not to leave well enough alone. She had no doubt that he still had a key to the building.

"Bit, our business was concluded the other day," Brook reminded him in a tone that broke no argument. "You made a choice, and now you—"

"Kuzmich knows that I was stealing some of the coins that I was mining," Bit replied desperately, though Brook couldn't fathom why he would call her. "I have Paula set up in a motel across town, but she has to go in for a chemo appointment first thing on Monday morning. She can't miss it, and Dima is going to grab her to prove a point."

"Not my problem, Bit." Brook had heard several sob stories like his over the years, and some of those people didn't have an out like he did. "Call up your buddy. I'm sure Special Agent Calabro will cut you some type of deal for turning on Kuzmich, and one that will include your sister's safety."

Another vehicle pulled into the parking lot. Surprisingly, she recognized the man. Knowing full well that Joe was keeping tabs on her as well as his truck, she made sure to meet Matt Henley's gaze through the windshield. She shook her head slightly that he shouldn't acknowledge her.

"Look, I need to—"

"I have more information on that target you asked me to keep tabs on," Bit quickly exclaimed in a desperate manner to prevent her from hanging up. "Please. Just wire me the money so that I can pay back Kuzmich. I'll get you the details and—"

"Not a chance in hell," Brook replied in anger, turning slightly so that Henley couldn't read her lips. The last thing she needed was for an independent crime journalist to get wind of a conversation regarding her brother. "Don't you fuck with me, Bit. We are done."

She disconnected the call before counting to ten, not that it did much good.

Bit apparently hadn't gotten her message the other day. He didn't have the right to dangle a carrot out in front of her, especially about her brother. Bit didn't possess any other information that could land her ass in hot water with Calabro or anyone else, and it needed to stay that way.

"Good afternoon," Matt replied as he walked by the front of his car, nodding her way in a rather impersonable manner that wouldn't have anyone thinking they were anything more than mere strangers.

Brook's cell phone vibrated since she still had the device set to silent. She didn't even bother to look at the screen before shoving her phone into the side pocket of her briefcase. Between

Bit and Matt Henley, her satisfaction with the day's events had gone to hell.

"Thank you," she murmured, brushing past Matt as he held open the door. "Have a good day."

The heavy smell of grease hung in the air, almost as if it were trying to vie for the top spot of her morning. First, the stale cigarette odor. Then came the odd bouquet of the cold wet outdoors. She'd take the delicious fragrance of seasoned fries any day.

"Everything alright?" Joe asked as he gestured toward the cup of coffee that was on her side of the table.

He'd somehow ended up claiming a private table in the corner. Given how busy the place was for lunch, that was quite a feat. She took her time removing her rain jacket and laying it overtop her briefcase that she'd set into one of the empty chairs. They had both chosen the seats that had them facing the front entrance, leaving him positioned on her right side.

"Everything is fine." Brook took a seat and pulled the mug closer, wrapping her hands around the warm porcelain. The design was old. There wasn't one thing in this place that had been updated since the eighties or nineties, and that included the stained curtains hanging over the windows. "Who was the man who just walked in ahead of me?"

Joe didn't even need to glance over at the counter, which was where Matt Henley had taken a seat on one of the stools. Joe slid a piece of paper her way that had been torn from his miniature notepad. He kept his hand over it while answering her question, though.

"Matt? His family owns one of the local farms, though he doesn't live here anymore. He moved to Pittsburgh after high school. Started some true crime channel on YouTube or something like that. Once it became a hit, he then moved to some other East Coast city. I'm not sure which one. He comes home every once in a while, but his visits are getting less and less. Honestly, he probably heard you were in town and caught the first flight here to check you out."

"I guess that's not surprising," Brook murmured, glancing down at the sheet of paper. Matt Henley's name wouldn't be on it. The first thing that she'd done after returning to her hotel room last night was check into his past. It had been posted in the about section on his channel that both of his parents still owned a farm on the outskirts of Sutton, which had just been confirmed by the sheriff. She'd also checked some of the other databases for confirmation, but she figured it was best to carry on the conversation as if she were in the dark. "Are both of his parents still on the farm?"

"Yes," Joe replied, even going above and beyond her question. He'd obviously been taking notes from her, and she appreciated his diligence in the face of his previous omissions. "Both are his biological parents."

"Let me see this list that you made," Brook replied, unsure of where Joe's hesitancy came from when he didn't immediately lift his hand off the paper. His indecision was so brief, she wasn't sure it meant anything of significance. "Look, I didn't mean to blindside you regarding Amanda's affair with Benny."

"Yes, you did." Joe tapped the piece of paper, but he didn't slide it toward her quite yet. "I don't have much of an excuse, other than I was young and stupid. Benny swore that his affair had nothing to do with Vicki's death, and I believed him. I still do. I realize that I haven't done anything to earn your trust, but I hope you can see this is me trying to do the right thing now."

Joe finally shifted his hand away from the paper. She waited a heartbeat before picking it up and reading the names aloud, leaving the rest of the discussion to die a natural death. She still needed him, and it wouldn't do to shut him completely out of the investigation. Regardless that he had covered for Benny, the residents of Sutton still trusted Joe's position of authority.

"Brandon Farina, David Molchalin, Jeremy Yates, and Timothy Milburn."

"I'd like to go on record that I don't believe any of them are capable of doing what I witnessed done to Vicki," Joe replied quietly, keeping their discussion contained to the table. "Jeremy…well, he's my cousin."

No wonder Joe had been hesitant to hand over the list.

The way he had leaned back from the table had her doing the same, though she'd also caught sight of movement out of her peripheral view. She tucked the small piece of paper into the pocket of her blazer before their waitress, who just so happened to be Meg, could see anything of importance.

It didn't take them long to place their orders, but their attempt for a peaceful lunch went straight to hell when Benny Morgan walked through the front door. The loud murmurs of conversation dulled to a few single whispers until Joe quickly stood from the table, but it was a little too late. Benny clearly blamed her for the unwelcome response from those who had considered him practically a saint.

To think the former sheriff's ire was due to her bringing up his son's involvement and not the fact that she was dredging up an old affair told her that a more severe response was on the horizon.

Joe had done his best to keep Benny from interfering with the investigation all morning, and the sheriff seemed to have lucked out in that area once again. Whatever had been said between the two men was enough to get Benny to rethink whatever confrontation he wanted to instigate with her. Both men exited the diner without a backward glance.

Brook retrieved the small piece of paper while she enjoyed her coffee, not having had a moment to herself all day. Her mood hadn't been helped by Bit's phone call, either. She hadn't expected any trouble after cutting ties with him, but he was desperate. The chances of him having additional information on Jacob was almost nonexistent.

Still, she hated the way doubt had begun to creep its long and twisted fingers into her conviction. The vision of Jacob's hands covered in blood followed by the tree branch tapping her bedroom window that fateful day returned with a vengeance.

Brook could feel the weight of multiple stares her way. Not knowing how long Joe would be, she retrieved her laptop and connected to the hotspot on her phone. She quickly ran the names through the system to confirm that they fit the profile.

Most of the full background checks that she'd requested had come through, with the exception of a few that were still pending. She still expected them all back by this afternoon, but she took the time afforded to her and ensured that there were no surprises. While she had her laptop opened, she went ahead and typed the names into the system that Joe had provided her.

The fact that Jeremy was related to Joe could prove a problem. Undoubtedly, Mitchell had relayed to his parents that Joe wasn't going to be immediately terminated from his position. Hell, Brook doubted that anything she said or did could have him fired, not unless those who voted for him opted for a recall. Such news had most likely already been passed to friends and family. Would such details regarding Joe's position provide Jeremy confidence that he wouldn't get caught if he turned out to be the unsub?

The man was now number one on her list to speak with, because Joe was obviously holding something back. Had Jeremy gone to high school with Vicki? Had the two of them been friends? More importantly, what had Jeremy's childhood been like?

Joe had walked through the entrance of the diner right about the time that Brook had closed her laptop. She planned to make quick work of the three interviews lined up this afternoon, with an additional stop to speak with Francis Walker. She had debated on whether or not to stop by his place of work, but she would rather he be in a comfortable setting. The most appropriate venue would be his parent's residence.

"You didn't tell me that you set up a meeting with Francis Walker and his parents." Joe didn't need to pull out his chair since it was already positioned away from the table. Benny hadn't returned to the diner, so she assumed that Joe had talked him out of any sort of confrontation. It didn't negate the fact that he'd stirred the pot with Joe, and she was now on the receiving end of his wrath. "You'll get a lot further with the Walkers if you allow me to—"

Brook held up a hand and leaned back in her chair when she spotted Meg returning with their food. They'd both ordered the BLT specials, which included a side of seasoned fries. Joe wasn't happy with the interruption, but at least he was smart enough to keep his mouth shut about her interviews in front of someone who was connected to the case.

It didn't help their situation that all eyes had been on them since Joe had returned from escorting Benny out of the diner.

"It was one of the topics that I wanted to discuss with you over lunch," Brook informed him as she laid a napkin over her lap. She maintained a civil tone, but she wasn't about to have her every move questioned by a former sheriff who had sought favors from a young twenty-something deputy. "Your presence will only have the Walker family on edge. What I would really like to know is how Benny was aware of such meeting, when I'm sure that Francis wasn't calling those around the neighborhood with his schedule."

For a brief moment, she wasn't sure that Joe was even going to supply her with an answer. She realized that he was in an awkward position with Benny and the residents, who now felt as if their lives were being torn apart all over again, but her investigation was bigger than Vicki Anderson. Apprehending the unsub would end up saving countless of lives.

"Sara Walker works at the only full-service gas station here in town. Not the 7-Eleven, but the small BP station on the corner. She was on break, taking a personal call. Someone overheard the conversation and—"

"Towns like this don't change, do they?" Brook said with a shake of her head, both in irritation and fondness. "Like I said, your presence isn't required for the Walker interview. I'm assuming the complete opposite is true with your cousin. Why don't we spend the rest of our lunch going over how your cousin is connected to Vicki Anderson?"

Brook didn't give Joe much of a choice in the topic of the upcoming discussion. Anything was better than thinking back to her upbringing. It had technically been typical in every single way, and the town had played a major part in it.

Of course, everyone had turned against her family after the truth had come out about Jacob. She'd almost chosen a nursing home in D.C. for her father, but she had her reasons for keeping him in Morton…selfish as those may be.

It was turning out that she and Joe weren't all that different after all.

# CHAPTER NINETEEN

**Brooklyn Sloane**
*November 2021*
*Friday—3:21 pm*

THE SOUND OF the ticking clock on the wall behind the desk was basically the only noise reverberating through the police station. The faint odor of brewed coffee from this morning had faded, and in its place was the smell of gun cleaner and disinfectant.

She much preferred the smell of coffee.

"...doesn't look good. Get him here now, Benny."

Brook continued to browse through one of the notebooks that she'd taken out from Vicki's backpack. Thankfully, there had been a pair of latex gloves tucked inside Brook's briefcase. She had already skimmed three notebooks, but there had been nothing that stood out in regard to a name or a set of initials.

Vicki's chemistry notebook told another story altogether.

At first, Brook had simply thought the young girl had mindlessly doodled during class. There were dollar signs written in pen over and over through at least ten pages, and then the scribbling had simply stopped. Had Vicki been obsessed with money? Had she needed cash for something important or had she simply been dreaming of something bigger than a small town?

"…serious. This isn't something that can be…"

While Joe attempted to talk some sense into the former sheriff, Brook stood up with the chemistry notebook in hand. She wasn't worried in the least that the two men would arrive for the interview. Benny was simply concerned about his son, and both of them were seeing how far they could push her before she pulled rank.

FBI always trumped local law enforcement, though. Benny and BJ would arrive at the station soon enough, even if she had to have the state police drag them both in kicking and screaming.

Brook made her way across the station, through the swinging gate, and pushed open the door. The behavior of three men who had just been questioned by law enforcement wasn't that hard to predict. None of them had provided anything other than confirmation that Vicki had sometimes bought marijuana from BJ. They hadn't even been aware that she'd lost her earring that day, nor had they known if she'd been interested in someone else besides Francis Walker.

"Relax, gentlemen."

Brook could see that her presence had them all nervous. Luke straightened from where he'd been leaning against his truck, while Sam threw his cigarette on the ground and used his boot to crush it into the gravel. John just came across angry that they'd even had to show up.

"I simply want to know if Vicki needed money or had recently come into some cash." Brook closed the distance between them, causing all three men to line up against Luke's truck. The weather was still quite gloomy, the ground was still wet, but the rain seemed to be on hold for a moment. "Did she mention needing money to any of you?"

Luke and Sam shared a confused glance, both shaking their heads in response. John was staring at her with a frown. He even lifted his baseball cap a little more off his forehead and stared at the notebook in Brook's hand.

"John?"

"I took chem with Vicki that semester," John replied, garnering nods of agreement from the other two men. Luke was the only one of the three who'd aged well. Sam had gained weight, while John had lost most of his hair, thus his choice of wearing a baseball cap. "That entire week she was drawing dollar signs in that notebook."

"Did you ask her why?" Brook wasn't sure that such a simple act had anything to do with the young girl's murder, but nothing should be overlooked when Brook was so close to unearthing the identity of the unsub. "Did she confide in you?"

"I did ask Vicki why she seemed so distracted in class, but she said that I should mind my own business."

"Did you?"

Luke and Sam were both staring at John with disbelief. Their expressions and body language were enough to convince Brook that this was the first time they were hearing about what happened in chemistry class. A bit of scribbling in a notebook normally wouldn't be anything of concern, but even they could realize the significance of such a small secret.

"Are you saying that someone killed Vicki over money?" Luke asked, preventing John from answering Brook's question. "Is that why you're so hung up on her buying weed from BJ?"

"You think BJ killed Vicki? I was wondering why you were

so focused on him." The revulsion in Sam's tone had Brook holding up her free hand, but he'd turned his attention to John. "Was Vicki selling drugs for him, man? Why didn't you say any—"

"Stop making assumptions," Brook directed, not wanting these men to spread anymore rumors than they already planned to do at the local bar. There were actually two bars—one of each side of town. "Nothing that I have discovered today indicated that Vicki was selling drugs. I'm simply trying to figure out why she was so obsessed with dollar signs when she should have been learning the periodic table. Were her parents having money problems? Did she need money for a car?"

"I didn't push Vicki for an answer, but I did see her using the pay phone outside of the main football gate a couple of times during that week." John's attention veered away from Brook to a vehicle that was slowing down to turn into one of the empty slots near Joe's truck. "Maybe she *was* trying to get a job, but I think she would have said something to us. I worked parttime at the movie theater and could have gotten her a job. Same with Sam over at the ice cream parlor."

"What time did you see Vicki at the pay phone?" Brook asked, pleased that she was finally gaining some ground. Such a random detail was easy to follow up on and could possibly lead her directly to the unsub. It would be relatively easy to gain access to the phone records from back then. "Morning? Afternoon?"

The engine of the vehicle that had parked next to Joe's truck turned off, and all that was left to hear was the ticking sound as the car cooled down. Brook was hoping for a quick answer, because then she would need to extend another warning to the three men in front of her. Benny and BJ had their full attention, and it was only a matter of time before accusations started to be made.

Now that her presence had sowed doubt amongst the tight-knit town regarding Francis Walker's guilt, the pitchforks would be drawn and pointed toward the one person who had gotten away with too much for far too long, all simply by being the son of the former sheriff.

"John? I need to know what time you saw Vicki using the pay phone."

"Um, morning. It was usually after cheer practice but before first period."

"I appreciate the information. The three of you are free to leave," Brook stated, continuing to stand in front of them until they got the hint. She wasn't moving until they'd vacated the parking lot. The last thing she needed right now was for the situation to get out of control on the steps of the town police station. "Have a good night, gentlemen."

Luke backhanded Sam's arm, giving the others permission to depart the area. It wasn't long until they were all getting into their vehicles and backing up onto the main drag. Luke and Sam went one way, while John drove in another.

Brook had immediately pegged Luke Harris as the leader of the three men from the get-go. He'd been the captain of the football team, married one of the cheerleaders, and appeared to be the one who maintained his reputation around town. He hadn't been very complimentary of Francis Walker, but there had been nothing in his statement nor his recollection of their high school days to give her the impression that she was wrong about her assumption of his innocence.

Just as she was about to turn and walk back into the police station, not really wanting to initiate any conversation with Benny and BJ out in this dreary weather, she caught movement from across the street where there was a small hardware shop. Only two vehicles had been parked in front of the building most of the day. Now there were three.

Brook tamped down her frustration at the sight of Matt Henley keeping tabs on the comings and goings of the police station. She mulled over her options before deciding to leave well enough alone…for now. He wasn't committing a crime, and anything she said would only make him more determined to shadow her every move while she was in town.

"Sloane, I don't see how my son's limited involve—"

Brook didn't bother to censor Benny's lack of respect toward her. The reason that he'd cut off mid-sentence was due to him following her gaze. He, too, realized who was sitting in the car.

"Son of a bitch," Benny muttered as he took off across the street without even bothering to look in either direction. "What do you think you're doing over there? If you so much as say one goddamn word on your…"

"Mr. Morgan, why don't we head inside," Brook suggested as she turned and didn't stop until she had the door opened to the station. "It looks as if your father might be awhile violating that man's first amendment rights."

BJ Morgan was the spitting image of his dad, only without the greying hair.

"I don't know how much help I can be. I didn't know Vicki all that well."

"You knew her well enough to sell her pot," Brook countered, still holding the door opened as she stared him down.

She'd given him the reassurance that he needed over the phone this morning so that she could get this interview out of the way. "You have nothing to worry about, Mr. Morgan. I'm not here for some petty drug charges involving your grow operation. All I want to do is hear your timeline of events in the days leading up to Vicki Anderson's murder."

The phone calls that John had mentioned seeing Vicki make the week of her death could have been to BJ. If she were desperate for money, which wasn't likely given that her two best friends hadn't mentioned anything of the sort, she might have turned to the one man who had the ability to hook her up with a reasonable amount of ready cash.

BJ was leaner than his father by quite a lot, though he had the same facial features. His dark hair hung to his shoulders with strands that had the appearance of pure grease. His mustache was much of the same and in desperate need of a trim. She'd expected him to reek of either cigarette or marijuana smoke after he'd brushed past her to step into the police station, but all she'd caught was a whiff of leather from his black jacket.

"If you'll take a seat in the guest chair at the far desk, I'll be with you in a moment," Brook instructed as she followed close behind him. She had made sure that her laptop was closed as she'd picked up her phone. Stepping away to make it seem as if she wanted to take a call in private, she then called Frank. She didn't mind if BJ overheard the request that she was about to make. As a matter of fact, it might make him a little bit more forthcoming with his answers. "Frank, I was hoping that you would still be in the office. I would like to put in a request for a list of calls made to and from the pay phone that would have been outside of the stadium gates of the Sutton High School football field the weeks leading up to Vicki Anderson's murder."

"Knowing that you can do it yourself from your laptop, I'm going to assume that this call is for someone else's benefit," Frank replied wryly, though there was a slight edge to his tone that had Brook straightening her shoulders. "I will go ahead and put in the request, though. You'll be busy interviewing one Jeremy Yates. He's forty-three years of age. On the older end of your profile, but get this—he works for a trucking company. Not as a trucker, but as a sales representative."

"Let me guess," Brook replied softly and with a bit of regret. "In the tristate area."

"You want me to contact one of the field agents in the Pittsburgh office?"

"Not yet. I want to wrap up some things before venturing in that direction. Besides, there's nothing to tie him to the murder."

"Brook, don't wait too long." Frank's friendly warning was taken under advisement. "The sheriff has personal ties to Yates. Hell, there are way too many personal ties in that town."

"I know," Brook replied quietly as she heard the door open at the front of the station. A quick glance revealed that it was Benny, though that wasn't surprising in the least. Matt Henley was probably driving around the block until he was in the clear of the former sheriff's sights. "I'll keep in touch and let you know if I find any connections."

Surprisingly, Benny hadn't gone over to Joe's desk. He made a direct path toward his son, coming to a stop directly behind the chair as if his mere presence was enough to get her to back down. Gone was the infectious smile, and in its place was nothing but a grimace of contempt.

"Let's get this over with."

Benny hadn't had the decency to wait until she'd disconnected the line. She leveled him a stare and continued speaking with Frank.

"The forensics report is due in the next hour," Brook lied as she continued to speak with Frank. He would understand her position and go with it. "Once we have that, the phone records, and confirmation on the other matter that we discussed, I should have everything that I need."

"I might as well use this time to catch you up on Ann's condition. She's conscious and they are weaning her off the ventilator. Harden is flying back to D.C. tonight."

Frank paused long enough for Brook to say something in return that indicated she was wrapping up the conversation, but she remained silent as the two men in front of her became even more impatient. That was fine by her, because such a strong emotion would have one of them inadvertently slipping up in their statements.

"I've been trying to keep tabs on the background checks you've been requesting, which is how I spotted the correlation of your profile with Yates." Frank must have been at his computer, because Brook could hear him pecking away at the keyboard. "It looks as if a few of them still haven't come back, but I'll check before I leave the office this evening. I take it you still plan to speak with Francis Walker?"

"Yes," Brook replied, glancing at the clock on the wall. She'd stalled long enough, but it had been enough time to cause BJ's anxiety to rise higher than before. He was beginning to realize that his father couldn't protect him anymore. "We'll talk soon."

Brook made her way around the desk and set her phone

down next to her laptop. She'd purposefully tossed down Vicki's notebook so that BJ couldn't miss her name printed on the top right-hand corner.

"You're wasting your time," Benny said, resting a hand on his son's shoulder.

She figured BJ would have normally shrugged it off. He didn't seem to be the touchy-feely type, but his insecurity had clearly gotten the best of him.

"You keep saying the same thing, Mr. Morgan." Brook reclaimed the desk chair and reached for her pen. "I'd like to speak with your son alone, if that's alright."

"No." Benny widened his stance. "I know the law, Sloane. I'm either staying or my son gets a lawyer."

"If that's how you'd like to play it, that's fine by me," Brook stated matter-of-factly as she met his angry gaze head on. "You might consider hiring one for yourself. After all, you did obstruct this investigation twenty years ago by withholding information regarding your son's illegal drug activities with the victim, along with the fact that you failed to disclose an affair that you had with the victim's mother. I can have the state police IG, a federal prosecutor, and a team of DEA agents here by tomorrow morning. Considering that you are currently obstructing an investigation which is now linked to my federal case, you'll be going to the Western Federal District Court of Pennsylvania under the 3$^{rd}$ Federal District Court of Appeals. I figure your attorney can meet you in Erie sometime tomorrow afternoon. It's your choice, Mr. Morgan."

# CHAPTER TWENTY

**Graham Elliott**
*November 2021*
*Friday—3:34 pm*

ORANGE EMBERS FROM the flickering flames raised into the air after one of the logs had shifted on the andirons inside the large hearth. The loud cracks of the escaping pockets of superheated air trapped in the split hardwood logs reverberated off the cathedral ceilings of the sizable room. The hand-carved cherrywood fireplace mantel juxtaposed with the stark white marble tiles was quite impressive and grand, and it had even been featured in Architectural Digest over eight years ago.

Long before Graham Elliott's daughter had been ruthlessly taken from him.

She'd always made fun of her mother for her need to constantly redecorate their family home, but he hadn't minded when such a trivial thing as décor had made his wife so happy. His years of service as culminated with him reaching the rank of Major General in the Marine Corps. His final assignment as Commanding General Marine Forces Special Operations Command (MARSOC) had been short-lived. His time in the Corps hadn't been easy on their marriage, but she had remained loyal by his side throughout every late night, each duty station, and countless deployments. The least he could have done in return was appreciate her talent for design.

Olivia had been so proud of her work on his personal office.

The built-in bookcases on all four walls had been filled with leatherbound classics that she'd handpicked herself. An original oil painting of landmark battle that held considerable meaning to him hung directly above the mantel. Dark burgundy leather couches and chairs surrounded an enormous hand-stitched 18th century Persian silk tribal rug that had been purchased by him in Saudi Arabia. To complete the ambiance, Thomas Jefferson's personal correspondence desk from Monticello had been restored with loving care and positioned in the back of the room to oversee the beauty of her choices.

Only she wasn't here to admire her work anymore, and neither was their daughter.

Graham shifted the desk chair slightly as he contemplated a phone call that had the potential to undermine the proposal that he'd given to Brooklyn Walsh. He could sense that she loathed when he called her by her biological surname, but he needed to gain a slight advantage when speaking with her, either in person or on the phone.

As he'd told her yesterday, he was a desperate man in need of the proper profiler and investigator.

Admitting such a thing wasn't in his nature. He simply wasn't an individual who usually held such a state of mind, and it set him on edge in a way that he hadn't been since before joining the Marine Corp at the tender young age of twenty-two. Serving his country had taught him discipline, value, and integrity.

Brooklyn had those qualities, as well…only for very different reasons.

He'd been monitoring her career with the FBI for quite some time now.

Brooklyn was aloof, unwavering, and stalwart in her quest to locate her brother. Graham could give her that opportunity free and clear of any roadblocks, if only she would return the favor. He'd seen to it that the case he had a personal interest in had been attached in its entirety, hoping the details would garner her interest.

He wasn't a man to base his future on a hope and a prayer, either.

He was merely counting on her ability to see what others couldn't in those files. If he were right in his suppositions, she would see what no one else was willing to admit about a possible serial killer preying on women in the service.

Brook had an intrinsic ability to place herself in the killer's shadow in a way no other profiler could, and that was a benefit to her career choice. Was it because she understood them as she did her brother or did those tendencies reside in her, as well? He doubted that anyone had ever posed such a question to her.

She had to wonder how two children could have been raised by the same parents, in the same household, with the same rules and turn out with two completely disparate moral compasses. Growing up with a boy who had turned into a serial killer had to have caused her a lot of psychological damage, but she seemed to have turned her hurt, anger, and fear into fuel for dispensing justice to those when it had completely escaped her.

It was quite admirable, really.

Why, then, was he about to give away his one advantage to help her?

The computer screen displayed the information that he needed to complete a single phone call that would save Brooklyn her consulting job at the Bureau. He could leave well enough alone and force her hand into taking his job offer. He'd done worse things over his life and career, but he hadn't been that man since his daughter's death.

She wouldn't want her murder solved as a result of blackmail.

Graham carefully set his glass of Kentucky bourbon down on the slate coaster before picking up the file that had been delivered to him by messenger earlier today. He'd requested information regarding the botched counterterrorism raid that had resulted in the death of two federal agents. It was what *wasn't* in the report that stood out, and the glaring judgement error had Jackson's name written all over it.

One phone call to a senior supervisory special agent who had served under Graham ten years ago had confirmed his suspicions. If Jennifer Madsen were to be provided with a direction by an anonymous source in exchange for leaving Brooklyn Sloane out of whatever exposé the reporter was writing, Graham would undoubtedly lose the incentive that would have Brooklyn agreeing to his job offer.

It was exactly what his daughter would have him do, though.

Without any more hesitation, Graham opened the bottom drawer of his desk to retrieve a burner phone sim card. He had an endless supply of them, for various reasons. Working contract jobs for different government agencies since his retirement had required him to be discreet.

It didn't take him long to punch in the number that he'd obtained for one Jennifer Madsen. She was currently staying in a hotel in downtown D.C., though the number he'd been given was that of her private cell phone.

She picked up on the first ring.

He proceeded to pour his advantage down the proverbial drain.

"Ms. Madsen, I have a proposition for you."

# CHAPTER TWENTY-ONE

**Brooklyn Sloane**
*November 2021*
*Friday—3:42 pm*

BENNY HAD GONE on for a good ten minutes or so about how his personal life had no bearing on the case, and that his son still had a right to legal representation. BJ had remained quiet, but he didn't seem to be in a hurry to bring someone else in on the interview. As a matter of fact, he'd remained in the chair as if he wanted to answer Brook's questions.

Guilty conscience, maybe?

"If your son would like to be represented by an attorney, that's his right. The phone is right there." Brook leveled BJ a stare that would get her point across. He wasn't focused on her at all. His concentration was solely on the red notebook that had Vicki's name printed on the cover in her own handwriting. "All I want to do is go over the week's events leading up to the night of the bonfire. Vicki bought weed from you that afternoon. All I need to know is if she was selling for you. Did she need money? Ask you for a loan?"

"You have no proof that—"

"Dad. Enough." BJ finally shrugged off his father's physical support. One would think he wasn't hitting forty in the next couple of months. "Listen, Vicki only ever bought a few joints off me from time to time. Maybe twice a month throughout that summer before school. We weren't really friends, and I have no idea if she needed money."

"Did Vicki ever dabble in other drugs?"

"No."

"Did she owe you money?"

"No."

"Did you and Vicki ever talk about anything personal, such as the fact that your father was having an affair with her mother?"

"No," BJ replied, shaking his head vigorously. "Like I said, we weren't friends. As far as I know, she didn't even know about the affair. Neither did I, until weeks after the murder."

Brook gauged the man's physical responses, not getting the sense that she was being lied to. One would think that she would have commiserated with him over their parents' indiscretion. Instead, she hadn't said a word to him, which was very interesting.

"Did you see Vicki with anyone unusual around town? Someone not in her circle of friends?"

"No."

"Where were you the night of the bonfire?"

"Some buddies and I drove into Pittsburgh." BJ hesitated, and he ended up leaving off the reason for his jaunt into the city. "We didn't get home until after three o'clock in the morning. We ended up crashing in my parents' basement. I didn't even know about Vicki until Dad got a call from the Johnsons the following afternoon."

Brook continued to ask the questions that were pertinent to

the case until Benny was comfortable enough to walk away from the desk. He gradually made his way over to Joe, who hadn't feigned his interest in the interview. The two were soon deep in conversation, allowing Brook to inquire about more intimate relationships.

"Vicki was having sex with Francis Walker," Brook stated, not saying anything to BJ that he didn't already know. Still, the switch in topics had him giving her his full attention. "Were you sleeping with her?"

"No," BJ said emphatically as he leaned forward. "I already told you, we weren't even friends. She was younger, and I had already graduated high school. She ran with the school jocks. Trust me, she wouldn't be caught dead with someone like me."

BJ recognized his poor choice of words. He ran his fingers down the sides of his mustache in the same manner that his father had a habit of doing before tapping his index finger on the desk.

"I didn't have sex with Vicki Anderson."

"Do you know if she was interested in anyone other than Francis Walker?"

"No."

"Did anyone seem unusually interested in her? Did you ever notice anyone staring at her longer than—"

"I've already told you that we weren't friends. I sold her some weed, she paid me in cash. End of story."

"No other conversation?" Brook asked, finding it hard to believe that neither one of them made any of their transactions in silence. "Are you saying that she bought from you in total silence? Not even a thank you?"

"Well, no…but—" BJ sighed in impatience. "We'd have

short discussions about what was going on around town. You know, the football coach getting busted by his wife for having an affair with the French teacher or the vice principal reeking of liquor by fourth period. It was never personal."

Brook continued to ask BJ questions that didn't result in any new developments. Twenty minutes later, she began to wrap up the interview. She even thanked him for agreeing to come into the station.

"That's it?" BJ asked hesitantly as he stood, straightening out his leather jacket. It seemed quite stiff, indicating that it had been a recent purchase. She gave him credit for not glancing over his shoulder at his father. "What about—"

"I keep my word, Mr. Morgan." Brook remained seated, wanting to go through some emails before she headed out to the Walker residence. It was important that she convey a message to BJ before he left the building, though. Chances were that he'd make sure word spread around town that would have the townsfolk relaxing somewhat about her presence. "I'm here for one reason and one reason only—to apprehend the individual who has been killing women in the tristate area. Again, I appreciate your willingness to help with the investigation."

"Son, let's go." Benny couldn't seem to accept that his son was no longer a boy who needed his father's protection. "Sloane, I trust that my son won't be hearing from you again."

Brook didn't bother to address Benny, who would no doubt steer clear of the police station while she remained in town. She didn't expect to be here for more than another day or two, at any rate. The case was coming together, and now she needed to figure out how it all tied together.

Once Vicki Anderson's murder was solved, so would the rest

of the cases that had followed suit.

"Agent Sloane?"

Brook had already opened her laptop, not expecting BJ to say another word. He and his father were standing near the front entrance, with Benny holding open the door. His anger was palpable that his son had stopped to say some parting words.

"Vicki *was* on the pay phone that afternoon when I drove into the parking lot." BJ shrugged, as if he hadn't thought anything of it at the time. "I heard you on the phone earlier. I don't know who she was talking to, and I didn't ask. It was none of my business. I parked in my usual spot and waited for her to finish the call."

Brook studied his facial expression, searching for the truth. Was BJ relaying his memories as they came to him, or had he simply wanted her to believe that he was helping her now that she was letting him skate on the drug charges? He seemed sincere, so she slowly nodded her appreciation.

"Thank you, Mr. Morgan."

Brook monitored the two men's departure, thankful that Joe hadn't interrupted her interview. She could feel the weight of his stare as she went back to work, utilizing the additional twenty minutes that would give her time to finish the list of questions that she'd composed for the Walker family.

Once again, the only sound reverberating throughout the station was the ticking of the clock behind her on the wall. It wasn't soothing in the least, and the irritating noise was a reminder that she didn't have much time before the unsub targeted his next victim.

Had her visit to his hometown altered his routine?

Only time would tell, but she was confident that the unsub

would be in custody before too long. The only reason the investigation might not go as planned was the man who'd been a detriment to the case in the first place—Sheriff O'Sullivan.

Brook grimaced at the fact that she was still missing around three background checks from Frank. She understood that he was waiting on information, as well, but the delay was holding her up in proceeding with certain interviews. She rechecked her messages.

"I'll want to meet with Jeremy Yates first thing in the morning."

Brook had begun packing up her belongings and placing them carefully inside her briefcase. The bag contained a lot of pockets, and she was able to secure her laptop, chargers, and files that she'd had out for the day's interviews without overstretching the material.

She heard the squeak of Joe's chair as he shifted his weight.

"Jeremy had nothing to do with—" Joe broke off his declaration. "Shit. I sound just like Benny, don't I?"

Brook fastened her bag and rested her hands on top of the soft leather, taking a moment to put herself in his shoes. She wasn't devoid of feeling. Far from it. She'd just been working non-stop, and her brief conversation with Bit hadn't exactly made her deposition any brighter. There simply hadn't really been a moment to get Joe's take on things, not that he'd been all that reliable so far.

"I'm due at the Walker house in ten minutes. Why don't we meet back here first thing in the morning? You can fill me in on your cousin, and we'll then compare him to the profile."

"You think I haven't read it? You think that I haven't been sitting here going over every detail?" Joe lifted one of the files that she'd given to him yesterday. "Jeremy fits almost every checkbox in your profile, only he wasn't in town that night. He has an alibi."

Joe's declaration was made with frustration and hope.

The mixture of such raw emotions indicated Joe's doubt of his cousin's alibi.

"Where *was* your cousin the night that Vicki Anderson was killed?" Brook asked as she slung the strap of her briefcase over her right shoulder. She would check her phone for messages when she was in the car, because she didn't want Joe to overhear her side of the conversation should she need to discuss Jeremy Yates with Frank. "And please don't tell me that he was at home alone…asleep."

"Jeremy was camping out in the woods."

"Locally?"

"Yes."

"With whom?"

Brook already knew the answer, but she wanted to hear Joe say it aloud. He had to have been in town the following morning, because he'd arrived at the crime scene after the Johnsons had called into the station.

"Jeremy was with me and my brother."

"And you were all awake, sitting around the campfire, and singing songs past midnight, right?" Brook waited for confirmation, knowing that she wouldn't get it. If Joe and his family were in the woods that night, chances were that Jeremy had ample opportunity to slip away from his tent in the middle of the night and make it back by sunrise. "At least tell me that the two of you shared a tent."

Brook had spent ten of the twenty minutes that she was

going through her email reading the background check on Jeremy Yates. While he met the majority of her checkpoints of the profile, they didn't have nearly enough evidence to make an arrest. There would still be quite a lot of groundwork that needed to be done before they made it to that point, which she planned to do with the rest of her evening after her visit to the Walkers.

"No, we didn't share a tent," Joe replied reluctantly, tossing the file back on his desk in disgust. "Jeremy and I are around the same age. I would know if he was capable of something like what had been done to Vicki and the others."

Brook didn't have the heart to tell him that he really didn't know what anyone was capable of, not even his closest family members. No one knew what someone else was thinking or feeling…or lack thereof. Psychopaths and sociopaths were manipulative and deceitful in ways that ordinary people couldn't comprehend, and Joe wasn't an exception.

She began to walk toward the door, not wanting to keep the Walkers waiting any longer than necessary. They'd been through enough over the last twenty years. Unfortunately, nothing that happened while she was here in town would change anyone's opinion of the family.

"Sheriff O'Sullivan?" Brook had paused at the swinging door to look back at his desk. He'd had his head in his hands, so she waited long enough that he eventually lifted his frustrated gaze and focused on her. "I don't need to tell you not to say anything, do I? I'm not only talking about Jeremy. By anyone, I'm referring to your parents, your brother, Benny, or any of your friends. I shouldn't have to go over the details of this being a federal investigation."

"You don't," Joe replied, holding up both hands as he leaned back against his seat. "I know what is riding on this, and nothing you've said will leave these four walls."

"Then it sounds as if we're finally on the same page."

Brook truthfully didn't have a lot of faith in the sheriff's role thus far, but she also wouldn't discount that he'd been forthright with Jeremy Yate's name when he could have easily remained silent on the subject. She'd entered quite a lot of names into the system from the yearbook that Tasha Dahl had provided this morning. It had been a tedious process, and sometimes suspects were overlooked in the progression.

"I'll see you first thing in the morning, Sheriff."

# CHAPTER TWENTY-TWO

**Brooklyn Sloane**
*November 2021*
*Friday—5:16 pm*

THE WALKER RESIDENCE was located toward the east end of town, away from the main cluster of neighborhoods. A simple dirt road maybe two hundred yards in led to a lawn that was full of junk, including two broken down vehicles that hadn't been moved in close to fifteen or twenty years if she had to hazard a guess. An engine block had been set next to one of the cars, whereas the other had been positioned on bricks as if the owner had at one time believed it had been salvageable.

The house was a two-story that hadn't been painted in decades. This home wasn't brick like most of the ones in the neighborhoods, and Brook had no idea how the siding remained attached to the frame. There was no screen door, though she wouldn't have had to knock on it anyway.

A woman in her early sixties was standing in the doorway with her arms crossed to maintain some body heat. The temperature had been dropping all day. The slight shiver of the woman's lips led Brook to believe that she'd been standing in the same spot for the past twenty-some minutes or more.

"Good evening," Brook greeted softly as she took the last

step onto the porch. The wooden structure wasn't in the best shape, but it was sturdy enough that the planks wouldn't give underneath her slight weight. "I apologize for being late. I was finishing up an interview at the police station with Sheriff O'Sullivan. You must be Mrs. Walker. I'm Brook Sloane, a consultant for the FBI."

"Did you find out who killed that poor girl?" Sara said with more fear in her tone than hope. It was clear that this woman had been disappointed in her life, time after time. Brook had to blink several times to erase the image of her mother. "Did you clear Francis' name?"

"Not yet," Brook replied gently, not wanting to give Sara false hope. "Do you mind if we take this inside?

Brook had been very careful not to mislead the Walkers. While Francis didn't fit the profile of her unsub, there was no guarantee that his innocence could be proven beyond a shadow of a doubt. Had she been dealing with anyone else, she would have stated that fact immediately, but she didn't have the heart to break whatever was left of this woman's faith in humanity.

"Of course." Sara stepped back, her disconcerted gaze taking in the front yard. "I apologize for the lawn. We're just trying to make ends meet, and my husband and I are working two jobs each. Francis helps when he can."

"There's no need to apologize for anything, Mrs. Walker."

Brook stepped across the threshold, not expecting a large dog to come barreling toward her from the other side of the house. He must have been out back and let in by the man who was following close behind. She braced just in time for impact.

"Diesel," the man exclaimed in a stern tone. His weathered features gave way to the fact that he was Francis' father, Earl

Walker. "Sit."

Diesel attempted to do as he was instructed, but his wagging tail made it rather difficult for him to follow the command. He was simply too excited to see a new face. He wasn't a purebred of any kind, and she guessed that he was a cross between several breeds, with his Rottweiler genes being more prominent.

"Sorry about that. He's not used to seeing strangers."

Brook figured that Diesel was more likely to lick an intruder than bite an arm or leg, and his behavior indicated that he was well cared for by his family. The unsub would never have an animal with a disposition such as this one.

"It's no problem." Brook took the time to give Diesel the attention that he wanted, waiting for the Walkers to invite her to take a seat in their front room. While the furniture was old, Brook was impressed with the interior's upkeep. It was in complete contrast to the exterior and displayed a loving home. "He's a sweet boy."

Brook would have expected the house to have an odor, especially given the dog and the weather. Instead, there was a familiar fragrance that hung in the air, reminding her of the lemon polish that her mother used to spray on the furniture. They had obviously taken a lot of time and care into making sure their home was presentable for her visit.

"Can we get you anything? Water? Coffee?" The man's uniform shirt had stains all over the fabric. He'd obviously come straight home from work. Brook had offered to arrive at a later time, but Sara's shift at the gas station in the next town over started in about an hour. "I'm Earl Walker, by the way. Francis just called, and he's running a bit late."

"Is everything okay?" Brook inquired, catching the concern

lacing the man's tone.

Mr. Walker tapped the side of his thigh, and Diesel immediately went right over to him. They had leisurely made their way into the living room, both husband and wife waiting for Brook to take a seat. She chose the right side of the couch, assuming Sara would take the left side while he took the recliner.

Surprisingly, they both sat on the loveseat.

Sara even shifted so that she was closer to Earl.

"Flat tire."

Those two words didn't need to be followed up with the fact that he feared it had been done on purpose. With the FBI's involvement in an investigation that hit so close to home, the residents were bound to react in a negative manner against Francis. If she were to guess, she'd say that some of BJ's friends weren't happy that she'd turned her sights on the sheriff's son.

"I'm in no hurry," Brook assured them as she set down her briefcase. She didn't reach inside the leather bag, though. They were already on edge, and they would take such an action the wrong way. Instead, she carried the conversation to ease the tension. "I appreciate the offer of a beverage, but I'm okay for now. You have a lovely home. My grandmother used to collect thimbles. I haven't seen such a grand collection since she passed."

Brook gestured toward the far wall that had rows and rows of vintage thimbles that had been collected over the years, causing Sara to display a fond smile. She squeezed her husband's hand in affection.

"It's been passed down in my family for generations," Sara replied, her gaze landing on an antique sewing machine with a bit of sadness. "I try to add to it every now and then."

"Sara used to be a seamstress," Earl replied with pride. "She made every single curtain in this house. Every few months we head down south to some of the flea markets and sell some of the clothes that she makes from bolts of material that she gets on sale down at the craft store."

"You're very talented," Brook replied with a small smile. Diesel's head tilted as something caught his attention. "Unfortunately, I didn't inherit my grandmother's talent at sewing. Neither did my mother. She was a great cook, but she couldn't—"

Diesel took off from his spot in front of the couch, heading down the same hallway that he'd originally come from with Earl. Seeing as Brook hadn't noticed any functioning vehicles out front, she could only conclude that they parked their cars or trucks out back.

"That must be Francis now."

"Before he comes into the house, I want to know…can you clear his name?"

Brook's heart ached for this family, because she understood exactly what it was like to be the scourge of a small town. Jacob's horrid deeds had caused every single person who they had ever considered a friend to turn their backs. The only reason her parents hadn't moved was due to her father's stubbornness. Her mother had suffered from so much loneliness, that Brook would have sworn at the time that she'd welcomed the cancer into her body.

"I'm here to find out who killed Vicki Anderson." Brook was very cautious on how she worded her response to Earl. "I believe that her murder is connected to others around the tristate area, and I—"

"Francis hasn't really left town, let alone the state," Sara replied, eagerly leaning forward with the information. "When we heard that you were in town and that you were here for the Princess Killer, we went ahead and looked up the dates that those women were murdered. He was here. We can vouch for that."

"That's good to know." Brook's phone vibrated in the side pocket of her briefcase, but she made no effort to reach for it. "Did the two of you know that he was seeing Vicki?"

"No." Earl had been the one to answer when Sara would have continued on about the sensationalized media reports about the serial killer. "We didn't, but he was pretty withdrawn that year. He'd been kicked off the football team as a senior, and he was never quite the same."

"I heard about Francis' altercation with the assistant coach."

Had Vicki's death been a spontaneous act of violence, Brook might have believed that Francis had been the one responsible. He'd been quick tempered as a young man. Getting into a physical disagreement with someone in a position of authority had been one of many reckless decisions that he'd made back then.

"Francis isn't perfect." Earl lowered his voice when the sound of the back door opened and practically vibrated through the house. "He got into a lot of scrapes back then, but he doesn't have it in him to kill someone."

"…we'll go for a walk soon, boy."

Francis had been murmuring reassurances to Diesel as he'd walked down the hallway and eventually came to stand in the wide arch of the living room's entrance. His first instinct was to glance at his parents, doing his best to get a read on the room.

He was nervous, and she couldn't blame him for all that he'd been through.

Benny, Joe, and the state police hadn't gone easy on him. Only those individuals knew what had been said and done inside that police station, which was way before the time of video cameras and documentation. She'd also only read the written statements, as she hadn't had time to go through the tapes that had been submitted into evidence twenty years ago.

"Mr. Walker, I appreciate you taking the time to meet with me." Brook stood from the couch, not needing to cross the living room carpet, which had been recently vacuumed. Francis had wiped the palm of his hand down his work pants and quickly closed the distance between them. Diesel followed close by his side, the caring action giving away that Diesel's loyalty rested with Francis. "I'm Brook Sloane. We spoke on the phone."

There was no need to provide him with a title or bring up again the fact that she was with the FBI. He was already nervous enough, and she'd like him to be somewhat comfortable in her presence. Going through the painful memories was going to be bad enough.

"Have you made an arrest?" Francis asked quietly, not giving her any indication that his anger might get the best of him this afternoon. If anything, he almost came across as defeated. "I heard that quite a few of Vicki's friends were at the police station today."

"No, I haven't made an arrest." Brook waited a moment, but he didn't make a move to take a seat. His uneasiness was more than apparent. "Please, may we sit?"

Francis was subconsciously rubbing the top of Diesel's head, and she decided to use an opening that usually wasn't quite so standard by the Bureau's protocol. She reminded herself that she wasn't an agent, and that it was her inherent instinct when examining crime scene photos that allowed her to construct a profile.

"Do you know what the percentage of serial killers who bond with animals are?" Brook asked, not waiting for him to take a seat.

She adjusted her blazer and made herself comfortable on the cushion. Francis didn't seem to know how to respond. More to the point, he'd taken her question as a trick question.

"The answer is way below one percent."

Sara had gradually leaned against her husband on the loveseat. She'd become comfortable enough that she no longer needed to lean forward to make a point, but not so comfortable that she'd released her grip on his hand.

"Francis, I only want the truth. If that's finding out that you are innocent of killing a young woman twenty years ago, then that is where the truth leads me."

"The truth didn't matter twenty years ago," Francis muttered in frustration, finally showing her an authentic reaction.

"I have no ties to this town, nor to any of the residents. I'd really like to hear your version of what happened back then, Francis."

Brook's request, along with hopeful expressions from his parents, had Francis taking a seat in the stuffed chair diagonal from the couch. He was wearing a light blue work shirt, along with dark blue pants that was clearly part of the uniform. There was grease underneath his fingernails, but she didn't believe it came solely from changing a tire. He worked with his hands on a daily basis, and it showed in the callouses that had been left behind.

"Everyone knew that Vicki and I were together that night." Francis met her gaze briefly before he glanced over at his parents. He was doing his best not to verbally say anything crass in front of them, and she nodded her understanding. "I took her home, dropped her off in her driveway, and then I came home. We'd made plans to meet up the following night, but then Joe and some state detective came knocking on the door the following day. They took me down to the station."

Brook had the surface details, but that wasn't what she'd come to discuss.

"Was there anything odd that stood out in the week prior to her death?"

Francis hadn't been prepared for such a question. His skepticism spoke to the fact that he'd never truly been asked for his side of the story. Benny and Joe had already made up their minds about Francis' role in the murder, but the state detective should have had a better handle on the investigation.

"What do you mean?"

"I know that Vicki bought marijuana from BJ Morgan at least twice a month. She wasn't paying attention in class, she was preoccupied according to John Taylor, and she'd used the pay phone outside of the football gates quite a few times in the days leading up to the bonfire." Brook was still waiting to hear back regarding the call logs, but that didn't mean she hadn't told Francis who she'd been talking to on the phone. "Did Vicki ever mention to you that she needed money?"

"No," Francis replied with a frown. Diesel seemed to notice his owner's unease, and he leaned against the chair. "Are you saying that she was *dealing* drugs with BJ? Not a chance. I would have known something like that."

"Did she seem preoccupied to you?" Brook asked directly, wanting to get a feel for Vicki's state of mind. "I know about her mother's indiscretion with Mr. Morgan. You were with her the most. Did she know about the affair?"

"Yeah. She was pretty upset about it. I remember telling her to talk to her mother, but Vicki said that she wasn't going to have to worry about it for long. You see, she was going to attend the community college after high school. She wanted to major in finance. Mrs. Anderson wanted her to go for nursing, and Vicki knew that they were going to butt heads when it came time to declare a major. I think she wanted something to hold over her mother. I'd planned to work—"

Francis caught himself before revealing too much. He pressed his lips together, his gaze once again sliding toward his parents.

Brook feigned a cough, and then she directed her attention toward Sara.

"Mrs. Walker, maybe I will have that cup of coffee, after all."

Sara had been monitoring her son the entire time, so she appeared quite startled by Brook's request.

"Of course," Sara exclaimed, patting her husband's hand after they released their grip on one another. Their love for their son was more than evident. "Cream? Sugar?"

"A bit of cream would be nice," Brook replied to keep Sara in the kitchen a bit longer. Once she'd rounded the corner, Brook got right to the point. "What did you plan to do?"

"We'd decided that she would go to the community college while I worked in the mine." Francis' statement had garnered a disappointing stare from his father. "The pay was good, and I would have been able to support us both while we lived in the apartments a mile away from campus."

"You wouldn't have agreed with such an arrangement, Mr. Walker?"

"Sara's father died in that mine." Earl shook his head in regret. "She didn't want Francis anywhere near it."

"Vicki's parents wouldn't have been happy about her and I moving in together, but it would have been our choice." Francis leaned forward and pulled Diesel closer to his leg. The pain and longing for the dog's unconditional love was more than apparent in the act. "I loved her, Agent Sloane. We loved each other. The reason that her parents hadn't known we were dating was because we knew they would disapprove. They wanted Vicki with a doctor or lawyer. Someone with money who could support her. Not a blue-collar worker."

"Were you or Vicki friends with Jeremy Yates?"

Brook had lobbied the question out of left field, but she'd done so on purpose to illicit a reaction. There was still quite a lot to do in order to link Jeremy to any of the crime scenes. It would go a long way to establish a connection with Vicki besides his ability to sneak away from a local campsite.

"Jeremy? I mean, yeah. I suppose. He was a lot older than us, but he was always hanging around the school. He wanted the assistant coaching job, but the only way to get it was to kiss the coach's ass."

"Francis Gene Walker," Sara admonished as she came back into the room with Brook's coffee. She also had a mug in the other hand, which she handed off to Earl. "I apologize for my son. I taught him better manners than that."

"Thank you," Brook murmured, taking the mug from Sara.

"What happened at the school for there to be an open assistant coaching position? Are we talking about the same assistant coach who you had an altercation with the year before?"

"Coach Thompson resigned the year that I got kicked off the team," Francis said with derision, not bothering to hide his feelings for the man. "He got a job at the community college and moved out of town. A lot of people wanted his position at the high school, and Jeremy was one of them. Why? Do you think Jeremy–"

"I'm simply asking questions and trying to piece together that week," Brook reassured him, once again disappointed that Joe would have kept something that significant from her. He had to have known that she would discover that his cousin had been on school property in the weeks leading up to Vicki's death. "Did you and Vicki go anywhere unusual? Did the two of you drive over to the community college?"

"No, but she did plan on skipping school for a day to check it out."

"Did you notice anyone unusual around?"

"No."

"What about Vicki? Did she mention anyone making her feel uncomfortable? Maybe someone was paying too much attention to her or mention the name of a person who she usually didn't reference?"

"No, to all of those questions." Francis continued to scratch Diesel behind the right ear. A sadness had settled over him, accompanied by acceptance. "We had everything to look forward to back then, and then it was gone."

Sara had let a small exclamation of sorrow leave her lips. Her emotional response had caused Earl to set his coffee down on the coffee table and pull her close to him. The minor reprieve allowed Brook to take a sip of her coffee. She didn't want to seem ungrateful after Sara had gone to the trouble of brewing a pot.

While it might not seem that the interview with Francis had provided a lot of information, Brook was satisfied with the outcome. Vicki's penchant for drawing dollar signs in the notebook could have stemmed from her decision to major in finance. As for her preoccupation in class, it had been most likely due to stress from knowing about her mother's affair. Tack on that she still had to tell them about her relationship with Francis, she didn't want to go to nursing school, and she planned to move in with him right after high school…well, that was a lot of stress for a girl that young.

"What can you tell me about Brandon Farina, David Molchalin, and Timothy Milburn?" Brook asked after she'd lowered her mug to rest on her knee. She'd crossed her legs in a casual manner to give the Walkers a sense of ease. "Did Vicki spend time with any of them?"

"Brandon and Tim were outcasts. They hung out together and basically shunned everyone else." Francis' shoulders had relaxed somewhat now that she had turned her focus on other men who Vicki had gone to school with twenty years ago. "They skipped school a lot. As for Vicki spending time with them, that didn't happen. Brandon and Tim never went to any school events."

"Were they even invited to those events or say the bonfire the night that Vicki was killed?"

"I couldn't say, but it's doubtful."

Brook was well acquainted with cliques, personally and professionally. Human nature didn't change just because people got wiser over the years.

"You mentioned that Brandon and Tim missed a lot of school. Did they have trouble at home?"

"Yeah, I guess you could say that."

"Brandon's father did the best he could," Sara interrupted, unable to stay silent. Maybe having been outcasted by those in town had her rethinking her own perceptions. "His wife up and left them after he got hurt in the mine. No one could believe that she would leave Brandon behind, but she did."

"Are you saying that no one has heard from her since? Brandon's mother simply left town and never came back?"

Brook had just read over Brandon's background check before leaving the station. She hadn't expected to get his back so soon, but nothing had stood out in a way that made her believe Brandon's mother had been missing or killed. She made a mental note to go through the information in a more meticulous manner.

Brook wasn't one to overlook something of such significance.

"As far as we know, that's what happened." Sara focused on Brook, presumably figuring out that there might be more to the story. "You don't think that Nancy was killed by—"

"I didn't say anything of the sort," Brook reassured her before any of them jumped to conclusions. "I'm simply trying to get a handle on all the people who were involved with Vicki, and it appears that Brandon and Tim ran with a different crowd. Francis, what about David Molchalin?"

"David was a complete loner. He kept to himself mostly. Honestly, I barely remember him. I think he hangs down at Lou's place on the weekend."

Lou owned one of the two bars in town. His was on the west side, if she wasn't mistaken. As for David, he was someone of interest. He had gone to school with Vicki, had lost his mother in a car accident when he was three years of age, and he had been raised by an abusive father. There were parts of the profile that didn't align with David Molchalin, though.

"What does David do for a living?"

"Odd jobs, but last I heard he was helping old man Seaver over on his farm," Earl replied when Francis and Sara didn't seem to know the answer. "He's not the reliable type, if you know what I mean. Can't hold a steady job."

"Alcohol?" Brook asked, wanting all the details on the four men who Joe had brought to her attention. "Or is he one of BJ's regular customers?"

"Alcoholic, like his father." Earl reached for the coffee cup that he'd set on the table next to the love seat. "The boy had a rough life."

Brook stayed for another half hour, gathering as much information as she could from Francis and his parents. He'd provided her with damaging information regarding Jeremy Yates, which she would bring to Joe's attention tomorrow. She wanted to spend the rest of the evening comparing Jeremy's life with that of the profile. He was the only one so far who fit the majority of the parameters of those she'd formed for the unsub.

Overall, the visit had been positive for both sides.

Francis and his father understood that no matter the outcome, life for them would never change. It had more to do with closure for them than anything else. As for Sara, she clearly still held out hope that those who'd shunned them so many years ago would welcome them back with open arms. In all the tragedy, she still held onto her faith in humanity.

It wasn't until Brook was backing out of their driveway that she spotted Matt Henley's vehicle parked on the side of the street. He'd been monitoring her every move since late last night.

Was he simply doing his job and trying to scoop the other journalists and reporters, or was there something more to his story? She'd already given her word that she'd see to it one of the agents gave an exclusive interview after the suspect was apprehended, but it appeared that such a perk wasn't enough for the man. Brook made a split decision based on several reasons, and she hoped like hell that it didn't backfire in her face.

# CHAPTER TWENTY-THREE

**Brooklyn Sloane**
*November 2021*
*Friday—9:42 pm*

"ARE YOU SURE that was the wisest choice?"

"No," Brook replied matter-of-factly, pausing to take a bite of her pizza.

She held the cell phone against her shoulder as she lifted the slice. She was able to catch the dripping cheese with her tongue before it landed on the front of her turtleneck. She sucked in some air as the hot, melted mozzarella and cheddar cheese burned her mouth. Once she'd carefully chewed a good portion of the bite, she explained her reasoning.

"Tipping off the major press agencies wasn't in the plans. On the other hand, having them here might force the unsub to make a mistake. Henley has been following my every move, and he's a threat to this investigation. Having some competition in town might keep him in line."

Harden remained silent as he listened to her rational. She understood his concern. She really did, because she wasn't a field agent. She was potentially putting herself at risk, as well as the woman who was the unsub's next target.

The odds were still in her favor.

"I made a judgement call."

"And one that I don't particularly agree with," Harden replied in irritation. "Jesus, Sloane. You're in some remote town with a sheriff who has done nothing but hinder your progress in the investigation. You're staying in a motel that has the security of a treehouse, and you—"

"I am doing my job," Brook interjected, dropping the slice of pizza back into the box. She grabbed one of the napkins off the small pile that she'd asked the delivery guy to bring with her order. He was the same individual who'd brought her dinner last night. "I'm going to spend the rest of the evening going over the background checks that Frank was able to send me. He was able to finish up quite a few of them."

Brook tossed the used napkin into the small trashcan underneath the desk.

"I pulled what I could off the software programs, but Frank was going to dig deeper into their family lives. He sent me a text a couple of hours ago saying that he was able to flag two, but he's been swamped with Ann's cases." Brook glanced at his email that she still had up on the monitor of her laptop. "Brandon Farina's mother abandoned her family and moved out west. I confirmed that she's still living near Los Angeles. I still have my sights set on Yates."

"What makes you think O'Sullivan won't give his cousin a heads up?"

"He very well could, but Agent Neville is making sure that doesn't happen," Brook replied with a half-satisfied smile. She waited a beat before breaking the silence. "You didn't think that I would follow protocol, did you?"

"Nothing about this investigation is following protocol, and you know it." At least Harden's tone had lightened somewhat, and Brook attempted to stem her unease that he'd been calling her for something other than checking up on the case. "I met Neville when he was in the academy. Young, but he seemed solid. Do I want to know how he's going to blend in with a population of under nine hundred people?"

"Everything is being done by the book," Brook reassured him as she reached for a water bottle. "I spoke to the Supervisory Special Agent in Charge, and he signed off on Agent Neville keeping tabs on Jeremy Yates until I was able to officially bring him in for questioning. He rents one side of a duplex off Main Street, and we staged a utility van breaking down in front of some of the shops opposite his property. It took some doing, but we finally got Neville set up inside for the night. He'll call me if Jeremy looks as if he's ready to run."

Brook pulled her cell phone away from her ear. Once she set it down on the desk next to her laptop, she made sure to hit the speaker button before unscrewing the cap on the bottle. She grimaced when the water spilled down the sides, having her once again snatching up a napkin to dry her hand.

"Jackson resigned today. Late this afternoon, to be exact."

Brook swore as she spilled more of the water.

She wasn't sure what she'd been expecting Harden to say, but it certainly hadn't been something to that effect. Truthfully, she hadn't given much thought in the last thirty-two hours to her problem with Jackson, Graham Elliot, or the fact that a reporter could blow Brook's entire life right out of the water.

"Why?"

"I'm not sure." Harden's displeasure at being left out of the know came through the line loud and clear. "You have nothing to worry about, though. Your background file has since been redacted, so anyone new coming in won't know your connection to Brooklyn Walsh. That basically leaves a handful of us."

She sat down in the chair, needing some form of support.

As Harden had mentioned, only three other agents within the agency were aware of her past now that Jackson was out of the picture—the Director of the FBI, the agent who conducted her background check, and the man on the other end of the line. He'd been her supporter from the moment he'd discovered her at the college, as well as going to bat for her against Jackson numerous times over the years.

Unfortunately, he didn't want her working on her brother's case, not that there was an official federal investigation into the six murders that the state of Illinois had shoved into their cold case section. Once Jacob had disappeared, it was as if he'd fallen off the face of the earth.

Brook had later learned in college how serial killers perfected their techniques, slowly modifying their standard operating procedures in order to go unnoticed by law enforcement and society as a whole. It was a horrifying refinement process, perfecting their craft. She never questioned Jacob's intelligence, and he most assuredly had discovered a way to stay hidden in the shadows.

"We need to sit down and talk when you get back to the office, Brook." Harden intentionally paused to hit his point home. "You can't keep this up."

Harden was basically saying that she was the only one who could fuck up her future at the Bureau. Only she wasn't willing to give up her search for her brother. The fact that no other murders since the death of her college roommate had been connected to Jacob had basically stalled out the state's investigation. The FBI had never been called in, and nothing Brook had said or done could convince Harden to allow her to work on the case in between her regular assignments.

"Are you back in D.C.?" Brook asked, purposefully shoving aside his request and steering the discussion away from her personal life. She had an uneasy feeling that Jackson's resignation wasn't due to some newfound sense of longing for retirement. "Frank said that you were due back tonight. I'll call you first thing in the morning if I can connect Yates to the other murders."

Harden was pushing her back against the wall when all he'd ever done in the past was leave her to her own devices. Well, for the most part. He didn't get to put a leash on her now.

"Keep things above board."

Harden wasn't pleased that she chose to ignore his request, but she was at a loss as to why he was still pushing against what she did in her own personal time. Granted, she colored outside the lines when it came to utilizing federal resources, but he'd always been willing to look the other way.

What had changed to have him so opposed to the way she'd chosen to handle her life?

Brook had been forced to look down at her phone when Harden said nothing else. Sure enough, he'd disconnected the line. She wasn't the apprehensive type, but that was the exact reaction she'd had to his call.

Had Bit said or done something to tip Special Agent Calabro off that what she'd requested had nothing to do with an active case? Or had Jackson decided to stick a nail in her coffin before he left his position at the agency?

Harden said himself that her file had been redacted, unless Bit had accessed the material through backdoor channels. He was more than capable of doing so, which was the reason that she'd gone to him in the first place.

"Shit," she muttered to herself as she held back from doing anything that would rock the boat. "Double shit."

She could easily reach out to Bit, but he'd be the first to hear the vulnerability in her voice. She couldn't allow him to believe that she could be manipulated in this situation. He was already desperate, and there was no telling how far he would go to pull her into his self-created problems.

Harden almost had her in the same position, because there was something more taking place at the agency than he was letting on in their recent conversations. She wasn't prone to paranoia, not even when the body of Pamala Murray had been discovered three years after Brook had caught Jacob with blood on his hands.

This was the second time in a week that her personal issues had interfered with a federal investigation. The next five or six hours should be spent piecing together alibis for Jeremy Yates. She'd already begun to establish a timeline based on his work schedule that Frank had been able to access before leaving the office.

Brook wouldn't be able to concentrate on such a timeline unless she was able to check with a particular source, but she had to be able to give something in return. She turned in her seat to face her laptop. Using the keyboard mouse, she pulled up her personal email and opened the message from Graham Elliott. His offer had been placed in bold, but she ignored the large number as she opened the first of seven files.

The majority of the criminal reports were from NCIS. Naval Criminal Investigative Services was a department within the Navy that investigated crimes involving members of the Navy and Marine Corps. According to the narrative attached, an ensign by the name of Austin Ridley had been arrested and convicted of involuntary manslaughter. He'd subsequently been dishonorably discharged and sentenced to thirteen years of hard labor in the United States Disciplinary Barracks (USDB) located in Fort Leavenworth, Kansas.

Why would Graham Elliott want her to look into a case that had already been solved?

Brook had her answer when her gaze landed on the name of the victim–Kelsey Marie Elliott. Farther down in the report, Graham and Olivia Elliott were listed as the deceased parents. Their daughter had apparently been in a relationship with Ridley, and the two had apparently been involved in a domestic dispute. The end result had been Kelsey receiving blunt force trauma to the head and Austin Ridley behind bars.

The only reason Graham would have sent his daughter's file to Brook was if he believed that Austin Ridley was wrongly convicted. She glanced over at the timeline involving Vicki Anderson that she'd drawn out on a large cardboard box that she'd confiscated from the station. On it was a line drawn straight across the middle with diagonal marks that retraced Vicki's steps the days leading up to her death. The visual presentation helped Brook understand what the young girl had been experiencing in her life.

There wasn't time to veer from the case, but she wouldn't be any good to Vicki by being preoccupied over something personal. Brook spent the next hour combing through criminal reports that Graham had attached to his email. An additional ten minutes had her discovering a pattern, though a lot of investigators and profilers would have argued against it…and with good reason.

Brook finally reached for her phone, armed with enough information that would serve as a quid pro quo. She went to her recent call log and pressed the number from yesterday. She wasn't surprised in the least when the line was answered on the first ring.

"You said your resources were as good as mine within the Bureau, Mr. Elliott," Brook confronted him before he had a chance to speak. "Prove it. Why did Jackson resign today, and what is Harden keeping from me?"

"I'm the reason Jackson took an early retirement."

Brook digested that news, no longer having an appetite for pizza.

She couldn't help but question why Graham would have done something like that for her when it went against his desire to have her work for him. Having dissected the last night of his daughter's life, she didn't have to wonder why he would want to own a consulting firm that took on cold cases gathering dust in backrooms of various law enforcement agencies.

"And Harden?"

Brook stood, unable to remain still any longer.

She walked over to the door and peered out the peephole. Matt Henley's vehicle was parked across the lot. He had no idea the headache his presence had caused or what she'd had to do in order to get Agent Neville set up inside the utility van on Main Street. Such a feat hadn't been easy. The young agent had been checking in with her on the hour.

"I just spoke with Harden on the phone, and I get the sense that he's keeping something from me. He's never cared what I do on my own personal time, and that has clearly changed sometime within the last week." The air in her room had become somewhat stifling, and she fought the urge to open the door. She turned away before giving into the impulse. "Why?"

Brook had expected to hear that the reporter who he'd mentioned yesterday had started reaching out to her coworkers or something to that extent. Never would she have guessed that the reason hit even closer to home than she could have ever imagined, and her stomach lurched as the nausea hit her out of nowhere.

"A body of a woman was discovered in Maine with her face dissected to the point that she needed to be identified through her dental records."

Brook pulled the phone away from her ear, needing a moment to process the information. She struggled to breathe in a way that hadn't happened since her last year of college. She always managed to blur out the faces of Jacob's victims, but it was impossible to do that with Cara Jordan. Brook had been the one to discover her roommate, her friend, and her confidant on the floor of their dorm room with her bloody flesh barely hanging onto her facial bones.

Brook somehow managed to prevent the scream that hit the back of her throat. She pressed her hand against her mouth to the point that she tasted her own blood. Ten seconds turned into thirty, and then sixty before she was finally able to lift the phone back to her ear.

"...you there? Brooklyn?"

The sound of her first name had her inhaling oxygen and

preventing her vision from obscuring into blackness. A feral rage washed over her, taking away the grief that she usually kept well hidden. The only saving grace was that Graham Elliott hadn't been here to witness such weakness.

"I'm here," Brook managed to say in a composed manner. She hadn't realized that she'd backed herself up against the door and slid down to the floor. Lifting both knees, she rested her elbows on them as she leaned her head back for some support. "I appreciate the answers. I did read over those files that you attached to your email. You realize that all seven cases resulted in arrests with the convicted offenders serving time."

Brook wanted nothing more than to demand more answers, but she would take a step back and get them on her own. She wouldn't rely on Graham Elliott, only to end up giving him hope that she would take on his daughter's case or go to work for him.

She couldn't grasp that a victim who fit Jacob's signature had been discovered in Maine.

Harden had obviously been able to keep a tight grip on the investigation, keeping it out of the press and from those in their division. It was the Boston field office that covered the entire state of Maine. Unfortunately, she didn't know a single agent who worked there.

"Is there anything else that you'd like to ask me?" Graham inquired in a softer tone than he'd utilized before. She didn't want his sympathy, and she certainly didn't want to be indebted to him. "I—"

"No, thank you. Let's discuss the files that you sent me."

Brook cleared her throat, although it did nothing to alleviate the burning sensation that had been left behind. She needed to pull herself together and finish this case so that she could take the personal time that she'd racked up over the years. She still had the upper hand when it came to Jacob, regardless that one of his current victims might have surfaced. She had to have been a recent one, given the physical state that she'd been found.

"All of the convicted killers say they're innocent." Graham went along with her lead, for which she was very grateful. "And before you point out that they all say the same thing, I know Austin Ridley. He did not kill my daughter."

Brook remained silent as she found the strength to push herself off the ground.

"The murders have nothing in common on the surface. Your daughter's case involved domestic abuse, one was mugging gone wrong, another was a drive-by shooting, and the list goes on," Brook pointed out, trying to focus on one thing at a time. There was nothing that she could do about Jacob right now, not until she was able to get her hands on the most recent victim. "What made you connect the cases?"

"So, you *do* see the correlation between them," Graham replied, his tone a bit more earnest than before. "All of the murders were within a one-mile radius from a base, all were women in their twenties, and every single one of them was a brunette."

Brook figured that Graham had pushed the authorities to call for a bigger investigation, but the fact that the murders had been committed in different states and all had been solved in the eyes of the law, not even his status could budge NCIS into declaring the deaths the work of a serial killer.

With that said, she wasn't even sure they *were* dealing with a serial killer.

"The women all have fathers who were in the service."

"No," Graham argued, taking her aback. "Jenna Spencer served in the Navy, but neither of her parents were in any military branch."

"Jenna Spencer joined the military to follow in her biological father's footsteps." Once Brook had begun to see a pattern, she'd noticed the case that stood out. It hadn't taken her long to locate the woman's obituary. "I can't be sure given the reports alone, but I'd focus on that angle. You are not dealing with a typical serial killer who focuses on the victims, but instead one who reasons away his tendencies by shifting the blame on the fathers. You could even be dealing with an act of revenge against those men."

"Are you saying that the killer is *in* the military?"

"No. I'm merely suggesting that the unsub is targeting his victims based on who their fathers are, Mr. Elliott," Brook corrected, resorting to a more impersonal manner. "I do believe it is an angle that you can convince NCIS to look into if you can get them to reevaluate the cases."

She was honestly unsure of almost everything at the moment.

There were too many directions that her thoughts wanted to take her, and she was unable to think clearly after the revelation that Jacob had continued his killing spree. She wasn't naïve enough to think he'd stop, but he had been so careful to keep his victims from being discovered.

Had something altered Jacob's routine, or had it simply been a fluke?

"I want you to take on the investigation."

Brook closed her eyes and tried to even out her breathing,

wondering how she'd lost control of the same routine that she'd had over the last seven years. She'd purposefully pushed things forward with the current investigation instead of waiting for Frank or another agent who could do the leg work.

There were still three weeks before the unsub took another life.

If she'd left well enough alone, she could have been back at her apartment, drinking a glass of her favorite cheap wine, and figuring out a way to apprehend Jacob. Instead, she was in a shoddy motel in a town with a population of under nine hundred people…one of them a serial killer.

"I made a commitment to the FBI, Mr. Elliott. I don't intend to break my contract," Brook informed him as she walked over to the large piece of cardboard that she'd hung on the wall in place of an inexpensive deer painting. "If you can get NCIS to share their files with me, I can speak with Supervisory Special Agent Harden. There have been instances where agents and consultants are lent out for temporary assignment to the military investigations agencies."

Brook honestly didn't understand why Graham hadn't gone that route in the first place. All the time that he had wasted leaving a business card with a simple number printed on the front in an attempt to try her patience had been for naught. It had obviously been a test, although she still wasn't sure the reason behind it.

Either way, their business had basically concluded with this phone call, and they could now both move on with their objectives.

"You have my offer, Brooklyn. I'm not willing to compromise."

"I'm not sure where you determined that there *is* a compromise to be had, Mr. Elliott." Brook didn't appreciate his attempt to drop the formalities. He was still a stranger, and whatever favor he had pulled for her with Jackson didn't alter their status. He didn't get the hint the first time, so she dug in her heels. "I gave you an alternative to your problem. Either you can take that route, or you can find another alternative, but know this—I didn't ask for your help with Jackson. There will be no quid pro quo."

Brook winced when she realized how crass and unsympathetic she'd come across about his daughter's death. She didn't have children, but she couldn't imagine such a loss. She'd gotten defensive, and she'd lashed out.

"I'm sorry. That was insensi—"

"You don't need to worry about Jennifer Madsen." Graham remained in control and never once indicated that she'd crossed a line. "She's agreed to drop her investigation into you in exchange for some information that I was able to provide her on Jackson. I'd still like you to consider my offer, and I didn't want you to agree because of undue pressure asserted for whatever reason. When you do agree to my offer, I want it to be of your own volition."

Brook wasn't sure what had changed, because she was almost certain that he would have done what was necessary to get her to agree with the details laid out in his email. She wasn't even remotely qualified to run a consulting service for cold cases for desperate families seeking justice for their lost loved ones. Hell, the majority of people didn't even have access to the monetary resources needed to fund such extensive investigations.

"Mr. Elliott?"

Brook could sense that he was about to disconnect the line, but she couldn't let their conversation end after she'd been so impervious to his grief. He'd given her the answers that she'd sought when he'd been under no obligation to do so.

He didn't respond, and she pulled away her phone to make sure the call was still connected. When the seconds ticked up to show that the duration of their conversation was still ongoing, she placed the cell back against her ear.

"I'm truly sorry about what happened to your daughter."

# CHAPTER TWENTY-FOUR

**Unsub**
*November 2021*
*Friday—10:02 pm*

EVERYTHING WAS UNRAVELING.

It was as if he were being suffocated, and it was all he could do not to become the beast that the town now feared. It was all her fault, and she needed to pay…she needed to die a long, slow lingering death filled with unimaginable pain.

He couldn't even hold his favorite pen in his hand due to the perspiration on his palm. Ever so gently, he set it down next to his journal. He'd written two words on the page and then crossed them out with purpose.

The media had dubbed him the Princess Killer.

He didn't view himself in that sordid way, but it didn't matter now. It was the public's perception of him, and that wasn't going to change, no matter the eternal truth.

He'd simply been giving those women a proper burial.

Why, then, were the reporters lying to the public? Who were the people behind the scenes directing the efforts of the media?

Those women had all mislead him, allowing him to believe that they had each been special in their own way. They hadn't been unique or innocent. None of them had been exceptional.

They had all been shallow, cruel, and downright wicked to their cores. Their deceptive subterfuges hadn't been lost on him, and he'd refused to lose his way.

All he'd done was seen to it that they had their own tales told for the world to see.

He'd exposed them.

Surely those who were there in person to see the ending unfold could see past the media's duplicities and lies? He'd always waited around to witness their understanding, though he'd done so from far enough away that the police couldn't recognize him in the gathering crowd.

It was important for the bystanders to witness how the women had misrepresented their places in his story. He was being painted as a sinner, and he couldn't let that stand.

It was time to prepare another shrine.

An unexpected shrine.

The vile and sinful queen of deception had to die.

# CHAPTER TWENTY-FIVE

**Brooklyn Sloane**
*November 2021*
*Saturday—1:24 am*

IT HAD TAKEN every ounce of control Brook had not to phone Harden back after she'd disconnected the call with Graham. Technically, he'd been the one to disconnect the line. She'd made a mess of that entire conversation.

There was no going back, though.

Graham wanted something from her that she couldn't give unless he followed protocol, and she wasn't willing to give up her position with the agency. The Boston field office would have reached out to the Peoria field office for their files regarding a string of murders that had been committed over the course of six years.

2000 to 2006, to be exact.

Jacob hadn't killed Pamala Murray the day that Brook had found him standing in the kitchen with his hands covered in blood. Her murder had come later, along with many others. Brook wasn't sure how Harden expected to keep her identity inside the Bureau under wraps now that the investigation had seen the light of day once again. Eventually, some eager agent would want to interview the sister or maybe even a profiler like herself. Wouldn't that be apropos?

There were too many things happening at once, and she wasn't even in D.C. to try and help do some damage control. She tried to reason with herself that maybe Harden hadn't mentioned anything to her because she was in the field. He wouldn't want her distracted from the case, possibly making a mistake that could put her life or that of another agent in danger.

She'd be lying to herself, though.

The body of the woman in Maine had been discovered two weeks ago.

It had taken Brook a good ten minutes after her call with Graham before she'd been able to locate an article online regarding the death of a yet to be identified twenty-two-year-old woman found in Maine. Two articles had been written for a local paper, but not enough information had been given out by local law enforcement for her death to have made national news. The investigators assigned to the case had obviously been instructed to keep the details under wraps.

Brook rubbed her eyes in exhaustion as she stood up from the chair. Late nights were nothing new to her, but too many events were taking place at once. She'd tried to focus on the background checks that Frank had been able to send her throughout the day, and she'd been able to make the case for a warrant to be served on Jeremy Yates' place of business. It was how she'd known that there were some dates in question. She wasn't confident that he was their unsub.

As for what she'd learned regarding Graham, Jackson, Harden, and now Jacob, doing nothing wasn't an option. Her funds were limited, especially after having paid Bit half his fee up front.

The net positive of it all was that she still had the other half in cash.

Brook made a rash decision, which she wasn't prone to do in stressful times. She'd quickly run down the cons of such a move, but she couldn't come up with one reason valid enough to stop her from pulling up a list of federal employees. After locating the name of interest, she had to then backtrack out of the site to log into one that allowed her to have access to personal phone numbers from select personnel.

Sylvie Deering was an analyst for the FBI who had inadvertently been put into a compromising situation right out of the gate due to her father's tax evasion scheme. He'd been subject to an investigation by the IRS for hiding money in his daughter's name without her consent. Regardless, Sylvie's bank accounts had been frozen, her security clearance had been revoked pending review, and she'd been relegated to a desk jockey position that had her shuffling meaningless administrative papers at Quantico.

The young woman wasn't cut out to be an agent, but given her current circumstances, Brook was confident that she would rather take personal time and do something different than sitting at a desk and staring at a wall for eight hours a day.

"Hello?"

Brook didn't flinch at the exhaustion in the woman's voice.

"This is Brook Sloane, from the D.C. office. I have a proposition to make, and it can't wait until morning."

Rustling sheets could be heard over the line, followed by the click of a bedside lamp. Brook figured the long pause was due to Sylvie putting on her black-rimmed glasses to get a better look at the time. She always had them on when Brook paid a visit to

Quantico for some reason or another.

"I'm not sure that you're aware of my situation, but my security clearance was—"

"My request is personal, and it has nothing to do with your security clearance," Brook stated, getting that concern out of the way. "I can't go into it right now, but I need to know all there is about a body that was discovered near a small town called Boothbay Harbor. I can offer you three thousand dollars plus expenses in cash for your personal time researching some information for me. I'm not in town right now, but I'm good for it."

There was nothing about the case that would have it labeled a top security issue. Local law enforcement would also be involved in the investigation. With the right questions and credentials, no one on that level would find such a request unusual in their day-to-day operations.

Brook walked into the small bathroom and grabbed a hair tie. Holding the phone against her shoulder, she managed to gather her long strands and secure them at the base of her neck while waiting for Sylvie to respond. She'd taken her clip out that she'd been using earlier to ease the tension headache that now seemed to have taken up permanent residence in her temples.

Brook tamped down her impatience, reminding herself that not everyone kept her odd hours. Sylvie had been awakened out of a sound sleep. It would take a moment to get her bearings and make sense of such a strange phone call.

"I'm not asking you to do anything illegal, Sylvie. I just need to know more about the investigation than I have time to research on my own right now." Brook exited the bathroom and found herself too preoccupied to sit back down in the chair. She walked over to her suitcase and grabbed the pair of shorts and t-shirt that she usually wore to bed off the top of her other clothes. "I can call someone else if you're not comfortable keeping this on the down low."

"Did you know her?"

"No."

Sylvie's apparent hesitation was the reason that Brook habitually took her time before acting on her impulses. She tossed her sleepwear on the bed.

"Look, I'm sorry that I woke—"

"I'll do it."

Apparently, Brook wasn't the only one making rash decisions tonight.

"Is this a good number to reach you?" Sylvie asked without hesitation, referring to the display number on her phone. "I'll put together a case file. I'll reach out to you when it's done."

Brook exhaled silently, not wanting her relief to be heard over the phone. Maybe she'd finally be able to focus and get some quality work done before she was scheduled to meet up with Joe in the morning. They had a long day ahead of them, and she was going to have her hands full keeping him in line. If she couldn't keep him on a leash with his family, then she would have no other alternative but to cut him out of the investigation entirely.

Such a move would hinder the flow of information, but she was too close to the unsub for him to fuck up their chances of making an arrest.

"Thank you, Sylvie."

"Three thousand plus expenses?"

"Yes. In cash. And please make sure that your expenses are

kept to a reasonable amount." Brook would have gone more into specifics of a meeting place, but she was cut off by an interrupting call. "I've got to go."

Brook pulled the phone away from her ear and switched over to the other number. She recognized it immediately, because she'd just saved it to her contacts hours before.

"Sloane."

"Yates is leaving his apartment," Agent Theo Neville stated, his deep voice discernable. "No incoming or outgoing calls to his known cell phone number."

They had gone over the tactics of what Neville would do in such a scenario. She'd parked his vehicle behind the police station. It wouldn't take him too long to reach it. With it being after one o'clock in the morning, he could easily get from the utility van to his car without anyone noticing or suspecting a thing.

"Emails?"

The federal surveillance warrant that she'd put in for had allowed them to monitor not only the man's cell phone, but also his personal and work electronic communications, as well. Unfortunately, social media private messaging took a bit longer to execute and required the internet service provider's cooperation.

"No."

Brook quickly walked over to her laptop and pulled up the email exchange that she'd had with the lieutenant of the Criminal Investigation Unit at the nearest state police barracks. She'd coordinated with him right after she was able to get Neville set up on Main Street.

Technically, she'd been in contact with Lieutenant Lawrence

since she'd arrived in town.

The detective who'd originally handled the case twenty years ago had retired many years ago, and she'd needed his personal notes on the case.

There was no other alternative than to have the lieutenant detain Sheriff Joe O'Sullivan. She'd truly believed that he would make the right choice, given the circumstances. She would still reserve judgement until she had a chance to speak with him, but she couldn't take any chances that he would assist his cousin in some way to evade capture and arrest.

Serial killers weren't prone to working well with others, but Yates also wouldn't want to surrender without making some sort of statement.

"Follow him," Brook directed as she sat down in the chair and began to lace up her black boots. They were the ones she'd worn to walk the crime scene earlier. The soles were basically flat, and she would be able to run in them if the situation warranted it. "I'll touch base with your supervisor and coordinate with the state police to provide you on-call backup. Once you have a location, ring me back. Do not attempt to apprehend this individual on your own under any circumstances. Maintain surveillance only."

Brook quickly disconnected the line and dialed the number that Lieutenant Lawrence had supplied her with in their email exchange. Neville was aware not to engage with the suspect unless he was given no other alternative. Once she had Yates' destination, she'd pass the address on to the lieutenant for additional backup.

"Lawrence."

The lieutenant seemed more alert than Sylvie had, and

Brook got right to the point.

"I'm not sure what prompted it, but Yates just left his apartment. Agent Neville is going to follow him at a distance and then text me the location. I need you to send someone to detain Sheriff O'Sullivan until I am certain that he did not furnish his cousin with information regarding the case."

"I already have a unit in the area," Lieutenant Lawrence replied. "I'll dispatch them to Sheriff O'Sullivan's residence and tell them to sit on him until they hear from one of us. I'll head toward Sutton with another unit as backup for Neville."

"I appreciate it," Brook replied, closing her laptop. "I'll send you the GPS coordinates the minute that I have them. Give Neville's cell phone number to your backup units, and also loop them in on any text traffic."

Brook quickly rattled off the information before disconnecting the line. She then hastily shoved her laptop into her briefcase. She'd never removed her holster. Her blazer was in the closet, and she didn't want to take the time to retrieve it. Instead, she grabbed her black dress coat that she'd thrown over the back of the chair.

As she went to slide her cell phone into the pocket of her coat, she was cut short by the vibrations. She viewed the address. It was one that she'd memorized earlier based on the one assumption she'd been hoping was wrong.

Jeremy Yates had driven straight to Sheriff Joe O'Sullivan's private residence.

# CHAPTER TWENTY-SIX

**Brooklyn Sloane**
*November 2021*
*Saturday—1:56 am*

THE NIGHT AIR was cold as Brook finished speaking with one of the state troopers who had been the first to arrive at Sheriff O'Sullivan's residence. The officer wasn't right out of the academy, and he'd understood exactly what was at stake when he and his partner had arrived as backup for Agent Neville. All three of them had secured the scene, and the two men who had been detained were waiting for her in the living room.

Brook slipped her hands into the pockets of her black dress coat right as two other cars pulled up behind the other vehicles at the bottom of the short driveway. Joe lived in the middle of the largest neighborhoods in town, which meant that all the unusual sights and sounds had acquired the attention of his neighbors. It didn't help that Matt Henley had turned up, parking his car across the street. He'd gone home at some point, because his vehicle hadn't been outside the motel when she'd left the lot. He must have heard about the call for additional units on the scanner.

Her investigation had been sidelined due to tonight's incident, and she put the blame solely on Joe's shoulders.

Lieutenant Lawrence opened the door to his unmarked vehicle, the red and blue swirling lights dancing off the wet landscape. While it wasn't raining at the moment, the highways and backroads were still damp and slick from the earlier storms. She was grateful for the reprieve.

"Agent Sloane?"

Brook didn't bother to correct the lieutenant. He was well aware that she was a consultant, and he was merely addressing her out of respect. She could usually read people, but she'd misjudged the mark on Lawrence. She would have pictured him former military maybe, or at least someone with OCD tendencies. He'd been quick to react with every request that she'd made, responded promptly to every email exchange, and answered his phone on the first ring of every call. Such actions were not that of a man who didn't care about his performance of his duties.

They shook hands.

She took notice of the absent tie, the stained white collar of his dress shirt, and the lint attached to the wool of his dress coat. He wasn't former military, and he wasn't a perfectionist. He was basically just good at his job.

"Agent Neville is inside the residence, but I wanted to speak with you about surveillance on another address. The owner is Brandon Farina." Brook slipped her hand back into her coat pocket. While she didn't believe that Farina was her unsub, he was now one of the only viable suspects. "I already gave Trooper Carlisle the address. Would you mind sending him over there to ensure that Farina doesn't make a run for it? The fact that we are standing in front of the sheriff's residence won't take long to make the rounds."

The unsub would never leave his hometown. He associated his mother with this area, with these people, and with his childhood memories.

The reason for the surveillance was due to the off chance the unsub would decide to take out his latest target before allowing himself to be taken down. He would have to travel somewhere to finish what he started.

"I thought that Jeremy Yates was your suspect."

"His actions speak for themselves, but I don't want to be caught making assumptions with this case." Brook went over her options. "Instruct the officer to detain Farina should he leave his residence for any reason. I'm hoping it won't come to that. If all goes well, I anticipate having things wrapped up in the next hour."

Brook had mentally gone over the background file that she'd received on Jeremy Yates. While he did fit the profile, there was something off regarding the events of his childhood. She'd even contacted Joe earlier in the evening to confirm Mrs. Yates history before her phone call with Graham Elliott.

Jeremy Yates' mother couldn't read.

It was one of the main reasons why the woman had dropped out of high school.

The unsub's mother had spent an enormous amount of time reading books to him, specifically fairy tales in which she most likely inserted herself into the key role. Taking that into consideration, she still hadn't been confident enough to strike Yates' name off the list. His actions tonight spoke against his innocence, regardless that he had an alibi for a few of the dates in question.

"I'll authorize the detail," Lieutenant Lawrence replied, motioning to Officer Carlisle that he was needed for an assignment. "I'll meet you inside once I'm done."

Brook nodded her appreciation as she turned and walked up the small sidewalk. The sheriff's residence was a two-story brick home, and well maintained. There weren't that many dead leaves in the yard, which indicated that he'd raked earlier in the fall season. He even had covers on some of the bushes for the upcoming brutal winter that was on the horizon.

One of the state troopers had stationed himself just inside the doorway. There was no entryway. The entrance literally led directly into the living room. Across the way, the officer's partner stood in front of what had to be the kitchen.

The wooden paneled walls made the living room appear much smaller than it actually was in size. There wasn't an overhead light, but rather two lamps set on opposite sides of the room on worn coffee tables. It wouldn't have surprised her to know that Joe had lived in this house for many years, most likely from the time that he initially became a deputy.

The sheriff was pacing back and forth in front of the couch, his anger palpable. He'd been keeping an eye on the front door, so she hadn't even been able to take a step toward him before he became confrontational.

"You had no right, Sloane."

"I had every right, considering your performance up to this point." Brook kept her tone steady, hoping that he would follow suit. She didn't want to deal with a knock-down, drag-out verbal clash right now. "You gave me your word that you wouldn't reach out to your cousin, yet he left his apartment in the middle of the night and landed on your doorstep. Why?"

She didn't wait for his respond as she zeroed in on Jeremy,

wanting to monitor his reaction. His cheeks contained a pallor to them that she assumed normally wasn't there. The fear in his eyes was evident, but she didn't catch a hint of anger toward her. His rage was solely aimed at his cousin.

"You gave your word? What is she talking about, Joey?"

Jeremy quickly stood from the couch in alarm as his words faded away. He wasn't speechless for long, though.

"Jesus Christ. You think that I killed Vicki?" Jeremy ran a hand through his hair, which had already been standing on end. His furious and outraged reaction had her rethinking the reason for his visit. She'd known that something was off with this entire stunt this evening, but she'd yet to figure out the reason. "You believe that I could do something like that? For fuck's sake, we're family. How could you—"

"Mr. Yates, why are you here?" Brook asked guardedly, noticing that Joe hadn't denied Jeremy's accusation. "I find it hard to believe that you suddenly got the urge to visit your cousin at two o'clock in the morning."

"Sloane, it was nothing more than a coincidence. Jeremy needed someone to—"

"Coincidence?" Jeremy asked, interrupting his cousin's explanation. He was still coming to terms with the fact that his cousin believed that he was capable of murder. "What the hell does that mean? Are you going to stand there and tell me to my face that—"

"Enough." Brook stepped forward and took her hands out of the pockets of her dress coat. She wasn't warm in the least, although Jeremy had a bead of sweat on his forehead. "Sheriff, I would like a moment alone with your cousin. I think all of us could use a cup of coffee, don't you?"

Brook had turned around and met the startled gazes of the two officers. They then shared a cautious glance with one another before slowing nodding their agreement. She couldn't see why they shouldn't also benefit from the situation.

"It seems we're all in agreement." Brook focused on Joe. She hadn't really given him a choice, and he understood how bad this situation looked for him. "Sheriff?"

Brook already had her black dress coat unbuttoned. She didn't need to make the adjustment as she motioned for Jeremy to reclaim his seat while she made herself somewhat comfortable on the couch. Her standing over him while questioning him about murder wouldn't result in many answers.

"Jeremy, I shouldn't have to explain your cousin's position. He's law enforcement." Brook left off that Joe had violated many of his job responsibilities during the initial investigation. Hell, he'd technically hindered her case, as well. Pointing out such flaws was futile. "I asked that he not say anything to you about the investigation."

"And you think that I killed Vicki?" Jeremy had been shaking his head back and forth almost subconsciously. "Which also means that you believe I murdered all those other women. I've heard the rumors that you're here because of that serial killer. You think he's one of us. You think it's me."

Brook didn't immediately reply when she caught movement near the area that led to the kitchen. Agent Neville had walked into the living room, and the slight shake of his head told her that nothing of significance had been discovered inside the residence. Joe had given Neville permission to search the premises, though they technically hadn't needed consent.

Jeremy's presence had given them all the probable cause that they'd needed for such a search.

"Jeremy, why are you here at two o'clock in the morning?"

"I found out yesterday that I'm up for a promotion, but it means moving to Philadelphia. It means leaving my family, and I don't know if I want to do that. My father's health isn't the best, and this town is all I've ever known. Joe is like a brother to me, and I wanted to get his take on things. I was having trouble falling asleep, and I know that he's a night owl. I just wanted to talk things through. That's all."

Brook could sense that he was still digesting the fact that he was considered a suspect in a string of heinous murders. She gave him a moment to process the situation, thus allowing her to mull over the past couple of days. She still had many more questions that needed to be answered, and Jeremy's head needed to be in the right space. Agent Neville was listening intently, though he'd preoccupied himself with the photographs on the wall so that Jeremy didn't feel that he was in front of a firing squad.

"The night that Vicki was killed, you and your cousins went camping. Did you leave in the middle of the night? Did you return to town without telling anyone and maybe join the bonfire?"

"No," Jeremy replied emphatically as he rubbed his hands up and down the fabric of his jeans. "I didn't leave the campsite and—"

"Enough." Joe had returned to the living room without the coffee. "Jeremy, stop answering her questions and ask for a lawyer. This interview is done until you have proper representation."

Agent Neville seemed surprised at the interruption, but Brook had known that Joe would only allow her line of questioning to go on for so long.

Family was family.

Unfortunately, Joe's reaction pointed toward his belief in his cousin's guilt.

"I want a lawyer," Jeremy said, relief heavy in his tone now that he sensed someone was on his side. However, he seemed to have missed Joe's reasoning. "I'm done answering your questions."

"So be it." Brook motioned toward one of the officers. "Would you please detain Mr. Yates? See to it that he gets his one phone call, and I'll meet you back at the station."

Jeremy began to protest, but Joe stepped in and began to explain the process to his cousin. She allowed it as she joined the other agent in front of a wall of family photographs.

"Nothing of interest inside the house?" Brook inquired softly while she studied the numerous framed pictures from over the years.

"No." Agent Neville pointed toward one specific photo of four young men, one of whom was Jeremy. "I spent the few hours that I had waiting for the subject to leave his apartment by going over your profile of the unsub."

"And?"

Agent Theo Neville was twenty-seven years of age. His father was African American and a decorated officer of the New York Police Department. She'd read over both of their files before personally requesting Agent Neville to help her on this assignment. Harden could believe all he wanted that she'd come unprepared, but he would discover upon his return to the office that she'd done everything by the book.

"I don't believe Jeremy Yates fits the parameters. His mother couldn't read, and aren't you basing this on the unsub's maternal issues?"

It appeared as if she'd chosen wisely, and it would be nice to have someone by her side for the rest of the investigation who she could confide in with thoughts on the investigation without fearing that everything she said was shared with the community at large.

"I sent two officers over to Brandon Farina's residence," Brook disclosed, noticing that Joe and Jeremy were still wrapping up their conversation. The officer was close enough to overhear what was being said, so she wasn't worried that the two men were conspiring with one another. "I don't believe Jeremy Yates had anything to do with the murders, but I can't ignore the circumstances, either. There are close to nine hundred people in this town, with seventy-one percent of them being male. Even by narrowing down their ages, it's quite an extensive list. A colleague of mine is doing what he can in between his other cases, but I get the sense my presence in town has everyone rattled…including the unsub."

"I can start to go through the rest of the names if your colleague provides me with the list."

Brook appreciated Agent Neville's determination, and she would absolutely take him up on his offer. First things were first, though.

"Sheriff?"

Joe remained silent as he closed the distance between them. He'd made his position clear the moment that she had stepped through his front door. He was no longer her ally, not that he ever was.

"Who is this between you and Jeremy?" The picture that

Agent Neville had referenced earlier was of four young men with camping equipment surrounding their feet. "You, Mitchell, Jeremy, and…"

"Justin."

"Justin?" Brook hadn't come across any Justin in any of the research that she'd done. She didn't like when she was surprised by something of such significance, especially on the night in question. "And who exactly is Justin?"

"He's a cousin who was visiting from San Francisco. He was the reason we went camping that year." Joe regarded both her and Agent Neville with more skepticism, if that was even possible. "Before you start to claim that I withheld more information from you, I did nothing of the sort. Justin died three years after that photo was taken in a carjacking attempt."

"I'm sorry to hear that." Brook took one more look at the photograph before stepping away. Her shift caused Joe to backtrack, but she didn't immediately head for the front door. "I think it best that you stay here. Your cousin will be allowed to make his one phone call, and I'll continue the interview once his lawyer arrives at the station."

Brook hadn't been giving him advice, and he seemed to understand that. Still, his reluctance was obvious in that he didn't immediately hand her over the keys to the station. She held out her hand, making it known that the subject wasn't up for debate.

"Sheriff O'Sullivan, no one is asking you to step aside from your duties," Agent Neville replied when Joe took longer to comply than she would have liked in this situation. "Should you get a call from someone in the neighborhood, respond as you normally would. When we're done with utilizing the station to conduct our interview, we'll let you know."

Agent Neville had handled the situation with the precision of a surgeon.

Joe walked over to the small table near the front door and picked up a set of keys. He handed them to Brook without brokering an argument before placing his hand on the doorknob.

"Jeremy has nothing to do with your case."

Brook didn't bother to reply as she palmed the keys and walked out of the house. The temperature had dropped even more in the short amount of time that she'd been inside Joe's residence. There was thunder rumbling off in a distance, and she noticed that one of the police cars had vacated the area to maintain surveillance on Brandon Farina as per her request.

"We'll ride to the station together," Brook said as she walked down the small pathway that led to the street. "We'll come back for your car when we return the sheriff's keys. I just need to speak with Lieutenant Lawrence before we head over to the station. Here."

Brook fished out her own set of keys from the pocket of her dress coat and tossed them to him. He caught them without hesitation.

Lieutenant Lawrence was on the phone, and he held up a finger to indicate that he needed additional time. She nodded respectfully as she caught sight of a state trooper who was about to get behind the wheel of his car. She called out to him right as he was about to close his door.

He was the one who'd been next to Joe and Jeremy as they spoke in private regarding a lawyer. She closed the distance between them while he unfolded his large frame from the seat. He closed the door so that Jeremy wouldn't hear their conversation.

"Was there anything said of significance between Yates and the sheriff?" Brook asked as she turned away from the wind. It had picked up in strength from earlier, and the biting cold was no better here than it had been back in D.C. "Or was the discussion simply about legal representation?"

"I guess Yates is close to the sheriff's mother. Sheriff O'Sullivan was trying to reach her while he was in the kitchen, but neither of his parents were answering their phone. I'm assuming they are asleep." Trooper Granger, according to his nametag, peered over his shoulder at Jeremy, who was currently in the back seat of the patrol car. He wasn't under arrest, and she hadn't requested him to be placed in handcuffs. "The sheriff mentioned a Ken Ellis. I've heard the lawyer's name before, and I think he's from around the area. Maybe Ellis is a family friend or something."

"Agent Sloane." Lieutenant Lawrence had finished his phone call and was walking in their direction. "My officers arrived at Brandon Farina's residence. Unless you want one of the troopers to knock on his door to verify it, they don't believe he's inside. There are no lights on. Granted, it's in the middle of the night. There is also no vehicle in the driveway."

"Garage?"

"No, it's empty. One of the officers peered into a side window."

Brook debated on whether to pay Joe another visit, but she decided that she didn't have to when she had another source at her disposal.

"Can you roll down the back window, please?" Brook asked Trooper Granger. "I'd like to have a word with Mr. Yates."

Trooper Granger didn't waste time as he opened the driver's side door and slid in behind the wheel. He turned over the engine so that he could roll down the back window. Brook leaned forward and made sure she had Jeremy's full attention.

"Where is Brandon Farina?"

"What time is it?" Jeremy asked, attempting to look over the seat so that he could read the clock radio. "If it's not two o'clock, chances are he's at Lou's."

Lou's was turning out to be quite popular.

"I'll tell the unit to be as discreet as possible."

Brook appreciated the lieutenant's assistance. Farina should be driving to his residence now, given that the bar closed a few minutes ago. She'd talk things over with Agent Neville on their drive to the station. It was time to bring more agents into the investigation. Though Jeremy Yates might not fit the profile, she got the sense that the situation was about to turn. Too many things were happening all at once.

The investigation was going much like her life was at the moment—at mock speed.

Brook thanked Trooper Granger and nodded toward Lieutenant Lawrence as he stepped away to focus on his phone. He had full knowledge on the rest of the night's events. He'd meet them at the police station.

It didn't take her long to reach her vehicle. She opened the passenger side door, noticing that her briefcase had been removed from the seat.

"I put your bag in the back."

"Thank you, Agent." Brook settled in and closed the door, though the inside of the vehicle wasn't nearly warm enough. "Brandon Farina is apparently at one of the bars in town, so

Lieutenant Lawrence is sending the patrol unit that way to monitor his movements. He's most likely driving home as we speak."

"The unsub isn't much of a drinker."

"You *have* read over my profile," Brook acknowledged with appreciation as she fastened her seatbelt. "The unsub would drink socially to blend in with society, but he wouldn't make a habit of frequenting a bar on a Friday night, nor would he ever allow himself to become inebriated."

"Call me Theo." Agent Neville expertly pulled the car around the lieutenant's vehicle, which he'd parked directly in front of her and half blocked her in against the curb. "I appreciate you asking for me specifically to help you out with this case. I'm the young guy in the office, and I'm usually given the white collar investigations that require a lot of paperwork."

"You are the only one whose parents are police officers, which means that you have inherent skills that the others don't, not that I'm knocking their abilities to do their jobs."

Brook shifted the vent toward her now that the air coming out of the slats was warming up to a comfortable temperature. They were in for a long night, and she wasn't going to stand for the station to remain as cold as it had been today. The first thing that she was going to do was turn up the thermostat inside the building.

"If Jeremy Yates isn't the unsub, and Brandon Farina isn't a match…where does that leave you?"

"It leaves me with two less suspects who I have to deal with," Brook replied, glancing over at Theo as he drove them underneath a streetlamp. "That doesn't mean they don't have information to share. There's a good chance they know him personally. I just have to ask the right questions to narrow the field."

"Doesn't everyone in this town know each other?"

"That's right," Brook replied, looking into the side mirror to ensure that the patrol car was right behind them. It wasn't a surprise to also see that Henley was bringing up the rear. He would have amazing photographs to display on his next video. "You're from the Big Apple."

"Don't tell me that you're from one of these small towns, because I won't believe it for a second."

"Don't make me second guess my decision to ask for you personally."

"Touché." Theo had navigated the neighborhood and came to a stop sign on a road that intersected with Main Street. "Did families name all their children with the same first letter where you grew up, too?"

"Some families did, yes," Brook replied distractedly, the same thought having been churning in her own mind since Joe had mention the other young man's name from the picture. "Such a tradition is normally done with siblings, not cousins."

Joseph, Jeremy, and Justin.

Why was Mitchell's name different from the others?

Brook held her fingers in front of the vent now that the air was relatively warm, ruminating over their names. She recalled from Yates' background check that his mother was the sister of Joe's mother. Who were Justin's parents and what were the familial connections between them?

"If you were to call your parents right now, in the middle of the night, would they answer the phone?" Brook asked as the pieces of the investigation began to fall into place.

"Always," Theo replied, shooting her a curious glance as he drove down Main Street toward the police station. "But not all parents are invested in their children. Where are you going with this?"

"I know the identity of our unsub," Brook murmured, her stomach tightening in apprehension that they might be too late to save another potential victim. "Unfortunately, I'm afraid we might have run out of time."

# CHAPTER TWENTY-SEVEN

### Mitchell O'Sullivan
*November 2021*
*Saturday—2:28 am*

MITCHELL LIFTED HER bound and gagged body from the floor to move her closer to the blazing fire. Her body was limp, but he doubted she would remain unconscious for long. When she awakened from her slumber, she would understand the meaning behind the small iron pails that he'd strapped to her feet.

As he laid her on the floor, a bitter taste flooded into his mouth over the wasted years that he'd had to endure under the roof of her house. Decades of deceit and lies woven in with the charade of posing as a family. She could never take the place of his mother.

His beautiful mother.

His memories of her had faded over the years, but he could still recall her sweet voice reading him fairy tales at bedtime. She'd loved his father with her entire being. She had been the focal point of their lives…until she'd died.

He recalled the day when he'd met Joe and his mother. They'd taken his father's surname, moved into their family home, and basically erased every trace of his mother. Mitchell had only been eight years old at the time. Joe wasn't at fault. He'd merely been a side character with no depth, not detail, and no truth.

Mitchell had been the one to suffer.

No longer.

Where was his sense of elation that usually came from exposing such evil?

It had never been his intention to create shrines that would honor the women who had attempted to delude him with pretenses over a perfect life. A life that his mother had so often said that he deserved. There was no future with them, though.

The shrines had been to display the irony of the unjust horrors that they'd committed on him. As for this woman in front of him, she was just like the others who he'd exposed throughout the years.

They were nothing but imposters.

Isn't that what the original tales had tried to convey to the children?

To warn them of the truth?

No one read the earlier stories anymore. They didn't want to accept the true nature of humanity. He hadn't, either, which was why he'd gone to such great lengths to find the perfect woman.

She was out there for him…somewhere.

It had taken him too long to figure out what needed to happen for him to find true happiness. He never would have had the courage to do what he'd needed had his hand not been forced to reconsider his life.

He, too, was to blame for not correctly interpreting the earlier classics.

All of that was about to change with the purge of evil that lay at his feet—his stepmother.

The lashes on her eyes began to flutter, and his heart suddenly began to race with the exultation he'd come to anticipate at completing a chapter of his life. He hastily leaned down so that he could get a better look at the woman who was about to get her just rewards.

"Have you ever read *Sneewittchen*?" His whispered inquiry jolted her into full awareness. She attempted to pull away from him when he brushed aside a strand of hair that had fallen over her cheek. Her frail endeavor left him smiling. "More commonly known as Snow White, where the wicked stepmother was forced to step into red-hot iron shoes that had been kept for hours over burning coals. Did you know that she was then forced to dance to her death?"

The faint whimpers that had been coming from her throat turned into guttural groans of denial that had him looking forward to the next few minutes when the flames of the fire would slowly heat the iron pails that he'd strapped to her bare feet. He would then stab her repeatedly in the abdomen so that he could witness the life drain from her soulless eyes.

"You'll get to experience her pain, as is your destiny." He was tempted to peel back an edge of the duct tape just to hear her beg for his mercy, but he was running out of time. "My life will change after tonight, my dearest stepmother."

He wrapped his arms around her legs and lifted the lower half of her body so that the iron pails rested over the hot, flickering flames.

# CHAPTER TWENTY-EIGHT

**Brooklyn Sloane**
*November 2021*
*Saturday—2:36 am*

"MITCHELL O'SULLIVAN ISN'T at his residence," Lieutenant Lawrence relayed a second time over the phone. "I've already called in for a warrant to search his residence and place of business. Two of my detectives will oversee the process. In the meantime, I'm heading to your location now."

"You'll want to step that up," Brook replied grimly, staring at the family home of the O'Sullivans from afar. The only saving grace was that Matt Henley had followed the patrol car to the station. "We've just located his vehicle. It's parked in front of the family home owned by Adam and Nora O'Sullivan."

Mitchell and Joe's parents owned a small piece of land not far from the Johnsons, which was where Vicki Anderson's body had been discovered next to an abandoned structure. The men would have known the area well back then from hunting and fishing the entire backcountry for most of their teenage years. Mitchell would have spent time as a pubescent boy envisioning the setting for one of his dark and twisted fantasies.

There hadn't been time to waste, so she'd called Harden on his cell phone. She'd needed the pay phone records to confirm her suspicions. The report had been held up in all the red tape, and he'd been able to cut through the bullshit by contacting the telecom's director of operations directly.

Vicki had been calling Mitchell O'Sullivan for advice on her choice of college majors.

At least, Brook assumed that to be the case. He owned the one and only accounting firm in town. It was small, catering mostly to the townsfolk who still owned the mom-and-pop shops in the area. He also traveled in the tristate area to conferences, giving him the ability to hunt and kill the women who he deemed not worthy of his love.

"Sloane." Theo was near the front of the car, his weapon already drawn. He whispered her name, though they were too far away from the house for anyone to hear them. "Do you hear something?"

Brook strained to pick up the slightest sound in the predawn stillness. Silence reigned, and not even the faintest rustling of leaves could be heard in the distance. The wildlife seemed to sense that danger lurked in the shadows, thus having them remain unusually still in their natural habitat.

"No," Brook murmured, scanning the edge of the tree line that was off to the right. She'd already discarded her dress coat to lessen any interference from the additional material. After tossing it on the passenger seat, she quietly closed the car door with only the slightest of clicks. "Do you still hear it?"

Theo slowly shook his head, all the while keeping his gaze on the house that sat atop a slight incline maybe a quarter of a mile down a single lane driveway. It was technically an old farmhouse, though the O'Sullivans hadn't utilized the land in that capacity.

"Do we need to worry about the sheriff?" Theo asked softly

as she joined him at the base of the long, gravel driveway.

"No. Lawrence already sent Trooper Granger over to the sheriff's residence," Brook shared quietly, motioning that they should cut through the grass in case Mitchell was monitoring the driveway. She withdrew her firearm from the holster attached to her belt. "Granger's partner will stay with Yates at the station. Sheriff O'Sullivan will be detained if he tries to leave his house."

Brook had called Joe to confirm that Mitchell's biological mother had died when he was only seven years old. His father, Adam O'Sullivan, had remarried a year later to a woman by the name of Nora Riley. She not only had taken Adam's surname, but her new husband has adopted Joe when he was six years of age. Had Brook known of the family connections beforehand, Mitchell would have been on her radar from the moment that she'd stepped foot in Sutton.

Joe had realized where she'd been going with her follow-up phone call, and his silence said it all. He just hadn't wanted to accept that the man who he thought of as his older brother could be so sick in the head. The irony of the situation wasn't lost on her.

"Go farther right," Brook whispered as she continued to scan their surroundings, as well as the front of the house.

Unless there were exigent circumstances to enter the family residence, their hands were tied without a warrant. Everything would then come down to what was found during the physical searches of property, bank statements, and the like. The fact that the sheriff hadn't been able to get ahold of his parents allowed them to be on the property for a health and welfare check. What it did not allow them to do was bust down the door unless they spotted signs of trouble.

She and Theo eventually closed the distance from the bottom of the driveway, through the yard, and to the front porch. There weren't any lights that she could see in the second-story windows, though there was a golden hue shining from behind some curtains in what she assumed to be the living room. The flickering of color indicated that there was a fire burning in the hearth, which she thought to be unusual.

No one with any common sense would allow a fire to burn unattended overnight.

Brook peered over her shoulder, hoping to find that Lieutenant Lawrence and the two troopers who had originally been detailed to Brandon Farina had arrived on scene, but all she could perceive was the predawn mists cloaking the distance. The cloud coverage restricted the moonlight and made it difficult to even distinguish her car from the bushes.

"Welfare check," Brook whispered in warning, garnering a nod of understanding from Theo.

She cautiously raised herself up on the first step, attempting to see past the drapes and into the living room. It was doubtful that a dining room had a hearth, although she had seen such a layout before in older homes.

Theo didn't immediately follow suit.

She wouldn't knock on the front door until Lawrence and the additional unit arrived on scene. Mitchell being at his parents' place in the middle of the night raised some red flags, but it wasn't enough to make an unwarranted forceable entry without exigent circumstances.

Unfortunately, her sudden presence in town could very well have shifted the perception and urgency of his fantasies.

Had he refocused his attention toward Nora O'Sullivan?

Technically, both the father and the stepmother bore responsibilities for their actions in Mitchell's mind. It would stand to reason that he would want to hurt both of them.

Brook carefully took the next two steps until she was on the main part of the porch. One of the boards had made a slight noise as she adjusted her weight, so she immediately stilled her motions. She waited a heartbeat before signifying that she was going to try and look through the window, past the drapes. Without even taking a step, a muffled yet horrifying shriek could be heard from somewhere in the house.

They now had their exigent circumstances, and they needed to force an entry to protect life and prevent threat of injury. There was no waiting for the lieutenant or the additional unit, and Brook and Theo had no choice but to somehow find an entry into the house to intervene with whatever scene Mitchell O'Sullivan had been attempting to recreate with his parents.

"Go around back," Brook directed sharply, closing the rest of the distance to the door.

There was no screen.

She tried the knob, not waiting to see if Theo had followed her instructions. When she found it locked, she pounded the side of her fist onto the hard surface. Best case scenario, Mitchell could possibly attempt to escape out the back. She didn't want to think about the worst case.

"FBI," Brook called out loud enough to penetrate through thick wood. "Open the door!"

Brook never had any intention of waiting the appropriate time. She'd given fair warning, and now she needed quick entrance into the house. Having been trained to a certain extent, she knew exactly where the weakness of the entrance was located on the door. She took a step back and used the base of her boot to breach the basic door lock barring entry.

The first attempt caused some minor damage to the frame, but she didn't stop at one. The muffled sounds were now high-pitched squeals that couldn't be mistaken for anything else but panic and pain. The second endeavor was successful, causing the doorknob to buckle to the side and the frame to splinter. Brook cross the threshold with her firearm at the ready.

The scene before her wasn't something that she would easily forget.

Nora O'Sullivan had duct tape around her mouth, wrists, upper body, and lower legs. She must have been positioned so that her feet were draped over the top of the burning fire. She'd managed to shift herself to the point that the buckets, pails, or whatever the hell had been secured to her ankles were now resting on the bricks on the edge of the hearth.

It wasn't until Brook got closer that she saw the blood pooling onto the floor from the woman's abdomen.

The room was clear, which meant that Mitchell must have gone out the back.

Brook trusted that Theo had that part of the house covered, so she had no choice but to quickly clear the nearby rooms before tending to Nora. The amount of blood that had already pooled didn't look good for the woman's chances of survival, but Brook didn't have any other option but to try and stem the blood flow once she'd ensured their immediate safety.

There was no sign of Adam O'Sullivan.

The living room was rather large, but nothing seemed out of place with the exception of an overturned rocking chair. There were no sounds coming from anywhere in the house that she could distinguish as she quickly made her way over to the couch. She snagged a quilted blanket and hurried back over to where Nora was no longer making any sounds.

Brook situated herself so that she had full visual of the room and entryway from what she assumed to be the kitchen. A stairway was to the left, but the upstairs was completely devoid of any light.

"Nora, if you can hear me, hang on," Brook said softly as she pressed the blanket over the wounds in the woman's stomach. The duct tape around her mouth was removed before Brook shifted enough to use her knee for pressure. She wasn't about to lower her weapon, but she also needed access to her cell phone. "I need an ambulance at…"

Brook rattled off the address right before she heard the board shift on the porch. She didn't bother to stay on the line. Someone had stepped in the exact same spot as she had previously, and she raised her firearm in preparation of doing what was necessary.

"Sloane."

"In here," Brook called out swiftly, easing the pressure of her knee when she was able to get a good grip on the blanket with her left hand. "Take over. I already called 911. I'm not sure we should take the pails off her feet until they are cool enough. Her flesh might have melted off inside them."

"Jesus Christ," Lawrence muttered as he hastily made his way across the large area rug and took over first aid. "Carlisle, get in here!"

"Does Theo have him in custody?" Brook asked, wiping the blood off her left hand using the side of her pants. "I'll go and search the rest of the house. Adam O'Sullivan has to be here somewhere."

"What are you talking about? Neville isn't out front." Lawrence motioned for the trooper to assess Nora's feet. She would probably be better off waiting for the medics to arrive, but Brook would leave that decision to Lawrence and the other trooper. "We saw the front door open and figured you already had the situation in hand."

"We made entry when we heard her screams. Stay with her," Brook directed Trooper Carlisle as she began to walk across the floor. He took over applying pressure on Nora's wounds. "Lieutenant, tell your other officer to circle around the house."

"Foster already started in that direction."

Brook couldn't allow emotion to cloud her judgement right now. If Theo hadn't apprehended Mitchell when he'd attempted to go out the back, then either he was still in the house or Theo was in some type of trouble.

Brook and Lawrence began to cautiously make their way through the house, bypassing the staircase. She made sure that the small bathroom was clear before moving onto the kitchen. It was quite dark, but the small light underneath the microwave made it possible to see that neither Mitchell nor Theo was in the room.

The backdoor to the kitchen was left standing open, allowing cold air from the outside to enter and suck all the warmth out of the house. Brook paused, giving time for Lawrence to take a position on the other side of the doorframe. He held his flashlight in his left hand while resting his right on top of his wrist with his weapon at the ready.

Theo hadn't entered the residence, or else he would have called out to alert her that he was making entry. His absence was indicative of the fact that Mitchell might have somehow gotten the upper hand. When she crossed the threshold, would she find her colleague lying dead on the ground outside?

Brook blocked out the bitter wind that seemed to have come alive in the past few minutes, as well as any contemplations that she wouldn't have had the ability to change anyway. It was how she'd managed in her personal life since she was a teenager, and it was how she would handle the current situation.

Lawrence stepped through the door first, his weapon drawn and at the ready. She followed suit, training her gaze on the shadows to her left.

There was nothing but darkness.

What moonlight had managed to break through the cloud coverage overhead wasn't nearly enough to allow them to take a step farther. Lawrence swept the beam of his flashlight over the area, catching Officer Foster about fifty feet ahead. He'd clearly already searched the left side of the property.

"Clear left."

"Shit," Brook muttered in distress. All three of them comprehended the severity of the situation. "Call in for backup. Find Adam O'Sullivan while you're at it. Foster, go around the other side and double check the area."

"Here," Lawrence said as he handed off his flashlight. "Take this. You and Foster can finish canvassing the area together. I'll call this in, as well as alert S.W.A.T. that we have a possible officer down and a hostage situation."

Lawrence knew as well as she did that there was no hostage situation. Mitchell O'Sullivan wasn't the type to take a hostage. Theo was either dead or unconscious somewhere on the property. As for Mitchell, he was in a position where he could watch their every move from the shadows of the surrounding darkness. With each minute, Mitchell's advantage would wane. The approaching dawn eventually would reveal him and flush him out sooner rather than later.

# CHAPTER TWENTY-NINE

**Brooklyn Sloane**
*November 2021*
*Saturday—3:52 am*

"EMS IS TWO minutes out," Lawrence replied, walking back into the living room. Another unit had arrived on scene, and the one of the officers would eventually ride in the ambulance to the hospital as a security detail. "Were you able to contact the Pittsburgh field office?"

"Four agents are on their way now. HRT is en route from D.C. by helicopter," Brook replied as she monitored Adam O'Sullivan being brought down the staircase. He'd been found beaten unconscious and tied up in his bedroom. "This entire situation went to hell way too fast."

Mr. O'Sullivan had black hair that had greyed on the sides. There was semi-dried blood on one side of his face, and he was rubbing his wrists as he stepped down onto the lower level. The horror written across his features was something very similar to how Brook's mother had reacted upon discovering that her son was a monster.

The man tried everything he could to reach his wife, but the officer finally got him to understand that her life was hanging by a thread. Adam started to cry, mumbling over and over again how sorry he was that he hadn't been able to stop his own son from doing something so heinous.

Brook had been the one to find him, and she hadn't had to ask a single question. His words kept tumbling out, explaining that Mitchell had come to the house at twelve-thirty. Adam and Nora had already retired for the evening, but it had been Nora who had gone downstairs to answer the door. Adam hadn't even realized that something was wrong until Mitchell had appeared at the bottom of the bed.

"We've searched the house and the grounds," Lawrence replied quietly, his gaze continuously darting toward the front door. Every second that passed without the EMS meant another drop of blood seeping away from Nora's chances of survival. "Both Theo and O'Sullivan are nowhere to be found. Once we have more manpower, we can start a grid search of the woods surrounding the property."

"Something isn't right," Brook murmured as she swept her gaze across the living room. "You sent Trooper Foster around the back of the house immediately upon stepping foot on the property, right?"

"Yes." Lawrence motioned toward the back of the house, where the officer was still stationed at the door. "He made a full sweep, double checking the area with you moments later."

Brook bit the inside of her lip as she processed the time of events. It would have been impossible for Foster to have missed seeing anyone attempt to run across the open backyard. Theo wouldn't have gone down without a fight, either. That alone would have delayed Mitchell from getting too far from the back door of the house.

"They're close by." Brook had come to the conclusion that

Foster couldn't have missed seeing Mitchell dragging Theo from the house. "They're still here, Lawrence."

Lawrence's skepticism didn't stop Brook from walking away. It wasn't long until she'd stepped out the back door, the cold night air enveloping her as she came to a stop in front of the officer.

"Did you hear anything when you first arrived on scene? I'm specifically referring to the first sweep."

"I did, but no one was visible by the time that I came around the corner," Trooper Foster admitted as he swept his flashlight over the tree line on the edge of the property. "There's been no sign of them since I've been out here, either. No visible tracks leading toward the back of the property, either."

Brook still had Lawrence's flashlight, so she clicked it on and retraced her steps. The light on the back of the house had been turned on to give them a better view of the area. Theo would have been approaching the back door with caution, so he would have slowed his steps as he moved around the corner of the house.

Brook would start there, and then see if she could find any indication of a struggle.

The beam of her flashlight jostled until she arrived at the area where she assumed Theo would have slowed his approach for his own safety. The grass had some indentions, but nothing noteworthy, especially considering she, Foster, and Lawrence had been through this region multiple times.

There was no sign of Theo's weapon, either.

A federal agent did not simply vanish without a trace.

It was practically pitch black around the side of the house, although Brook could spot one of the other officers monitoring as much of the side property as he could from the front yard. Another unit must have arrived after she'd left the living room.

Brook swung her flashlight in the direction of the trees, noting the distance once more.

She slowly stood and turned around to face the siding, using the wide beam to scan the worn vinyl. Starting from the corner of the house, she slowly moved her wrist until…

Blood.

There was a smear of blood on one of the vinyl siding.

Brook almost called out to Trooper Foster, since he was the closest officer. She immediately decided against it. If Mitchell was close by, she didn't want him to hear her alert the others. She took a few more steps, but there was nothing more to be seen on the house. Lowering the flashlight, she studied the ground.

The grass was still quite wet from the earlier rain. Between the weather and the previous searches, it was hard to distinguish anything amiss.

Brook decided to walk the entire length of the house anyway before she doubled back. When she reached the double doors leading down into the storm cellar, she came to a complete stop. They had canvassed every part of the basement inside the house. They had left no hiding place unturned, and there hadn't been any sign of either Mitchell or Theo inside the basement.

Brook and Lawrence had canvassed the lower level themselves.

Only she couldn't recall seeing this exit from the basement.

Brook glanced to her right, but the officer in the front yard was no longer visible.

Knowing exactly where Trooper Foster was stationed, he

would see what she was about to do with her flashlight. She turned it off and on multiple times in his direction. It didn't take him long to appear around the corner of the house.

Brook waited until he was close enough for her to motion toward the storm cellar doors. She could have sent him back into the residence to request more backup, but she risked being isolated if Mitchell attempted to flee. He had to have seen the sweep of her beam across the doors from below.

She shifted to the side so that she wouldn't be exposed when the left side entrance was opened by Foster. He'd already holstered his flashlight, drawn his weapon, and had his fingers wrapped around the rusted handle. If she were right, the O'Sullivans had plastered or bricked off any entrance into the house, most likely for security reasons. The space was probably no more than six feet wide, which meant that Mitchell would be at the base of the stairs or very close to it.

The wet grass had shown no signs of a body being dragged, so chances were that Theo was still ambulatory. Lawrence had been right, after all. Mitchell had been desperate enough to take a hostage. Everyone had limits.

Foster threw open the door as she shined her light down into the black hole.

"I'll shoot him! Make way or I will shoot the bastard!"

Mitchell's loud declaration had caught the attention of the officer near the front of the house. He was no doubt alerting Lawrence and any other officers who had made it on scene. The distant sound of a siren could be heard approaching, but it was that of an ambulance.

"Mitchell, it's over," Brook called out, keeping the flashlight on his face to prevent him from seeing how many weapons were trained at his head.

Unfortunately, he had the upper hand. He was using Theo as a shield, and the federal agent was bleeding quite profusely from his right eye. His hands were handcuffed in front of him, which could have only happened once the two men had made it down into the storm cellar.

"Do you hear that ambulance?" Brook asked loudly as Foster backed up enough so that he was about a hundred and twenty degrees from where Mitchel and Theo would have to exit. The trooper was experienced enough to realize if they were forced into a shooting that they would want to catch the perp in a crossfire, but also leave themselves a clear backstop against the structure. "Your stepmother is alive, Mitchell. You didn't finish your story."

It wasn't in Mitchell's profile to take his own life. He wanted to live out his fantasy. Being cornered by the authorities wasn't something that he'd considered, and he would attempt to find a way out of this, knowing full well that he would need to leave his life behind.

Jacob certainly hadn't had an issue with abandoning all he'd known to continue on with his purpose, and Mitchell would be no different. The only deviation between the two was that Mitchell was the one trapped and standing at the foot of a storm cellar.

"Back up," he directed with such conviction it was as if he'd convinced himself that he had the upper hand. "I won't hesitate to shoot him in the head."

"If you do that, you lose all your leverage." Brook didn't alter her tone, needing him to believe that she was just as confident as he was in this situation. "The best thing that you can do right now is lower your weapon, let Agent Neville climb out of the storm cellar, and surrender yourself before this ends in a way that will never allow you to finish your story."

Brook figured that Foster was probably wondering why she kept bringing up endings and stories, but she needed to feed into Mitchell's illusion. Theo's life depended on it.

"You won't allow him to die, which means that you will back up and let us out of here."

There was no way that she or Foster would be able to get a clean shot while Mitchell was protected down inside the storm cellar using Theo as a shield. Lawrence had come around the side of the house with two more officers, letting her know that the backup they'd requested had arrived on scene. They were all approaching with caution, guns drawn as she continued to negotiate.

"Fine. You and Theo come on up here, and then we'll talk about your surrender."

"We'll talk about the fact that you're going to let the two of us drive out of here," Mitchell countered, waiting until the beam of her flashlight indicated that he had room to maneuver. The last thing she'd witnessed before she stepped back away from the entrance was Theo preparing himself to climb the stairs. "Go. Slowly. I will shoot you in the head if you so much as look back at me."

Theo must have put up one hell of a fight earlier.

Brook had slowly backed up, positioning herself at the opposing hundred and twenty-degree angle that Foster had done for himself earlier. Lawrence and the other officers were approaching with caution along the side of the house, and she was relieved when they began to spread out behind her. The last thing they needed was for any of them to be caught in a crossfire, escalating situation tenfold.

By each of them being spread apart as widely as possible, Mitchell would have a hard time keeping both in his line of sight. If they had to shoot, one of them would theoretically have a clear line of fire, and Mitchell would only be able to target one of them.

For each step that Theo had taken up the stairs, Mitchell had followed suit. There was no chance for either her or Foster to get a round off and connect with the subject without hitting the hostage. They had no choice but to see how things played out once the two men were completely out of the storm cellar and above ground.

"Back up. Get those officers out of here."

Brook and Granger both cautiously did as Mitchell instructed, and their acquiesce had him easing his finger off the trigger. Her sole attention was on his weapon, which was currently being held against Theo's right temple.

"How does your story end, Mitchell?" Brook asked, knowing full well her question would distract him long enough for Theo to make a move. While her focus was on the firearm, she couldn't miss the way Theo's gaze kept darting to the ground. It was only a matter of time before he was able to give them a clear shot of the suspect. "Tell me."

"My parents had everything," Mitchell called out, though she couldn't see his face. He was cleverly keeping himself hidden behind Theo. "Everything. Then Nora came along, and nothing was ever the same. It's my duty to give my mother the story that she deserved. Don't you see? She would want that for me. Those women weren't—"

"Now!"

Theo suddenly bent forward, using the lower half of his body to push back against Mitchell's hips. He'd instinctively fired his weapon, but he'd lost his balance due to Theo's actions. It was pure chaos from there.

Theo dropped completely to the ground, while Mitchell managed to swing his gun to the right and get another shot off in the same moment that she and Foster squeezed their own triggers. The surrounding officers all fired multiple times before he fell backwards into the open storm cellar.

The thud of Mitchell's body hitting the cement floor below reverberated out into the darkness.

"Go, go, go!" Lawrence instructed his officers while he rushed to Foster's side. The trooper had fallen forward on his knees, grabbing at his chest as he attempted to rip off his bulletproof vest. He must have been hit by one of the stray bullets that Mitchell had fired from his weapon. "Breathe, Foster. Your vest caught the bullet. You're fine. Breathe."

Two of the other officers were already shining their flashlights down into the storm cellar while another of them was already halfway down to secure the scene. The likelihood of Mitchell O'Sullivan surviving the multiple gunshots and then the fall were next to nonexistent, though stranger things had happened.

"I wish I could say the same for you," Brook muttered as she knelt beside Theo. He wasn't remotely fine. His right eye had suffered a lot of damage. "Don't move. An ambulance just pulled up to the scene."

He'd rolled over, most likely in an attempt to even out his breathing.

She had to blink a few times to rid her own eyes of the tears that had collected over seeing the damage done to the right side of his face. She doubted that he could even see out of his eye due to all the blood, and she hoped like hell that he wasn't going to suffer some type of permanent injury.

"I need a medic over here!"

Brook reached for the keys to her own set of handcuffs. They were universal, and she quickly managed to release his wrists. He still hadn't said a word.

"Theo, are you hurt anywhere else?"

Someone made mention that several more ambulances were on the way.

"My pride, maybe?" Theo groaned as if talking made his head hurt worse. "Did you just smile at me?"

Brook might have cracked a grin, but she wasn't sure why he would make such a big deal out of it. Frank had mentioned something about it before, as well. There wasn't much in life to smile about, was there?

She glanced over her shoulder in hopes of seeing that one of the medics was making their way toward them. Sure enough, a woman with a bag was headed their way, which meant that an officer must have gone with Nora and the other EMT to the hospital.

"O'Sullivan surrendered, you know. He came out the back door with his hands in the air. Right when he went to turn around, he ambushed me. We scrambled for my weapon. He got the upper hand and coldcocked me."

Lawrence was still near Foster, helping the officer remove his vest. There was also a bit of commotion inside the storm cellar, and Brook could hear the drifting voices of the officers inside confirming her belief that Mitchell O'Sullivan was dead.

His reign of terror had come to an end.

"It happens," Brook reassured Theo, shifting to give the medic room to work. "We weren't dealing with some mindless idiot. O'Sullivan was manipulative, meticulous, and depraved in a way that we will never understand."

By this time, Lawrence had left Foster in another officer's care as he began to make his way over to the storm cellar. She could hear multiple vehicles approaching the house, and one of them even drove into the yard to give them additional light until a forensics team arrived on scene with their equipment. Another ambulance pulled up beside the patrol car.

"My eye is fucked up pretty bad," Theo muttered in apprehension. "Really fucked up, Sloane."

"I'll meet you at the hospital," Brook said to him, not wanting to give him false hope. The butt of his weapon had done some real damage to his eye socket, and she wasn't sure what the extent of impairment would be to his vision. "I've got to call both field offices to fill them in on what happened out here tonight."

Brook was able to extricate herself as another medic rushed forward and another went to tend Foster. Lawrence was calling her over, pulling her attention to the storm cellar. She wanted to witness for herself that O'Sullivan was dead. She'd done to him what she hadn't been able to do to her brother.

She also didn't experience one ounce of guilt.

Her therapist would have a field day with that admission, but that was for another day.

Brook came to a stop beside Lawrence, who was staring down at two officers who were now stationed around the body.

One of them had kicked Theo's weapon to the side, but he'd left it on the ground so that the forensics team could take photographs and bag it for evidence.

Mitchell O'Sullivan's sightless eyes stared up as blood still flowed from the side of his mouth. The fabric of his sweater over his chest was blood-soaked, and a wide pool of blood surrounded his head where it had slammed against the cement.

"You alright?"

"Yeah," Brook replied softly, not bothering to acknowledge that it had been a hell of a close call. In truth, her heart was still racing. If she were to bring up her hand, it would almost certainly have a tremor. "I don't think that I'll be asking to venture out into the field again anytime soon."

Lawrence grunted in humor at her response.

"What are you talking about?" Lawrence shoved his hands in the pockets of his trousers and then rocked back on the heels of his dress shoes. "You're a natural."

"…get an exclusive. Agent Sloane! Agent Sloane!"

"The press is going to have a field day with this one," Lawrence said in disgust, not even bothering to glance toward the front of the house. Matt Henley wanted his exclusive. He no doubt had heard the request for more units and medics at the O'Sullivan residence. "I can read the headline now—The Princess Killer Dies in Shootout."

"I don't care what they say in the press." Brook continued to stare down at the motionless form of Mitchell O'Sullivan. "All that matters is that he doesn't get his happily ever after."

"I like the pun, Sloane. I like it a lot."

# CHAPTER THIRTY

**Brooklyn Sloane**
*November 2021*
*Sunday—6:26 pm*

BROOK REMAINED IN her car underneath the awning as she finished her phone conversation with Frank. She'd spoken with Harden yesterday, giving him a verbal account on everything that had taken place at the O'Sullivan property. The conversation had been brief, but civilized. She hadn't let on that she was aware of the investigation going on up in Maine. Such a confrontation could wait until she was in the office tomorrow morning.

"Harden sure as hell won't be sending you out into the field for a while," Frank said with a laugh. "I'm friends with Benning, out of the Pittsburgh field office. He said he'd never witnessed a case go from zero to sixty in such a short amount of time."

A massive headache had set up residence in her temples. Technically, it was the same one that had started days ago. She'd spent the last thirty-some hours coordinating paperwork between the agency and the Pennsylvania State Police, giving debriefings to several points of contacts, writing up press releases, and visiting the hospital before heading out on the long trip home.

And those were only the tasks related to her professional life.

Graham Elliott's background check, or lack thereof, was currently sitting in her inbox. Half of it had been redacted due to special assignments that he'd served in the Marine Corp. She hadn't bothered past the second page, because there wasn't going to be anything in there of interest. His past was mostly classified beyond her level of access.

"Benning wasn't even there," Brook replied wryly, resting her elbow near the window of her door. She pressed her fingers against her temple to ease the throbbing. "He arrived after the fact."

Images of Theo flashed in her mind, and her stomach lurched at the fact that he was most likely going to lose sight in his right eye. That was a signed death warrant for a field agent. He'd be relegated to desk duty, because he wouldn't be able to pass a field-readiness physical. By the time that she had left his hospital room, he'd already instructed the nurses that he didn't want any more visitors.

"I should have requested a more senior agent." Brook bit her lip hard enough to get her train of thought back on track. She shouldn't have brought up one of her many mistakes from the past few days. There was nothing to gain, and she was bound to make many more in the near future. "Will you please give the interview for me?"

Brook had a promise to keep. She would have said that Matt Henley was the bane of her existence, but that role in her life was already taken.

"Fine, but you owe me." Frank's next words were muffled, but he must have been talking to his wife. Brook was about to tell him that she would see him in the office tomorrow, but he spoke first. "Hey, in all the excitement, I forget to tell you about

Jackson. He resigned. Word has it that Harden might actually be up for that promotion. Then there is…"

Frank's mood had improved since he'd received word that Ann might be released by the middle of next week. He'd even spoken to her himself, and she was slated to make a full recovery. Theo hadn't been so lucky.

"Frank, I've got to run," Brook said right as she heard the distant sounds of sirens. They were a reminder of the weekend, but it was a common noise people expected to hear when living in the city. Either way, it provided her with an excuse to cut their phone conversation short. "I'll see you in the morning, alright?"

"Sure, sure," Frank replied in understanding. He must have caught the irritating sound, as well. "Brook, you handled everything by the book. Things sometime happen that are out of our control."

"I appreciate the support, Frank. Have a good night."

Brook disconnected the call and leaned her head back against the headrest. What she really needed was a glass of wine and a hot shower. She went to tuck her phone into the side compartment of her briefcase when she remembered that she'd had two voicemails.

One of them she'd already listened to from Sylvie. She'd managed to get information on the murder of the young woman in Maine. The case file was ready and waiting as soon as she had an email to send the report. Brook was appreciative of the fact that Sylvie had known she wouldn't want it traced to her work address.

The other was from an unknown number.

Brook decided to quickly listen to the message as she began

to collect her briefcase and purse. She'd even tossed her wallet on the seat after she'd fueled up a few hours ago.

"Agent Sloane, it's Bit."

Brook stifled a groan as she shoved her wallet into her purse. The sirens were practically right on top of her, so she wasn't surprised when two police cars came to an abrupt halt across the street.

"I get why you won't take my calls. I do."

The officers flung their doors open, one of them quickly issuing orders to the other three.

"I want you to know that I'm going to reach out to Agent Calabro tomorrow. I'm going to come clean about Kuzmich now that my sister can receive her treatments. I got the call this morning. You're the only one who knew about it, so I'm assuming that you're the one who paid the hospital in advance. I don't regret what I did with getting involved with Kuzmich. I was able to keep us afloat, but I have to keep her safe now. That means turning against Kuzmich and going into witness protection."

Brook monitored the scene in front of her as she listened to the rest of Bit's message. She *had* called the hospital and paid for his sister's treatment in advance. She'd taken up the majority of her savings by doing so, but she didn't regret her decision. She wouldn't go so far as to say that she had an epiphany while in the waiting room of the hospital, but there was nothing wrong with doing a good deed or two. In truth, it was her way of alleviating her guilt over requesting a young agent fresh out of the academy to assist her on a major case.

"I don't know what changed your mind about the money, but I wanted to call and say thanks before I turn myself into

Calabro. I also wanted to return the favor, not that it even comes close to what you did for my sister. Anyway, the guy who you had me…"

Another vehicle came out of nowhere, stopping abruptly alongside a patrol car without any thought to the traffic behind him. It was an unmarked vehicle, and she recognized the homicide detective from a previous case that she'd worked on around two years ago. She hadn't seen him since then, and he'd gained a bit of weight. Unfortunately, his presence meant that whatever had taken place inside the building hadn't been a simple robbery or domestic assault.

A sense of dread overcame Brook, causing her to quickly collect her belongings. She'd dropped her phone on the floor in the process before she could end the voicemail. Due to the message having been on speaker, she could still hear Bit's voice.

"…should know that he's in D.C. I still had some alerts set up for facial recognition on the city's street cameras. I don't know if he's someone from one of your cases or not, but he is definitely here. Anyway, I just thought you should know. Take care."

Brook struggled to breathe.

It was as if she was being suffocated, and she couldn't get her mind to work. She attempted to focus on what was transpiring across the street, where an officer was already checking the identification of people coming in and out of the building.

She didn't believe in coincidences.

Brook took ahold of the disdain and loathing that had been festering inside her for decades as if it were a life raft. Jacob's visit to their father in Illinois, the murder up in Maine, and now his visit to D.C. was just a warm-up.

Her brother had returned, and he wanted her to know it.

He now had the upper hand.

Brook canvassed the area in her usual fashion, though this time she was prepared to set her gaze on the one man who had refused her the life that her parents had given her at birth. She'd purposefully kept everyone at a safe distance, from colleagues to neighbors. While she spoke to the doormen on a daily basis coming and going from the building, she made sure that it was nothing more than polite exchanges.

Had Lou refused Jacob entry into the building?

It wasn't like her brother to react spontaneously in anger.

As Brook continued to mull over what he wanted from her, because that would be the only reason he was in D.C., she managed to find her phone. Once she had her emotions collected, she opened the car door.

Not wanting to be bogged down with too much baggage, she only collected her briefcase and purse. Hoisting both over her right shoulder, she exited her vehicle with her FBI credentials at the ready. She wouldn't need her access card into the building. The rain was coming down steadily, but she didn't bother with an umbrella.

She walked with purpose across the street, holding up her identification.

The officer didn't hesitate as he backed up and reached for the door handle. The entrance had been prevented from closing by a simple door stopper so as not to automatically lock behind someone. The moment that she stepped over the threshold, a bit of tension released from her shoulders.

Lou was standing in front of his station while speaking with one of the officers. It was evident that the doorman was giving his statement. The relief that washed over her due to his presence was overwhelming. He called out to her the moment that he saw her walking his way.

She didn't bother to wipe the raindrops off her face.

"Miss Sloane, it's horrible. Just horrible," he insisted as he reached for her hand. She held up her credentials to the officer. "Mrs. Upton was…"

"Are you the tenant who resides on the twenty-third floor in the condo on the southeast side?" the officer asked as he reached for his radio. He leaned in to read the small print of her identification, most likely distorted from the rain that she'd gotten on the plastic. "Brooklyn Sloane."

"That's right." She had to swallow twice before she could get her voice to work. It helped that Lou had squeezed her hand in grief, as well as reassurance. "Can you please tell me what happened here?"

"A woman by the name of Lorraine Upton was found murdered," the officer explained before Lou could find the words. The older man had to have been the one to find her body. "Detective Hughes, I have a Special Agent Sloane in the lobby. She lives in the other condo located on the southeast side."

Once again, Brook didn't bother to correct the officer over her title. Hughes would remember her, though. He'd allow her to view the crime scene based on mutual respect.

"Lou, when you finish giving your statement, see if you can find someone to cover for you. Go home. Be with your family."

"You'll find out who did this, right?" Lou was still in shock, but he trusted her word over the officer standing in front of them. "I already gave them the security footage."

Brook didn't have the heart to tell him that Jacob wouldn't

have allowed himself to get caught on tape. The video that Bit had gotten his hands on had been nothing but a fluke, but Jacob's visit to their father still might be something that she could use at a later date.

"Get him a cup of coffee," Brook directed the officer quietly without addressing Lou directly. She wasn't going to give him false promises. "He takes it with cream."

Brook hated that she'd known such a fact, because it meant that she'd been fooling herself for the last seven years. She had allowed these people to get close to her.

Had that been Jacob's plan?

Had he wanted her complacent just so that he could knock her back to reality?

Brook had to show her credentials once more in order to get onto the elevator. As the doors closed, she noticed the security camera installed in the corner of the foyer. The stairs would have had the same surveillance. As for the hallway in between the condos, those were camera free due to the privacy concerns of the tenants.

The numbers above weren't ticking by as fast as she would have liked, and she was doing everything she could not to think about Mrs. Upton. How many times had the older woman asked Brook to stop by for tea? Brook's work schedule hadn't been the only reason that she'd turned down the invitation throughout the years, and now it appeared that her efforts to maintain some distance seemed quite foolish.

Brook cleared her throat in an attempt to compartmentalize the facts, finally taking the time to brush the wet strands away from her face. Jumping to conclusions wasn't going to help her mental state. There was a chance that Jacob had nothing to do with her murder. It could have been someone who thought she had money and it was a robbery gone bad. Lou did his best to guard the entrance from solicitors and strangers, but he was only one person.

Mistakes happened all the time.

She should know, especially after this weekend.

The ding of the elevator revealed that she'd arrived on her own floor. How many times had she come home and checked the tape on her door? Each time she'd discovered that it hadn't been tampered with, the reprieve had been a relief. It meant that she had time to gain the upper hand on her brother.

It appeared that time had come to an end.

"Miss Sloane."

Detective Hughes placed a hand on the side of the elevator to keep the doors open. He waited for her to step out, and the grim expression on his face told her all she needed to know—it hadn't been a robbery or anything of the sort.

"You might want to drop your things off at your place," Hughes suggested grimly, looking her over from top to bottom. "You'll want to dry off, too. No need to contaminate the scene."

"I'm dry enough," Brook replied in a tone that broke no argument. "I'll just leave these by my door. Give me a moment."

She had many reasons to prevent him from following her into her condo.

For one, he'd witness the check she would do for the tape on the doorframe.

Two, if Jacob was the one responsible for Mrs. Upton's death, he would have left something for Brook on her bedside table.

Three, the white boards and the numerous information

pinned to her dining room wall might raise some eyebrows.

Brook would decide after walking the crime scene if she should mention her brother. She'd been so careful to separate herself from that young girl who still hadn't found the answers to the questions that she'd sought all these years—how could two siblings be raised in the same household, by the same loving parents, and turn out so completely different?

"It doesn't look as if the victim put up much of a struggle. There were no signs of a fight. She might have even known her attacker, especially given that no one saw anything suspicious in the lobby."

Brook wasn't going to point out that he hadn't been here long enough to know such a thing, but that wouldn't start them off on the right foot. She had to be careful how she handled the next five to ten minutes. She didn't want to be cut out of the investigation. As of right now, this was a simple homicide.

"Cause of death?" Brook asked as she approached him after leaning her briefcase and purse against her door. An officer was stationed in the middle of the long hallway between the two condos, and he had somewhat of a clear view of her belongings given that the long corridor was slightly curved on either side. Besides, she wasn't worried that Jacob was still in the building. He'd never make such a drastic mistake. "Please keep an eye on my bags."

"Yes, ma'am."

"It's too hard to tell with all the blood, but I'm going to go with a severed carotid artery from the gapping slit in her throat." Hughes hadn't caught her wince, and she was grateful that he was one step ahead of her. There was no crime scene tape to seal off the area yet, but he handed her a pair of gloves that he must have had in the interior pocket of his suit jacket. "We'll have to get a positive ID of the body through dental records, though. There's nothing left of her face."

Brook tried to stay in the here and now. She even began her counting exercises that Dr. Swift had recommended. They'd done miracles for her in the past, and they did nothing to help her now. Hughes gestured toward the cane that was on the floor just inside the doorway. She wasn't sure how Hughes had gotten the idea that Mrs. Upton had known her attacker, but Brook kept that opinion to herself.

It was more than evident someone had forced the woman backward into the foyer.

The strong odor of copper was overwhelming the deeper they walked into the condo. It was the same layout as Brook's place, only flipped. She began to put on the latex gloves, not that she would need them. She had no intention of touching anything.

"Are you going to take this over?" Hughes asked as he came to a stop just shy of the large area rug in the living room. "If so, I'll cancel the call to our forensics unit."

She couldn't give him an answer. She was too busy fighting against déjà vu. What had been done to Mrs. Upton had been done to many other women, usually younger.

Brook swallowed the bile that had hit the back of her throat.

What had been left of Mrs. Upton wasn't recognizable. As was Jacob's signature, he'd taken a knife and practically carved the flesh right off the woman's face. The slit in her throat made it difficult to determine if she'd bled to death or choked to death. She certainly hadn't died quickly.

Jacob had wanted to make a point, and Brook had received

his message loud and clear. The last words that he'd said to her still rang in her mind, and she would never forget them.

*You don't get to be the normal one, Brook.*

The one time that she'd made an attempt at a normal life, he'd brutally murdered her college roommate. She had no idea where he'd been for the last seven years or why he'd chosen now to make an appearance, but she was no longer the scared little sister who was afraid of her brother.

"Agent Sloane?"

"No," Brook replied after she'd had a moment to process her next step. Jacob had once again ripped her life to threads, only this time she wasn't going to hide anymore. "I just drove in from Pennsylvania. I had a case there, and I'm still wrapping up the paperwork. This one is all yours."

She would have retraced her steps back to the door, but she forced herself to stop and take in the rest of the condo. Antique furniture gave the place an elegant feel, and there was even a china cabinet that displayed the antique porcelain teacups that Mrs. Upton had been so proud of collecting over the course of her marriage. She'd certainly mentioned them enough in passing, and now there was no one left to cherish them.

"Are you okay? I just assumed that you'd be alright seeing—"

"I'm fine." Brook had only gotten one glove on, so it didn't take her long to remove it. "The way her cane was left in the entryway indicates that she was taken by surprise. My guess was that she left the door unlocked, and the intruder walked right in and overwhelmed her. Good luck with the case."

There was no question that Harden would take over the crime scene once word reached him of the horrific details. Add on the fact that the murder had taken place in her building, on her floor, to her neighbor, and her supervisor would know immediately that the authorities were dealing with Jacob.

Only she wouldn't be allowed anywhere near the case.

Harden would use the excuse that she could compromise the investigation, refusing to acknowledge that she was the best chance law enforcement had to apprehend her brother. She would never be able to change his point of view on the case, which left her little choice.

Brook didn't even bother to acknowledge the officer who was still stationed in front of the elevator. She'd gone numb inside. She supposed that she should be grateful that she could turn off her emotions at will. The last time that she'd found herself in this situation, the medics had to give her a sedative.

She reached the door of her condo and leaned down to pick up her purse and briefcase. A casual glance over her shoulder revealed that the officer was facing the entrance to Mrs. Upton's condo. Brook took the opportunity to examine the tape in the top corner of her doorframe.

It had been completely severed in half.

Once again, she had to swallow the bile that rose from her stomach to the back of her throat. He had invaded her personal space once again, only this time she'd been ready. He might have been able to disable or manipulate the security footage for the building, but she'd gone to great lengths to ensure that her own security system consisted of cameras that were invisible to the naked eye and recorded off site. She'd purposefully not had them connected to the panel by the door. Seeing as she hadn't received an alert, it meant that Jacob had disarmed the main unit.

Brook didn't even bother taking her keys out, knowing that Jacob would have left the door unlocked for her. Sure enough, the knob turned without any resistance. She slowly walked inside and set her bags down off to the side. She heard the ding of the elevator right as she had turned around, satisfied that the officer had been too preoccupied with whoever had arrived on the scene.

Closing the door, she took a moment to lean up against the hard surface. The numbness inside of her was starting to fade, but thankfully it wasn't being replaced with panic, anxiety, or even dread. In their place were contempt, fury, and determination.

Nothing was out of place.

Then again, she hadn't expected anything to be touched or shifted from its location. Jacob was too good for that. He would have simply casually walked through her condo, looking upon her life with amusement.

Fortunately, it did not seem that he'd tampered with the white boards or the information taped to the wall of her dining room. Such a discovery would have given him pause. She also hadn't written anything down regarding his visit to their father, and she had the USB with the footage tucked into her briefcase.

She'd left her dress coat in the car, but the blazer that she had on was soaked through to her skin. After stripping it off, she tossed it to the floor as she collected her phone from the side pocket of her briefcase. She didn't look forward to placing the call, but she had to have everything set in motion before Harden got word of what had happened today.

As she began to walk toward her bedroom, she managed to multi-task and scroll through her recent call log. After finding the number that she was searching for, she pressed it right as she had entered her bedroom.

Graham Elliott answered on the first ring.

She only had to say one word.

"Yes."

The long pause on the other end of the line should have given her some satisfaction. Graham was obviously taken aback by her abrupt change of heart. Unfortunately, every ounce of her energy was now focused on the hardback book that had been so strategically placed on her bedside table.

*Harry Potter and the Sorcerer's Stone.*

"I'll be in touch," Graham responded quietly, as if he'd sensed that it wasn't the time to hash out the details.

The line went dead.

Brook slowly lowered the phone from her ear. Her life was once again about to be turned upside down, only she would be ready this time around. She'd spent years honing her craft at profiling, and she'd left no stone unturned when it came to her brother. While she hadn't expected him to take the life of a neighbor who Brook had tried so very hard to keep at arm's length, Jacob hadn't been able to stay away from her.

Whereas he'd brought malevolence into her world, the tables had just been turned.

Jacob Matthew Walsh's life was about to be touched by evil…and it would be done so by her own hand.

# CHAPTER THIRTY-ONE

**Jacob Walsh**
*November 2021*
*Sunday—9:39 pm*

RAIN. How he detested this type of sloppy weather.

The slight breeze off the gulf coast with the heat of the sun warming his skin was much more preferrable than this bitter, revolting climate. How his younger sister spent her every waking moment in such a miserable place like this was unknown to him. Was it her way of trying to prove that they were different?

Brook wanted so badly to believe that they were nothing alike.

Oh, how he'd missed her.

He hadn't realized how much until he'd walked through her condominium. Giving her these years to establish a sense of self had been important, and his patience had paid off in spades. The place had screamed of loneliness and detachment. There hadn't even been a single framed photograph on the walls.

Instead, she'd attempted to profile him as if he were nothing more than one of her many other homicide cases.

He was so much more than that.

He was a part of her, and she had no idea that she'd proven

it by becoming as obsessed with him as he was with her.

"Here is your caramel macchiato, sir."

Jacob had been waiting patiently by the counter of Brook's favorite café. She came here every morning on her way into the office for a large caramel macchiato. He'd been monitoring her for the last several weeks. He'd been quite surprised when she had disappeared on Thursday, not returning to her apartment after a full day of work. Her routine rarely varied, and he'd become curious about where she'd gone off to in such a rush.

"Thank you," Jacob murmured in appreciation.

He took his purchase and made his way over to an empty table that looked out onto the deserted sidewalk. The vile weather had even created somewhat of a cold draft near the seat he'd chosen, but it allowed him to have a somewhat clear view of the turmoil occurring down the street. There were still police vehicles, vans, and media converged outside of Brook's building.

Was she inside with the homicide detective examining the scene?

Jacob could only imagine what she thought of his handiwork. Quite the masterpiece, if he did say so himself. He preferred younger women who believed their family lives were perfect, but Lorraine Upton had surprised him with stories about the life she'd had with her husband.

The older woman had been extremely talkative as he'd escorted her into the building. He hadn't even bothered with the pretense of being someone else. He'd explained that he was Brook's brother, and that she'd given him a key to her condo while she was out of town on assignment.

Lorraine Upton hadn't even thought twice as they had walked through the foyer. He'd made sure that the doorman was busy helping one of the tenants collect coupons for his weekly trip to the grocery store. Once they'd reached the elevator, the rest had been a breeze.

Of course, he hadn't planned on killing the older woman. It was only after he'd canvassed his sister's condo that the idea had come to him. He found it quite amusing to leave her such a present that she would remember so vividly. Of course, Mrs. Upton hadn't thought it amusing when he knocked on her with one of Brook's kitchen knives in his hand.

Even altering the security footage had been effortless. The technological equipment that one could buy nowadays made things so much easier. He wasn't worried about the street cameras picking up his movements, because he'd studied their placement. He'd made himself known when he had deemed it appropriate, and he'd avoided any others that would give away his location to the authorities.

Little did they know just how close in proximity he was to his sister.

Jacob leaned back in his seat and sighed in contentment as he savored Brook's favorite beverage. He grimaced when the sweet taste washed into the back of his throat. It was a bit too potent for his liking, but he enjoyed trying the things that gave her pleasure.

Would she appreciate sampling his pastimes?

Only time would tell.

## ~ The End ~

*USA Today Bestselling Author Kennedy Layne continues the psychological thriller series that will have you redefining evil…*

kennedylayne.com/longing-for-sin.html

Brooklyn Sloane has left her job as a consultant for the FBI to take on her first cold case in the private sector. Doing so allows her the freedom to work the one case she's never professionally been allowed to touch – a ruthless serial killer, who just so happens to be her own brother.

Privately, she's hunting her only sibling, but alongside her team, she's seeking justice for those without a voice. But there is always the anomaly…

Seven arrests. Seven trials. Seven closed cases.

Brook has discovered one thread that ties them all together. Soon, as the investigation begins to unravel, the evidence all points to one disturbing truth – the real serial killer has never stopped hunting innocent victims, planting evidence, and causing others to pay for his violent crimes. Unfortunately, he isn't Brook's only concern. As she divulges deeper into her brother's reign of torment, she finds herself falling down a dark rabbit hole where she lands on a web of deceit. Who wins is unknown, for their chilling lies can make for very convincing truths.

# Books by Kennedy Layne

## Touch of Evil Series
Thirst for Sin
Longing for Sin

## The Widow Taker Trilogy
The Forgotten Widow
The Isolated Widow
The Reclusive Widow

## Hex on Me Mysteries
If the Curse Fits
Cursing up the Wrong Tree
The Squeaky Ghost Gets the Curse
The Curse that Bites
Curse Me Under the Mistletoe
Gone Cursing

## Paramour Bay Mysteries
Magical Blend
Bewitching Blend
Enchanting Blend
Haunting Blend
Charming Blend
Spellbinding Blend
Cryptic Blend
Broomstick Blend
Spirited Blend
Yuletide Blend
Baffling Blend

Phantom Blend
Batty Blend
Pumpkin Blend
Frosty Blend
Stony Blend
Cocoa Blend
Shamrock Blend
Campfire Blend
Stormy Blend
Sparkling Blend
Hallow Blend

### Office Roulette Series
Means (Office Roulette, Book One)
Motive (Office Roulette, Book Two)
Opportunity (Office Roulette, Book Three)

### Keys to Love Series
Unlocking Fear (Keys to Love, Book One)
Unlocking Secrets (Keys to Love, Book Two)
Unlocking Lies (Keys to Love, Book Three)
Unlocking Shadows (Keys to Love, Book Four)
Unlocking Darkness (Keys to Love, Book Five)

### Surviving Ashes Series
Essential Beginnings (Surviving Ashes, Book One)
Hidden Ashes (Surviving Ashes, Book Two)
Buried Flames (Surviving Ashes, Book Three)
Endless Flames (Surviving Ashes, Book Four)
Rising Flames (Surviving Ashes, Book Five)

## CSA Case Files Series

Captured Innocence (CSA Case Files 1)
Sinful Resurrection (CSA Case Files 2)
Renewed Faith (CSA Case Files 3)
Campaign of Desire (CSA Case Files 4)
Internal Temptation (CSA Case Files 5)
Radiant Surrender (CSA Case Files 6)
Redeem My Heart (CSA Case Files 7)
A Mission of Love (CSA Case Files 8)

## Red Starr Series

Starr's Awakening (Red Starr, Book One)
Hearths of Fire (Red Starr, Book Two)
Targets Entangled (Red Starr, Book Three)
Igniting Passion (Red Starr, Book Four)
Untold Devotion (Red Starr, Book Five)
Fulfilling Promises (Red Starr, Book Six)
Fated Identity (Red Starr, Book Seven)
Red's Salvation (Red Starr, Book Eight)

## The Safeguard Series

Brutal Obsession (The Safeguard Series, Book One)
Faithful Addiction (The Safeguard Series, Book Two)
Distant Illusions (The Safeguard Series, Book Three)
Casual Impressions (The Safeguard Series, Book Four)
Honest Intentions (The Safeguard Series, Book Five)
Deadly Premonitions (The Safeguard Series, Book Six)

## About the Author

First and foremost, I love life. I love that I'm a wife, mother, daughter, sister… and a writer.

I am one of the lucky women in this world who gets to do what makes them happy. As long as I have a cup of coffee (maybe two or three) and my laptop, the stories evolve themselves and I try to do them justice. I draw my inspiration from a retired Marine Master Sergeant that swept me off of my feet and has drawn me into a world that fulfills all of my deepest and darkest desires. Erotic romance, military men, intrigue, with a little bit of kinky chili pepper (his recipe), fill my head and there is nothing more satisfying than making the hero and heroine fulfill their destinies.

Thank you for having joined me on their journeys…

Email: kennedylayneauthor@gmail.com

Facebook: facebook.com/kennedy.layne.94

Twitter: twitter.com/KennedyL_Author

Website: www.kennedylayne.com

Newsletter: www.kennedylayne.com/meet-kennedy.html

Printed in Great Britain
by Amazon